THE HIGH SCHOOL QUEENS TRILOGY BOOK ONE

HIGH SCHOOL QUEENS

YOU MAY NOT KNOW WHO I AM, BUT YOU'LL REMEMBER MY NAME. THE MARKED QUEEN.

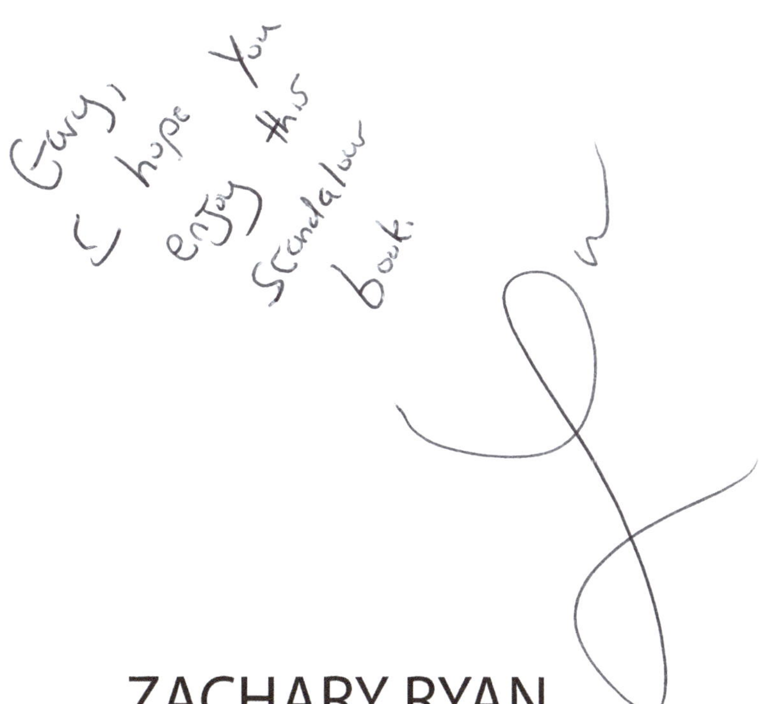

ZACHARY RYAN

Copyright

Editing by KP Editing
Cover design by KP Designs
Published by Kingston Publishing Company

ISBN: 978-1-64533-098-1
EBOOK: 978-1-64533-099-8

Table of Contents

Copyright....3
Table of Contents....5
Chapter 1....9
Chapter 2....13
Chapter 3....17
Chapter 4....20
Chapter 5....24
Chapter 6....28
Chapter 7....32
Chapter 8....37
Chapter 9....40
Chapter 10....44
Chapter 11....49
Chapter 12....52
Chapter 13....56
Chapter 14....60
Chapter 15....64
Chapter 16....68
Chapter 17....73
Chapter 18....76
Chapter 19....80
Chapter 20....84
Chapter 21....88
Chapter 22....92

Chapter 23 96
Chapter 24 100
Chapter 25 104
Chapter 26 107
Chapter 27 112
Chapter 28 115
Chapter 29 119
Chapter 30 123
Chapter 31 126
Chapter 32 129
Chapter 33 133
Chapter 34 137
Chapter 35 141
Chapter 36 145
Chapter 37 149
Chapter 38 154
Chapter 39 158
Chapter 40 161
Chapter 41 164
Chapter 42 169
Chapter 43 172
Chapter 44 175
Chapter 45 179
Chapter 46 183
Chapter 47 186

Chapter 48........190
Chapter 49........194
Chapter 50........198
Chapter 51........202
Chapter 52........205
Chapter 53........209
Chapter 54........213
Chapter 55........217
Chapter 56........221
Chapter 57........225
Chapter 58........229
Chapter 59........233
Chapter 60........237
Chapter 61........241
Chapter 62........245
Chapter 63........249
Chapter 64........253
Chapter 65........258
Chapter 66........261
Chapter 67........264
Chapter 68........267
Chapter 69........270
Chapter 70........273
Chapter 71........279
Chapter 72........283

Chapter 73 287
Chapter 74 290
Chapter 75 292
Chapter 76 295
Chapter 77 297
Chapter 78 300

Chapter 1

They've always said a Queen would know her rule on the kingdom she's built, by the reaction of her worshippers. Danielle walked down those halls of Johnson Prep, with her perfectly-manicured brown hair, flawless make-up, and designer clothes, that hugged her petite frame in all the right places. She watched as her peasants whispered as she walked past them. She knew she was feared and adored by her people. The only problem was, she had a new Queen trying to take her throne. She had dealt with other girls before, but The Marked Queen had her own flare to bring to the war. Spring has always brought a sense of new beginnings, why not have a full out bitch war for the kingdom? Danielle knew that the best way to keep her secrets safe, was to expose someone else's.

Danielle held up the new post by The Marked Queen, and put it on the cork board for the whole school to see. Right in the middle of the busy hallway. She knew people were wondering what was said on that single sheet of paper. She had to admit, she was impressed with the attention this new Queen brought to the school.

Danielle looked at the new post herself and read it out loud. Those were the rules when you had been marked.

Who doesn't love an innocent pregnancy scare on a Sunday afternoon? Clara, you must have been sleeping during your father's sermon on the Devil's temptation. Or maybe, you were too busy thinking of all the positions Troy planned to do. Troy, I'm proud you're stepping up to be with Clara during these hard times. I just hope Vanessa doesn't mind sharing you. Remember boys and girls, a couple of minutes of sinful pleasure, is a lifetime of scandal. -The Marked Queen.

She turned around to see people whispering, and shocked to see the latest post. She saw Vanessa slap Troy across the face and run off screaming. She turned to see Clara hugging her stomach, and looking completely mortified. Danielle rolled her eyes. She didn't think the post this day was that scandalous, but it got The Marked Queen off her back…for now.

She saw Aman coming up to her with his camera ready to record the whole thing. She rolled her eyes. She has always hated him for his stupid vlogs. "Danielle, what secrets are you trying to hide?" he asked.

"For an Indian, shouldn't you be busy in the chemistry lab or something?" She crossed her arms and raised an eyebrow.

Aman turned off his camera. "Really, an Indian Joke? I thought you were better than that," he said. Aman was an Indian-Muslim. His parents came to America when he was five-years-old. He kept his black hair slicked back. He was slim, but he was starting to form muscles, and Danielle had to admit, he did have beautiful brown eyes.

She laughed. "If I recall, you've also been marked. I don't see you exposing your secrets either."

He knew she had a point there. "We've all got secrets we're trying to keep hidden. Why not be the first person to break that mold, and take down The Marked Queen?" He paused. "Unless, you're okay with her having control of *your* school."

Danielle didn't get a chance to respond before Delilah came up to Aman. "Or, you could talk about your secrets on your weekly videos. We could all be the bigger person," she said. Delilah was Danielle's best friend since they were in elementary school. She had dirty blonde hair, freckles, emerald eyes, and didn't fit the mold of being super thin. She was thicker than most girls, but beautiful in her own right.

Aman rolled his eyes. "Bitches, all of you." He turned and walked away.

"And this is why you don't have a girlfriend," Delilah screamed.

Danielle laughed. "Thank you for coming to my honor. He's always trying to get views and hits." She was impressed with Aman's empire that he was starting to build for himself.

"Did you hear we have a new kid in the school?" Delilah asked with a smirk. She turned and pointed to the new kid at his locker.

Danielle followed her finger to see a guy at his locker. He looked scrawny with dark hair, hazel eyes, and stubble. She also saw who he was talking with. "Clearly, he doesn't have enough class, because he's mingling with Tucker and Bethany." She rolled her eyes. "He's not that cute anyway."

"Already pining over the new boy in the school? Don't you think you should give him a full day to realize that you suck their souls, like you suck dick to keep the wrinkles away," Jasmine said, walking up to them. Jasmine and Danielle have been the two most popular girls in their class and have never gotten along. "Besides, aren't you too busy being The Marked Queen's bitch?"

Danielle turned and smiled at Jasmine. Jasmine was a shorter, thicker, and mousy-voiced creature that Danielle had the displeasure of knowing. She thought Jasmine's pixie haircut made her look more like a lesbian, than an edgy girl. "At least I'm interesting enough to be marked. I don't think I've ever seen you have to post anything."

Jasmine crossed her arms. "Maybe because I have no secrets to hide."

Danielle and Delilah both laughed. "We've all got things to hide." Danielle leaned forward. "Yours are just not that juicy to expose," she whispered. Danielle turned to Delilah. "We've got class, and I've done my fair share of charity work for the day." Danielle made sure her charity work comment was pointed right at Jasmine.

They walked away from Jasmine. Jasmine felt a little insulted by Danielle's comments. It was true what Danielle said. She hasn't been marked, but she does have a lot of secrets. Everyone might have been feared to be marked, but they were lying when they didn't get an adrenaline rush from their name being spoken on everyone's lips.

Chapter 2

"What was that all about?" Andrew asked, looking at Tucker and Bethany. Tucker was Andrew's locker neighbor and Bethany and Tucker were dating. They seemed like nice people, and he hoped this new school would give him the chance to start over. He had done enough damage in his life, and he wanted to finally act like a normal high school student.

Tucker was a short, acne plagued-glasses, wearing-heart-of-gold nerd. He had curly blonde hair and blue eyes. He would be cute if he actually took care of himself. It was truly a tragic life lesson about the boys in high school. If they knew their potential, then they wouldn't be lowering themselves to date, Bethany.

Bethany was adorable with her basic brown hair, American Eagle outfits, and her desperate need for attention with her peers. She was president of the prom committee, and she was in student government. She was as boring as her outfits. It wasn't surprising when the two wallflowers fell in love. Now, they were trying to get a third to join their pathetic group.

"The Marked Queen decides that every Monday she would choose a student to be marked and expose someone's secrets. She makes them read it out loud to the whole school," Bethany said. She was more focused on the prom committee than The Marked Queen.

"So, she's a bully?" Andrew asked. He understood that New York City was the type of place for people to backstab each other, but he didn't think he would have experienced it on his first day. He came from a small town, and maybe it was better he lived in the city. He could hide in the shadows until graduation.

"I think it's awesome. She goes after the popular kids who think they're so much better than all of us," Tucker said. He realized soon enough, that they were too busy going after each other to worry about the "bottom dwellers," as Danielle liked to put it.

"So, people fear this person?" Andrew asked.

Bethany shrugged. "If you have nothing to hide, then you shouldn't have to worry about The Marked Queen. She came around at the beginning of the school year. She's been on a roll, and I think it's good for people to be on their toes."

"I guess I'm used to violent bullying," Andrew said, with a shrug.

"You have to understand, that this is Johnson Prep. You must be smarter and slyer than your competition. We don't believe in violence here. It's kind of beneath us," Bethany said.

Andrew nodded. "I guess I have a lot to learn at this new school."

Tucker smiled. "Well, now you have two new friends. Why did you move to the city anyway?" he asked Andrew.

"We moved because my dad got a new job. He thought it was good for me to be social with people, other than the small town that I lived in." He knew it was the lie that everyone would believe. He didn't want to admit the real reasons why his father took him to the big city. He knew there was temptation everywhere, and he had to accept that it would be hard for him.

Tucker smiled. "Well, welcome."

"You can think of us as your welcoming committee," Bethany said with a smile. She was happy to have another friend in the fold. She just hoped he didn't get dragged away by the rest of the kids at this school. She knew that it might have seemed glamorous, but she knew that it wasn't worth it in the end.

Bethany should have known the only reason she wasn't invited to a party was that only the cool kids get to have friends. She might have had Tucker on her arm, but that didn't give her any street cred. Cling all you want to a society that you would never be a part of. We all knew you were just trying desperately to think you are better than all of them.

"Thanks," Andrew said with a smile.

"I've got to get to the photography studio before the first bell," Tucker smiled. Bethany and he walked away from Andrew leaving him at his locker.

He was about to open his locker when Aman walked over to him. "Welcome to Johnson Prep. I'm Aman. Tell me about yourself."

Andrew reached out and blocked the lens of the camera and pushed it down. "I'm not doing interviews for whatever the hell this is."

Aman turned the camera off. "Come on. You're the new hot guy of the school. Don't you want people to know who you are?"

Andrew turned to him. "I don't care what people think of me. I'm good at keeping a low profile. We only have three months of school left, and then we graduate. It's all I'm focusing on." Andrew opened his locker and saw a piece of paper drop out.

"You're going to regret not being in my blog. Everyone wants to be famous, whether they admit it or not," he said, walking away from him.

Andrew ignored him as he picked up the piece of paper. He looked at what was written on it.

Welcome to Johnson Prep, the new kid. Let me be the first of your welcoming committee. If you haven't figured it out yet, I can be your best friend or worst enemy. Let's see how you do here. Are you going to be like the rest of these insecure bitches trying to get power and dick? Or, are you going to be like the testosterone-filled boys looking to score with one of the slutty cheerleaders? The choice is yours, my dear Andrew. Always remember one thing; we've all got secrets that we will protect from getting out into the world. I'm just wondering what yours could be? -The Marked Queen.

"I guess there goes the idea of me keeping a low-profile," he said to himself. He looked around at the kids gossiping to each other. He thought this would be his fresh start after the year he'd had, but he didn't know if this would make him stronger, or make him relapse again.

Andrew, you shouldn't have been so worried about going back down a dark path again. We would find out soon enough what monsters live under your bed. The Marked Queen took an interest in you. You should probably take her suggestion very carefully, or you could be the next one to do her bidding.

Chapter 3

"You missed a great showdown this morning," Aman said, walking up to Calvin. Calvin was putting away his baseball gear after practice. We couldn't begin to describe how dreamy Calvin was. He was built for the gods with his sandy blonde hair, blue eyes, puppy-dog smile, and a scar on the left side of his face. He knew damn well how to be mysterious and sexy all in the same breath.

Calvin rolled his eyes. He knew Aman loved gossip more than the next person. "Sorry, I missed whatever secret The Marked Queen decided to expose today. I had practice this morning. You do know that states are right around the corner."

Aman loved that Calvin was so invested in his baseball career, but he wished Calvin was invested in the drama of the high school, too. "You act like you're above it all."

Calvin laughed. He threw his bag over his shoulder. "It has nothing to do with being above it all." Calvin looked around to see that everyone had already gone to the locker room. It was common for Calvin to be the last player on the field. "I don't need anyone finding out about the skeletons in our closet."

"No one is going to find out. We're careful." Aman quickly leaned forward and gave Calvin a chaste kiss.

Calvin raised an eyebrow. "You actually gave me a kiss in public. I'm pretty impressed."

Aman pushed him. "I hate dating you."

Calvin laughed. He loved this side of Aman. He knew that Aman had a personality he perceived for all his viewers, but he enjoyed when he let the walls down. These were the moments that he truly knew that Aman was special to him.

"I'm just worried that The Marked Queen will find out about us," Aman said. He knew that was a constant fear, because he didn't know who this Queen was.

Calvin reached over and pulled him into a hug. "You need to stop worrying about what people are going to think. If it gets out, then it gets out. We can finally stop sneaking around."

"What about your baseball career?" he asked.

"So?"

Aman stepped back. "I get that your parents are okay with you being gay. They've accepted me into your family, but my parents aren't that cool. You get that, right?"

"And, I haven't come out because my dad wants me to be a baseball star. I get what it's like to have to live a double life," Calvin said. He would never get the Muslim culture, and he wasn't sitting here trying to get to know it. All he had to do was understand the position that Aman was in.

"I need to go edit this new vlog before tomorrow," Aman said. He was done with this conversation.

"Are you seriously walking away from me?" Calvin asked. He crossed his arms and looked at his boyfriend.

"You know that me coming out will never happen. I wish you would stop trying to push me."

"I would never ask you to come out, Aman. I have loving parents, and it scared me shitless. I'm not going to ever make you come out of the closet unless you're ready."

"But we don't know if we have that chance. We all have knives over our head because of this Marked Queen bitch."

Calvin knew that Aman was worried when The Marked Queen started coming around at the beginning of the year. They both thought it was someone that would eventually blow away. The problem was, she was gaining more power each day. He sighed. "You need to stop freaking out so much. We're good people. If we keep it on the down low, we'll be okay."

Aman wished he could keep a low profile. He had fans that he couldn't let down. He had the biggest target on his back. He also knew that Calvin did too. He was the baseball star of the school, and people always wondered why he never dated anyone.

Aman, we already knew why he wasn't dating anyone. The all-star baseball player has a secret other than his training regime. It was so tragic that he had to disappoint so many girls, and tell them the only person he wanted to play catch with was a vlogger.

"I don't think we get the luxury of low profiles," Aman said.

Calvin leaned forward and kissed Aman on the lips. He put a sense of love and urgency in this kiss. He wanted Aman to know that no matter what happened in the world, they still had each other.

Sweet Calvin, everyone wished you could see that notion was only for fools. They said the only person you should protect was yourself. When would you learn this lesson yourself? You both might have enjoyed these tender moments, but Aman was right. The Marked Queen was looking for her next scandal, and she didn't have to look too far. Who knew that baseball was like a soap opera? We all should have guessed that there was more injecting on the field than just steroids. We hoped you enjoyed these moments together, because we all had a feeling that they were turning into your last together in the closet.

Chapter 4

They said the worst type of people were the ones that peaked in high school. The high school jocks ended up being fat guys that work at Walmart, while the beauty Queens became your future sons spank bank material. The question we all had on our lips, was what would become of Danielle and Delilah? The beauty Queens of the school knew a thing or two about bitch battlefield. But what would happen to them once they were shown the door to the real world?

"I need to get at least a C on this test, or my parents are going to be so pissed," Delilah said, taking her seat next to Danielle.

Danielle rolled her eyes. She had enough of Delilah's complaining. She knew that if Delilah really applied herself, then she wouldn't be failing this class. Danielle, you should have known as her best friend that she had other things she spent her time doing, but that was for another time. "If you want me to tutor you, then I can. I have no problem coming to your house after school."

"Why don't we go to yours?" Delilah asked. She hadn't been to Danielle's house in two years.

"We're still remodeling. My mom can't seem to make up her mind on how the house should look." Danielle tried to play it off. She knew once her mother left her father, that things had changed. She knew how to keep up appearances, and she would survive the next couple of months.

Delilah shrugged. "Your mom does love interior designing. I remember when I came over in eighth grade, and she freaked out when I put my feet on a chair."

Danielle laughed. It seemed like a lifetime ago when things were easier. It was always a bitch slap to the ego when you realized that your life now, was worse than the past. Aren't you supposed to be growing in life? "Yeah, those were the days. She's still the same woman." Danielle shrugged.

Ms. Linder walked around with last weeks' math tests. The nerds were obviously the ones getting the high scores. The burnouts were pleased with their mediocre grades and thinking of using their test as paper for their joint later. The cheerleaders shrugged off their poor intelligence just looking to join a sorority and get their M.R.S. Degree.

"Good job, Danielle. I'm seeing improvement in your scores," the teacher said, handing a 94 to Danielle.

She turned to Delilah. "We might need some more work on you," she said, handing a 65 to Delilah.

Who would have thought the Queen bitch had the smarts, too? She sure seemed flawless. We were all dying to know what secret The Marked Queen had over you, Danielle. They said D's get diplomas, but we aren't sure that applies to you, Delilah. It seemed you won't be walking down the graduation aisle with your friends this year. Don't worry, we heard you connected more intellectually with a third grader. Maybe they should send you back to where you were most comfortable?

Delilah leaned over and saw Danielle's score. "You're so fucking lucky."

"I actually studied. My father always raised me to know that a woman with brains is deadlier than a woman with beauty. We all can be dumb whores, but why not be a smart bitch?" Danielle had the perfect mentality for a modern-day woman. We applauded her for knowing that it was time for a man's world to be destroyed. Besides, a company takeover by two women, was way more fun than by two silly boys.

Delilah felt so stupid at that moment. She looked at her paper. She had tried her hardest on this test. She wanted to believe that she was improving herself. She kept her emotions in check because there was no point in crying right now. She didn't need anyone to see her weak.

Delilah turned to Danielle. "I think I'm going to talk to Principal Grand after class. I feel like he could help me with getting my grade up."

Danielle raised an eyebrow. "Why not go to Ms. Lindner?"

"Because she hates me. I know that she looks at me like I'm just some stupid little girl."

Danielle reached over and squeezed her friend's hand. "You aren't stupid. I know you're struggling in math, but you have a talent out there for you."

Delilah was grateful for Danielle in her life. She knew that she was lost in the world, and it freaked her out that she was graduating in a couple of months. She knew that she had her passion for writing, but she was just so doubtful that she didn't know how to improve anything else.

"Maybe you should come over and help me study. I just don't want to look like a complete idiot."

"You aren't an idiot. I think you're too focused on getting a date for prom," Danielle said. She knew that Delilah was more focused on getting Flynn to take her to the dance.

"Flynn will ask me. I know it."

"I'm going alone this year," Danielle stated. She didn't see any of the guy's in her high school class as mature enough to date. It was also because she had an older gentleman caller waiting for her.

"Really? I don't think I could ever be strong enough to go alone. I feel like everyone needs a date." Danielle looked back at Bethany who was looking at her math book. "Even Bethany has a date."

Danielle rolled her eyes. "Please, the bottom feeders always have a date. Desperation works in many ways. She picked a virgin, because no one else would put up with her stuck up and inexperienced vagina."

Delilah laughed. "I guess you do have a point there." She paused. "I hope Flynn thinks I'm cute and smart enough." She held up the test. "Because this makes me look like a dumb bitch."

"I'll help you get your grades up, but not for you to date Flynn," Danielle said.

One thing you never saw at Johnson Prep was two girls supporting each other. It was a refreshing break from the constant backstabbing. Danielle took Delilah under her wing, but Danielle, do you think Delilah would always support you? You girls seemed to forget that The Marked Queen was out there ruining lives. Who said she wouldn't keep your friendship out of the blood bath?

Chapter 5

It seemed Delilah's only asset was her looks, because clearly her brain was deformed since birth. Here she was trying to get Principal Grand to give her a pass. "I just need help in this class. Could you transfer me or something?" Delilah asked.

Principal Grand was, how do we say, soft on the girls of Johnson Prep. Principal Grand kept a reputation that he was hands-on with the students, and wanted them to feel safe. The problem was, that this mid-forties man really did enjoy getting to know them. Sure, he played right into the boys and girls issues they had with their daddy, but he only wanted to hear that word come out of a certain someone's lips.

He sighed and looked at Delilah. He had recently dyed his gray hair black. He had been putting on some weight since his wife had left him, and he wore glasses to make him more distinguished among his colleagues. "I don't get it." He looked over her files. "You have great grades in English, Creative Writing, and History. You're only failing Math and Chemistry."

"I've tried to get a tutor. I study all of the time, but it's not working." She wanted to break down in tears, but she knew that she couldn't come off whiney.

"We only have three months left in the year. I can't transfer you out of the class."

"Is there something that you can do?" she asked. She needed to graduate. She knew damn well how humiliating it would be if she was forced to stay another year.

He thought about it for a moment, and he knew that she was trying. "Why don't I see about getting you some private time with Mrs. Lindner? If she sees an improvement in your grades, then we can raise it high enough to graduate with the rest of your class."

"What about chemistry?" she asked.

"I'll talk to Mr. Warren about extra credit or something."

She clapped her hands. "I knew you were the person that I should have gone to."

"You've always been my favorite student."

Delilah raised an eyebrow. She turned to see that the door to the office was closed. "Is the door locked?" she asked.

Principal Grand always knew when Delilah came into his office, it was best to keep the door locked, and make sure no one disturbed them. "I've already cleared my plans, and you know that I'm not foolish enough to leave that door unlocked.

Delilah smiled with glee. "Good boy." She got up from her seat and walked over to sit on his lap. She ran her fingers through his hair. "I do have to admit that I miss the gray hair."

He raised an eyebrow. "I thought this would make me look younger."

She rolled her eyes. "When will men learn that they should age gracefully?"

"Jenny hated the way I looked," he said.

She placed a finger on his lips. "What did we say about ex-wives?"

He nodded. "We should never bring them up."

"Exactly." She leaned forward and kissed him on the lips. There was no romantic chemistry or love. It was pure lust, and they'd been doing this for months. Who knew bumping into each other at the grocery store next to the frozen produce would cause such a steamy stir?

He pushed her off him. She got up and went down on her knees. She looked at him with a wink. "What are the rules?" she asked. She always liked to be in control, because this was one of the only things she was good at.

"I have to be quiet, and we can't fall in love."

"No one can find out, or we're both screwed. Can you get my grades up?" Delilah asked.

He nodded. "Yes, I can."

She winked. "That's what I like to hear." She unbuttoned his belt and unzipped his zipper. She pulled out his manhood, and she decided to enjoy herself. Who said that a true love story couldn't start this way?

It was a tale old as time, but with an interesting twist. People always suspected the teachers of having affairs with the students. No one ever thought that the principal could be doing the dirty, also. I must say, Delilah, you did have a talent for making the man that ruled your school, your own personal bitch.

She had finished her extra credit homework for Principal Grand. She stood up and wiped her mouth while he got himself proper again. He was flush, and he needed to compose himself. "I don't know where you learn to do the things you do, but I can never complain."

Delilah smiled. "I'm glad that I'm good at something."

"I'll talk to the teachers by the end of the day, and we will get it all sorted." He paused. "I sure will miss you though, once the school year is over."

"Who says it needs to be over?" Delilah knew that she needed to play with his hopes. She learned a long time ago, that the only way to succeed in this world, was to wrap the men around her finger.

He blushed, and he felt himself getting ready for another round at the thought of continuing this after she graduates. "We will see what happens."

They heard the bell go off. "I better get to class before I'm late." She walked to the door and unlocked it. "Thanks again." She winked and walked out. This gave a whole new meaning to the term, teacher's pet. I thought you were supposed to give them an apple as a gift, not a taste of your cherry pie.

Chapter 6

Andrew walked into the kitchen to see that his father was making dinner. Mark, Andrew's dad, smiled when he saw his son come into the room. "How was your first day?" he asked.

Andrew took a seat at the kitchen island. He leaned across and grabbed a tomato. Mark was cooking pasta for dinner, because it was Andrew's favorite. "It was interesting, to say the least."

Mark turned around after stirring the noodles. "How was it interesting?"

Andrew looked at his father. They hadn't had a chance to talk since they moved to New York. His father quickly went into work, as Andrew unpacked everything. "Why did we move here?"

"It's a fresh start for both of us."

"But, New York City? Dad, this is a breeding ground for bad decisions." Andrew was trying to make up for the bad mistakes he has made in the past year. He wanted the old Andrew to be gone, but he didn't know if this city was going to let him.

Mark turned around and looked at his son. "You had a rough year. You lost your mom, and you tried to find comfort in other ways. I saw how destroyed you were, and I saw how much people watched you."

"It was a small town. People love to gossip and know everyone's business."

"Exactly my point." Mark wanted his son to fully understand why they were there. "I had too many people looking at me with pathetic eyes. I saw people whispering. I knew exactly what they were saying. 'That's Taylor's boy. He's lost his way since her passing.'"

Andrew never denied that it was a good thing they moved out of town, but he didn't get why it had to be New York City. "Why a city? Why not another small town?"

"Because here, you can be invisible." Mark walked over and sat down next to Andrew. "You won't have a target on your back. You can grow and focus on yourself. I know what would have killed your recovery, even more, is having spectators."

Andrew knew his father was right. He could keep his head low, and he didn't need to worry about other people knowing his past. He sighed heavily. "I guess I can be a wallflower here."

Mark smiled. "Nothing wrong with being under the radar. I was a wallflower when I was in high school."

"But mom was popular?" Andrew asked.

Mark nodded. He got up to check the pasta. He knew going down memory lane about his late wife would be hard. He didn't want his son to see him cry. "She always teased me back then. She was playful with me. She never made me feel less than her. I saw her around her worshippers, but she never truly connected with them, like she did with me."

"Why did she connect with you so much?" Andrew asked.

Mark turned to look at his son. "I saw her crying once in the library. She didn't get something, and she had worked so hard for it. She kept up a shield, so people couldn't get in. She let me in because she knew I would never hold it against her."

"Wow, high school still hasn't changed," Andrew said. He thought about the people at his new school. He could tell that they were keeping their secrets close to their hearts.

"It's weird thinking back to high school. We all cared what people thought of us. We created this character for ourselves, so people wouldn't find out the real us. We wanted to connect with people without getting hurt," Mark said, while wiping his hands and leaning against the stove.

"We're at the point where it's like the hunger games. We don't lose our lives, but we lose our reputations," Andrew paused. "I think that's more important to some people."

"It's why most movies and books are based in high school. It's supposed to be the most influential years of your life."

"Do you believe so?" Andrew asked.

"I met your mother during that time. I think I wouldn't have learned the lesson of being open to people without her."

Andrew knew that his mother was a courageous woman, and the world lost an incredible soul. He knew he wasn't doing her proud, and he was trying to make up for it. He prayed that she would be smiling from the heavens, not frowning.

"Keep your head down, and you'll be fine. It's only three months until you graduate. You can do this."

Andrew thought about Tucker and Bethany. He felt like they were good friends to have. He remembered what Aman said about everyone wanting to be famous. He knew that he was wrong. It was good when people didn't know your secrets, and he wanted to keep it that way.

"I think I'll find a couple of friends and try to have a normal high school experience."

Mark nodded. "It's New York City, I don't think there's such a thing as a normal experience here."

Andrew, you should have listened to your father because he was giving you all the best advice. He was right about so many things. People protected their secrets and created personas to make people adore them. You wanted to keep your head in the sand, but everyone had a feeling that wasn't going to last. The Marked Queen was intrigued by you, and she would find any way of getting to know the monsters under your bed; so be careful because we knew the real truth in your heart. You would never admit that you relished when people whispered about you. It was the love that you had been trying to get for some time now. Boys and girls, you should never believe anyone that wanted to keep a low profile. Why be a peasant when you could be royalty?

Chapter 7

Aman was busy texting Calvin and was becoming a little flustered.

Aman: *Hey babe, sorry I can't come to the movies tonight. My mom needs help and doesn't want me to leave the house.*

Aman texted Calvin in response to Calvin wanting to go see a movie that night. Poor Calvin, when would you learn that you were dating mommy too?

Calvin groaned and ran his fingers through his hair. Something wrong, sweetie?" Audrey asked.

Calvin was sitting at the counter with his mom and dad while they were cooking dinner. Calvin's little sister was in the other room watching cartoons. "Aman and I were supposed to see a movie tonight, but he can't because his mom wants him to stay home."

Audrey turned to look at her husband, Paul. "Cal, we told you that dating him would be hard. It's not easy for him to be out like you are," Paul said.

Calvin looked at his dad. "I'm not even out, dad. You told me that I had to stay in the closet. I want to be out to the world," he said. He came out to his parents a year ago when he and Aman had their first kiss. Calvin had always had a suspicion. He believed he was more focused on baseball, but he realized that he would rather suck than lick.

"We love you for who you are. We have no problem with you being gay. Your uncle is gay," Audrey said. When her brother came out, she instantly loved him. She knew that gay people had so much hardship from society already, that they should be able to count on family.

"But we know that baseball isn't very LGBT friendly. We want you to succeed in your career as a catcher. We don't want your sexual orientation to ruin that for you," Paul said. He would never deny that he wished his son was straight, because it would be an easier life for him. He also knew that his son would be able to overcome anything.

Calvin looked at his parents. "Why can't Aman see this? We're open about my sexuality and my relationship with him. You guys have welcomed him in with open hearts, and he should understand that he has a family here." Calvin didn't get why Aman didn't think he had any support system.

Audrey leaned over and squeezed Calvin's hand. "You don't get it. He's Indian-Muslim. Those two cultures don't believe in homosexuality."

"But it's the 21st Century," Calvin argued.

"But you're a white male with loving parents who accept you. You're still in the closet yourself," Paul said. "Have you told any of your friends?"

Calvin rolled his eyes. "Do I even have real friends? Everyone is so focused on keeping the perfect image at school. Look at Aman, he has to keep up this happy go lucky persona for his YouTube channel."

"We all have to keep a mask on when we're out in society. When you find someone, you can take that mask off with, then that's true love," Paul said.

Calvin looked at his father. "I don't really care for you being all romantic."

Audrey and Paul laughed. "I learned to be soft with your mother." He paused. "You haven't even told Danielle? You guys have been close since you were in elementary school."

"She knows that I like guys, but she doesn't know about Aman and me."

"Why not?" Audrey asked.

"I love Danielle, but she's trying to keep up a strong front since her parents' divorce." Calvin knew that she was still trying to be the Queen bee of the school, even though she's lost her empire on the home front.

Audrey and Paul looked at each other. "Danielle's dad isn't paying for anything?" Paul asked.

Calvin shrugged. "She doesn't talk about it much." He felt his phone go off. He saw that it was a text from Danielle. "She wants to talk now. I better go see what she wants."

"Just remember that it will get easier with him. You have your baseball career and it will help you in the long run," Paul stated.

Calvin put on a forced smile as he left the kitchen to go up to his room to talk to Danielle. He called her, and she picked up on the second ring. "What a fucking day it's been," Danielle said.

Calvin chuckled. "It's not fun being marked by the Queen."

Danielle groaned. "Whatever."

"What does she have over you?" Calvin asked.

"What do you think?" Danielle asked. She didn't even know why he asked. He already knew the answer to that.

"Oh right," he paused, because the new kid came popping into his mind. He only heard a little bit from Aman. "So, what do you think of the new kid?" he asked.

She didn't think much. She didn't even remember his name. "He seems dark and mysterious. I don't know. The only problem is, that I saw him with Tucker and Bethany of all people."

Calvin laughed. "I think you need to give them a break. They aren't horrible people."

"Oh please, you're only nice to them because they did a great job on your yearbook spread."

"It's not my fault that I look good in front of a camera."

"I hope whatever guy you fall for breaks that confidence in you." She paused. "Or you could tell me who your mystery boyfriend is." Danielle knew that Calvin was seeing someone. She saw it right on his face the moment it happened.

"I told you that we have to keep it in the closet. We both can't make a spectacle of our relationship."

"I wish he went to our school." She thought for a moment. "Does Aman know you're gay?"

"No, I only told you." It was the same lie he'd told over and over again. He saw a movie about the main girl hooking up with a college guy, so he went with the same story about the mystery boyfriend he had.

"I wish you could come out. I just want you to be happy and loved."

"It's the same with you. We all are trapped in our own closets, but who knows? Maybe the Marked Queen will blow the doors off all of our safe spaces."

She rolled her eyes. "Don't get me started on that bitch. I better go help my mom."

Calvin saw his phone receive a text from Aman. He wanted to talk about his new video. "Yeah, I've got to go too. I'll talk to you later." He hung up and called Aman. He thought about what he said to Danielle. They all had closets they were hiding in, and he needed to accept that some people weren't ready to come out. Sweet Calvin, when would you learn The Marked Queen didn't care if you weren't ready? She wanted people to fear her, and she would make all of you bitches her prime example of why you shouldn't disrespect her.

Chapter 8

"What do you mean, it's not fitting right?" Jasmine asked Susan.

Susan was stupid enough to be friends with the pathetic Queen. Jasmine had been nice to her freshman year when Susan transferred to the school. Jasmine knew that for her to be on top, she had to get minions. No one knew why you would choose Susan as a minion. It wasn't like Susan was ugly or anything. She had red hair, green eyes, and pasty white skin. She also was forgettable. She made more of a perfect before model in a plastic surgery commercial.

"Jasmine, I'm sorry, but I can't button it up. I think you might need to go up a dress size."

Jasmine turned around and looked at Susan. "I will not go up another size. I'm a fucking 4. I will not be heavier than that bitch, Danielle. We're both the same weight."

"It's okay to be bigger," Susan said.

Jasmine had enough of Susan's bullshit. She slapped her across the face. "Big girls are pathetic scums of society. I will be loved, and I can only do that if I'm skinny." Jasmine knew that for her rule to happen, she needed to keep her weight down. She was tired of people overlooking her. She was done being the forgotten one. "I'm not the 'pathetic Queen' that they call me."

Susan nodded, and felt the pain in her cheek slowly start to fade away. "What do you want me to do?" she asked.

"Buy the damn dress. I'll have to lose some weight. This is my fucking prom dress after all," Jasmine said. It was a black dress with an exposed back, plunging neckline, and a slit to show off her legs.

Susan nodded. "I'll get them to ring it up for you."

Jasmine smiled. "Good, I need to take care of something first." She walked toward the bathroom. She closed the door and took off the dress. She leaned over the toilet and put two fingers in her mouth. No one was surprised that this Queen liked the taste of bile. We all had a bad taste in our mouth when she walked into the room.

She was right after all; no one liked a fat Queen. Jasmine, your problem wasn't the fact that you were fat. It was the fact that no one could stand your horrid personality. Even The Marked Queen was loved by some people, were you?

She stood up and wiped her mouth clean. She walked out of the stall and over to the mirror. She fixed her make-up, and made sure that she didn't leave any evidence. She knew Susan would suspect, and she couldn't have her minion asking questions.

She came out of the bathroom to Susan standing there. "Are you all right?"

"Yes, I just had to use the bathroom."

"I heard vomiting noises."

Jasmine crossed her arms. "Are you implying that I puked? It was the sound of the toilet, you idiot."

Susan thought she heard her throw up, but she didn't want to make Jasmine angry. She hadn't made a lot of friends here, and she hated to admit Jasmine was her only one. She knew Jasmine was a sweet girl under all that hatred, and she hoped eventually, people would be able to see it.

"They're waiting for you to pay at the counter," Susan said.

Jasmine smiled. "Good. I know once Calvin sees me in this, he'll be dying to go to prom with me."

"Are you asking Calvin to prom? Wouldn't he go with Danielle? Aren't they super close?" Susan asked.

Jasmine looked at her with such disdain. She wished she picked up a smarter girl. "Calvin feels sorry for her."

"Have you talked to Calvin?"

"No, but he will come to his senses." Jasmine knew once she had the most popular boy on her arms, that would seal her fate as the next Queen of the school. She knew that her secrets were kept under lock and key. She needed to get the guy and take down the bitch.

Susan clapped. "I can't wait for you."

"It's time that I ruled this school," Jasmine said. She knew that it only mattered once prom came who the real Queen was. She was tired of Danielle having control, and it was time for her to be taken down a peg or two. She needed to find out the secrets that The Marked Queen had against her. It was all love and war, and she couldn't wait to see how it all turned out.

Our stupid, worthless, Jasmine-- when would you learn that you are no match for Danielle? Maybe you should have spent your energy on becoming Queen of the cafeteria. We heard you do love your desserts, and no one could miss those back rolls. Also, if you were trying to wear a black dress to prom to make you look slim, you had another thing coming. Jasmine, they called you the pathetic Queen because you had no clue, that to be Queen, you had to be adored, not pitied.

Chapter 9

After a long day of hard work serving the commoners, a Queen needed a good night's rest. Most Queens had their share of rooms in their castle to lounge in. Too bad for Danielle, her kingdom was a two-bedroom apartment in the Bronx. Who would have thought this mean girl with high fashion lived a life of poverty?

Danielle walked into her house, where her mom was currently getting ready for work. Lily looked up at her daughter walking in the door. She smiled. "It's good to see you're finally home." Lily walked over and kissed Danielle on the cheek.

"I've put some food in the fridge for you. I'm working the late shift at the diner." Lily grabbed her apron.

Danielle smiled. "It's fine," she paused. "I was wondering if you could pick up my shift Friday night?" Danielle wanted to go to Jordan Caraway's party.

Lily sighed. "Danielle, you can't keep missing work so you can go to these high school parties." She touched Danielle's dress. "I know you want to keep up this persona, but you need to realize that we aren't rich anymore."

Danielle smiled weakly. "Mom, I gave up that fairytale a long time ago. I thought Dad would have left us some money."

"He left you money once you turn twenty-one, but he decided that he didn't need to support us anymore."

"Because he has a new wife to focus on," Danielle said. She tried to keep her anger to herself. She hated seeing photos of her father with his new wife splashed all over social media. She thought he would have the dignity to not rub it in their faces.

Lily touched Danielle's face. "He still loves you. You have to remember that."

"Really?" She looked around at their crappy apartment. "But he's forcing us to live like this. He's making us feel like we're his dirty secret. You were his wife, not his whore."

"And you don't think I know that? He pays for this apartment, your school, and he gives you an allowance." Lily knew Ethan was a heartless asshole. He had all the money in the world, but he couldn't admit he was wrong. It was why Lily got nothing after the divorce.

"But we should be living on the Upper East Side, not the Bronx." She rolled her eyes and took a seat on the couch.

Lily walked over and sat down in front of her. "You will see that this is the best for you. You need to realize that this will humble you. You can't be a human being without a struggle in your life. Look at the kids around you. You've gotten a gift with this."

Danielle looked at her mother. "This isn't a gift. We used to live a life of luxury. We used to have anything we wanted at our fingertips. Now, we have nothing."

"Except each other. I was more worried about what our house looked like instead of you. I had you because it was part of the social standing." Lily smiled, because now she had an actual relationship with her daughter. "We've struggled, but we're here now. It's going to be okay."

Danielle gave her a weak smile. "I'm happy you found clarity, but I still go to Johnson Prep. There's no such thing as understanding there. Once people find out that I'm poor, then I'll be the bottom of the barrel."

"So?"

"I'd rather not have my last couple of months in high school be horrible, and you know this." Danielle wished her mother didn't find her peace after she lost everything. She was happy her mother wasn't crying herself to sleep anymore, but she still vied for the luxuries her previous life afforded her.

"You still think social standing means the world?"

Danielle raised an eyebrow. "It's high school. Social standing means everything if you're going to be remembered."

"Once you graduate it won't matter anymore."

"I know that. I'm not going to lose my reputation at school because you decided you wanted to be happy in your own life." Danielle stood up and walked past her mother.

Lily stood up. "I was doing what made me feel proud of myself. I won't apologize for standing up for myself."

Danielle turned to look at her mother. "I'm proud that you became strong, but you could have had an affair like every other housewife."

"There's nothing wrong with being poor!"

Danielle laughed. "Then you really have lost it." Danielle walked away from her mother. She was done with this conversation. She walked into her room where she kept all her fabric on the wall with dress designs. She had her sewing machine in the corner, and she looked up at her prom dress design. She tried her hardest to accept that this was her new life. She had to make amends that she would never have a personal shopper, private car service, or no worries about making sure the bills were paid. She took in a deep breath and tried to calm herself. She focused on sewing her prom dress, because even though she didn't have the money, she still had taste.

We were so proud of you, Danielle. Who would have thought the Queen of fashion and making people feel less than, was one of the people she looked down on? You would continue to make us believe that you had it all, but we knew it was all about to be pulled from under your feet. We hoped you knew how to design a new life for yourself, because we had a feeling The Marked Queen was about to take this one from you.

Chapter 10

Who doesn't love a Johnson Prep Friday night party? It had everything you needed: drugs, alcohol, sex, and scandal. You had to be careful here, or you were going to be the talk of the school on Monday. Jordan Caraway was known around the school as the Queen of the parties. She made sure everyone begged for another. She might not have been a bitch, but she was like every other mean girl. She was looking for love since she didn't get it from the people she really wanted it from. It was perfect that her parents were never home, because she got to host all the parties she wanted. She took the role of hosting the parties when her sister graduated last year. It was the only reason seniors talked to the junior.

Danielle, Delilah, Aman, and Calvin were standing around talking to each other as they watched the social climbers enjoying their taste of royalty. Danielle rolled her eyes as she drank her champagne. She thought it was pathetic to watch the commoners partake in the lines of coke on the table. "You would think they would have the dignity to do that in the bathroom," Danielle said.

Calvin laughed. "Danielle, you shouldn't judge. They're just having fun."

"Whatever." She took a sip and enjoyed the taste. She missed the taste of wealth and class, and she only got it when she came to Jordan's parties.

Aman pulled out his camera. "This would be perfect for the vlog."

Calvin grabbed the front of the camera lens. "The point of these parties is to keep them in this apartment. You know the rules."

"No camera or video." Aman put his camera away. He was trying to think of a new vlog, but he was coming up blank. He knew that he had a deadline soon, and he was completely stuck. Aman, you could always just steal someone else's success. Wasn't that how you got here in the first place?

Danielle turned to see Andrew walk in with Bethany and Tucker. "Why the hell were they invited?" she asked.

Delilah, Aman, and Calvin turned to see who Danielle was talking about. "Doesn't he know that Bethany and Tucker aren't popular?" Delilah asked.

"This is the problem with new kids. They don't know who to stay away from, maybe someone should inform him?" Danielle put her glass down.

Calvin grabbed her arm before she could walk away. "Your bitch is coming out."

"How about I talk to him?" Aman asked. "I need to anyway." He walked away toward Andrew, Bethany, and Tucker.

"Andrew," Aman said, walking up to them.

Andrew looked at Aman. "Hey, what's up?"

"I know you said no, to my idea of doing an interview the first time, but I thought maybe you would reconsider," Aman said.

"Andrew, you shouldn't do it. Aman likes to make everyone a spectacle, and he'll twist anything to make it better for his viewers," Bethany said.

Aman turned to look at Bethany. "You're just mad that you got embarrassed from my prank."

Bethany rolled her eyes. "I need a drink." She grabbed Tucker's drink and they walked away.

Aman turned to look at Andrew. "Everyone in this school is buzzing to find out more about you. What do you say?" Aman asked.

Andrew knew his father brought him here to keep him under the radar, but he thought maybe it would be a good idea. He had nothing else to lose. He thought about what his father said. He could create a new persona for himself, and he would be known for more than just being the recovering drug addict. "Sure, why not?"

Aman smiled. "Perfect." Aman and Andrew started talking about the ideas or topics they would talk about in their vlog.

"It looks like Aman found himself a new friend," Danielle said to Calvin.

Calvin kept his jealousy to a minimum. He knew that Aman only wanted to talk to Andrew for his vlog. He just hated that someone could hit on Aman, and he couldn't say anything about it. It was the drawback of fooling around behind a closed closet door. "It's fine," Calvin said. "I'm going to grab myself a beer."

"Grab me another glass," Danielle said.

"Flynn's over there," Delilah said.

Flynn was the hot nerd, unlike Tucker. Flynn was mysterious, intriguing, sweet, and the perfect man to bring home to mom and dad. He had curly brown hair, a crooked grin, strong jawline, and brown eyes like a puppy. He was the only one at Johnson Prep that had high morals, and he was determined to leave with a path to his dreams. A person without a secret was boring to us, but some people wanted to live mundane lives.

"Go talk to him," Danielle urged.

"About what?"

Danielle rolled her eyes. "I don't know. Maybe about your writing class. You did say you were working on a new short story."

"But he could find that boring," Delilah said. She didn't want Flynn to think all she wanted to talk about was writing. She didn't want to come off as the book nerd. Delilah, you were too sweet. No one saw you as the book nerd. If you wanted to give him a different impression of yourself, we heard you had a great relationship with the principal.

"Just talk to him and stop being stupid." Danielle pushed Delilah toward Flynn.

Delilah sucked it up and walked over to Flynn. Danielle watched as Delilah and Flynn started talking. She smiled because she saw the hearts in their eyes. She remembered when she met Dan for the first time. She would see him in a couple of days once he got back from his vacation.

Calvin walked back over with a drink for Danielle. "Some party, huh?" Calvin asked.

Danielle shrugged. "It's a nice distraction from our daily struggles."

"What do you mean?" he asked.

"Look around. People are talking to each other about bullshit topics. People are doing drugs and drinking alcohol to forget their problems. We're all escaping and trying to be someone different. It's the point of a party. We've all got things to bring us down, but we can cut those ties when we come here," Danielle said.

Calvin smiled when Aman turned around and looked at him. This was one of the few times Aman was able to come out and stay out. "I guess you're right. We do all need an escape from reality."

Too bad the party eventually had to end, and you were brought back to the problems you were escaping. Danielle felt her phone go off. Your time at the party had been cut short. We all hoped you enjoyed your time flying high, but your anchors missed dragging you down.

Danielle pulled out her phone and read the text from a mystery number.

My, my, that's such a cute dress, Danielle. You've always been so secretive about the designer who makes all your outfits. Didn't know his name was JC Penny. It makes sense, truly. Off the rack clothes for an off the rack personality. Don't worry, every Queen needs a peasant, and I've always had a soft spot for you. I would say maybe you'll get the Cinderella ending, but I think a Marie Antoinette one is more your speed. Get your popcorn ready boys and girls, this Queen is about to realize the only kingdom she rules is the trailer park. - The Marked Queen.

Danielle locked her phone and put it away. She grabbed her glass of champagne and took a sip. Enjoy your champagne, because we bet they wouldn't have it in social exile once your secret comes out.

Chapter 11

Aman walked into his house after the party, knowing that he had passed his curfew by two hours. He walked into the living room to see his parents Amara and Taj sitting there reading books. Amara looked up first. "You were supposed to be home two hours ago. We called you several times," Amara said.

"I know. I'm so sorry. I lost track of time." Aman knew his parents wouldn't be pleased with his excuse, but he was trying to savor all the time he could with Calvin. He knew it was harder to see him with baseball season in full swing. He needed all the training with scouts watching him.

Taj slammed his book on the table. "Don't give us any damn excuses. You were supposed to be home a long time ago. We've set these rules in place to protect you."

Aman crossed his arms. "Protect me from what?" He didn't think there was anything wrong with staying out until midnight. He got home safely, and no one tried to attack him.

Amara stood up. She walked over to him. She pulled him into a hug. "You don't get it. You're not like the other kids in your school. You have to remember the world we live in. People instantly hate you because of your race and religion."

Aman looked at his mother and father. "No one has a problem that I'm Indian-Muslim. Who cares if I'm out there having fun? I'm a senior in high school. I should be able to have the same freedoms as my other friends."

"You think you get the luxury of white privilege?" Taj asked. He shook his head. "I thought I raised you better than this. Maybe that YouTube channel is getting to your head."

"I've made money off that channel. I have over four million subscribers, and it's slowly going up."

"Because I paid for them," Taj said. "I thought you would make this a good instrument to start a business. I want you to have training before you go to college. I didn't want it to distract you from your studies, or what's important to you."

"This is important to me," Aman said. He really wished his parents could see that he loved being in front of that camera. He had people who truly loved him commenting all the time. He wanted nothing more than to be a YouTube star.

"The goal is for you to go to business school, find a wife, and make babies. You're our only son. Your sister found a good man, and she's making this family proud. Are you?" Amara asked.

Aman shrugged. "I don't know what else you want from me. I'm trying to give you what you guys ask of me, but I'm trying to live the life I feel like I should be living."

"That's your problem right there. You don't get it that you don't get the same freedoms as your friends," he sighed. "Maybe it was a mistake sending you to Johnson Prep."

Aman shook his head. "I won't be late for my curfew again. I'll keep my grades up. I'll do whatever you guys want me to do. I just don't want to transfer right before graduation." He also didn't want to leave Calvin.

Taj nodded. "Go to your room. We will talk more about this later."

Aman hugged his mother and went up to his room. He sat down in front of his computer. He felt his phone go off. He looked to see that it was a text from Calvin, asking if he could hang out tomorrow since he didn't have practice.

Aman: *I can't hang out. Parents are pissed I stayed out past midnight.*

Aman texted back angrily.

Calvin: *You're eighteen. You're legally an adult. They don't have control over you anymore.*

Aman wished Calvin could understand where he was coming from. He knew dating a white guy would make things difficult. Calvin didn't get why Aman had to keep sneaking around. Calvin was ready to tell the world about their relationship. Calvin would only lose his baseball career, while Aman could lose his family.

Aman: *I'm sorry.*

Calvin sent an angry emoji, and Aman didn't respond. He knew Calvin was upset, but he didn't bother to dive into those emotions at the moment. He took a deep breath, connected his camera into his computer, and he started going through some of the videos from the day. He was hoping he could make a solid video to make himself go trending again.

Yes, why don't you just be loved by the faceless subscribers that you assumed knew you so well? Poor Aman, didn't you understand that no one cared about the pain behind those eyes? We all knew daddy was too busy fronting the bill for your little "career." You had better be ready for the day he found out that his proud son was actually a proud Mary. The Marked Queen did love a good behind the scenes of her subjects, maybe you would be her next piece.

Chapter 12

Young love was something so precious and pure. The smile on the guy's face when he saw the girl of his dream. The girl pushing her hair behind her ear, so she looked innocent. It was the joys of love that we all dreamed we would have ourselves. Johnson Prep was filled with young love, and our newest couple was Delilah and Flynn. We heard they had a grand conversation at Jordan's party on Friday, and they wanted to finish that conversation with some Sunday coffee. Delilah, you were a busy girl. Coffee with a boy and pie with the principal. How do you find the time to keep up your grades…oh wait?

Delilah was going over her short story that she planned to turn in tomorrow at school. She wanted someone's feedback, and she felt connected to Flynn. Sure, she had a crush on him, but he also was the best kid in the class.

Flynn walked in wearing a sweater vest, glasses, and khaki pants. Could this kid be any more of an aspiring artist? We all thought guys in high school were trying to look like jocks, not be beaten up by them. Flynn saw Delilah and smiled. He walked over and sat down in front of her. "Sorry, I'm late. I wasn't expecting the trains to take so long."

She shrugged. Flynn was at Johnson Prep on an academic scholarship. His family lived in Brooklyn, and they both worked in real estate, but they knew Johnson Prep was the school to help him succeed in life. "It's fine. I just was going over my reviews for the short story."

He sat down and ordered himself a coffee. He pulled out a writing notepad and his own story. "Do you want to exchange stories, and we can talk after we're done?"

"Yeah, I would like that." Delilah gave him her story. Delilah was never the girl to get nervous. She wasn't nervous when she gave a speech in front of the whole school on the dangers of drug use. She wasn't nervous when she got caught by her parents sneaking out of the house. Hell, she wasn't even nervous when she went down on Principal Grand for the first time. She felt butterflies in her stomach giving her story to Flynn.

She took his piece, and she started reading. She would look up, time to time, to see his face. She thought it was adorable when he was concentrating, he would pout. She saw his brown eyes and hair, and she wanted to run her fingers through his curls.

She shook her head. She knew he would never go for a girl like her, and she had brought him here so she could improve her writing. The only class she actually had an A in was her creative writing class. She wanted to feel dignified that she was good at something other than swallowing on her knees.

Delilah read Flynn's story about a girl facing her past and deciding if she will stay with the man she's with now, or the man she let go. Delilah was so engrossed with the story, that she completely forgot where she was. She laughed, cried, and rooted for the girl to make the right decision that she was left empty at the end.

She looked up at Flynn who was staring at her. "That's not fair," she said.

"What?" he asked.

"You can't end this story on a cliffhanger. The reader needs satisfaction that she chooses a guy. It's not right that you leave it in the open."

Flynn laughed. "I want people to use their own experiences to think of the person she would choose."

Delilah rolled her eyes. "I think it's the writer being lazy."

Flynn grabbed his paper. "I will not sit here and be attacked for my writing."

Delilah laughed. She knew Flynn was only joking by the twinkle in his eyes. "What did you think of mine?" She asked. She hoped he would like it. She wanted to impress him more than anything else.

"I really enjoyed it. I like the character development with the hint of scandal. I want to know if this girl is going to expose the principal for their affair. I think it's a heroic journey she goes on from being the vapid girl to actually caring." Aw Delilah, you really didn't have to go far for the inspiration of your story, did you? We were pretty sure, you were also not going on some heroic journey. We liked you the way you are now, a vacuous girl with very low dignity.

Delilah smiled. "Thank you. I'm trying to do something more meaningful. Mr. Rozengota wanted us to dive more into our dark side, and I want to play around with that."

"Where did you come up with the idea?" Flynn asked.

Oh Delilah, please do tell him how you came up with the idea. "A writer never tells a person how she got her true inspiration. We all keep it close to our chest."

He nodded. "Yes, we are all fighting for the spotlight."

"I don't want to fight for the spotlight with you. I enjoy bouncing ideas off each other."

"I like my time with you too," Flynn said, which caused Delilah to blush.

They spent the rest of the afternoon throwing ideas back and forth with each other on how to improve their stories.

Delilah felt confident after she walked away from their coffee, more inspired than ever. She wanted to go home right then and write even more. She could feel herself falling for Flynn, because he was honest and good. She hadn't had that in a long time, and he was the first guy to make her believe she could be something.

Delilah needed to be careful who she trusted. She might have assumed Flynn was her partner in the writing world, but she needed to think again. Desperation was the true source of any writer, and they would do anything to see their words published for the world's delight.

Chapter 13

"It was that damn first sip after my mother's funeral," Andrew said. He looked around at the people that were staring at him. "My dad wanted to argue with me about drinking, but he had just lost his wife. He wanted his son to find solace in this tragic day. I was sixteen, and I didn't have her anymore," Andrew said. He tried to keep his composure in a room full of strangers.

He knew he was the youngest at this AA meeting. He had heard all the stories of why alcohol and drugs had ruined their lives. He was blessed that he could bounce back from this. He didn't ruin his life, but he knew deep down, that he let his mother down. He destroyed her image of him, and he was no longer her perfect little boy.

"Why do you think you turned to alcohol?" Demi asked. Demi was the leader of this AA meeting. She had been sober for over ten years. She had long, black hair styled in a couple of long braids. She had a sleeve of tattoos. She was an artist, and she took to alcohol and drugs after a bad break up. She saw Andrew, and she instantly wanted to take him under her wing.

"I think because I wondered why my mother enjoyed it so much." Andrew laughed. "She had liver cancer. She always had a glass of wine at dinner, she would be hungover too many times to count."

"Do you think your mother was an alcoholic?" Demi asked.

Andrew looked at her. He didn't want to admit it to a room full of strangers, but this was where he felt most safe. "I truly believe that maybe she was."

"When did it become more of a problem?" she asked.

"For me or her?"

"She's gone now, so we need to focus on you."

"I think when I got drunk that night. I didn't cry anymore. I felt free in those moments. I could understand why she chased after this magical liquid. I understood why she truly believed that she needed to escape." Andrew hated his mother for so many months as she was dying. He wanted nothing to do with her. He remembered always blaming her for causing so much pain in this family.

"Is that what you were doing?" Demi asked. "Were you trying to escape from it all?"

Andrew looked around. He felt the tears start to fall from his eyes. "I hated her. I told her so many times she should have been strong enough to fight off her desires. Was I not good enough to put down the bottle?" Andrew looked at Demi for the answers. "Was I not worth it?"

Demi got up and walked over to sit in front of Andrew. She grabbed his hand and squeezed it. "You now know that she couldn't be strong enough. It's a disease, and she couldn't fight it."

He shook his head and laughed. "I feel the opposite. I was strong enough to quit. I saw that my father was completely destroyed by my habit. Do you understand how many nights he had to call 911 on me? Do you understand the look of sheer worry he had when they had to pump my stomach? He thought he lost me," Andrew said.

"But you made it out stronger."

Andrew looked up at the ceiling. "But I kept doing it. I kept enjoying the bottle without giving a fuck."

"What was your turning point?" Demi asked. "What made you start to get sober?"

Andrew looked at her. "I'm not ready to talk about it," he said. "I want to keep some things to myself."

She nodded. She got up and walked back over to her seat. She smiled. "I think that's enough progress for today." She turned to look at the rest of the group. "I think we've all made enough progress for the day. We will meet up again next week. I hope you guys live a good week, and I'm only one phone call away."

They all started to get up and walk toward the door. Andrew grabbed his jacket, when Demi walked over to him. "I'm impressed with how open you were today. Not a lot of people would breakdown to a room full of strangers."

Andrew smiled. "I think it's the first time that I actually felt free. These people didn't know me when I was at my worst."

"But, they understand when you hit rock bottom. We've all had to eventually share that moment in here. We hope you share yours too."

Andrew nodded. "I'll eventually tell that story. I just don't think I'm strong enough yet."

Demi opened her arms, so that he could get a hug. He welcomed it. He exhaled the breath he was holding in, and it felt so damn good to just connect with a human. "How's your new school going?" she asked.

"People try their hardest to keep the real them from the world's stage."

"Will you?" she asked.

He shrugged. He felt his phone go off. He looked to see it was Aman wondering when they would meet to do the interview. "I just want people to know me in a different light."

Demi smiled. "You shouldn't be ashamed of the person you are. We've all made our share of mistakes, but people will understand."

"I don't think people at my school are as forgiving."

Demi nodded. "Have faith in people," she said. She walked away to talk to other people about this week's meeting. He looked at his phone, and he texted about a meeting on Tuesday. He would revamp his image, and he would keep his past close to his chest.

Andrew, we all wished you were the moral compass of this story. We wanted you to make it okay to share your secrets, but you took the easy road out. You were going to protect your secrets, and you would do anything to do that. You should have learned by now that people's secrets controlled them, and The Marked Queen used that to her advantage. We hoped you enjoyed strings attached to your body, because you just adopted a puppet master.

Chapter 14

Jordan came storming up to Danielle and slammed a piece of paper into Danielle's chest. Jordan's dirty blonde hair was pulled into a ponytail, her blue eyes were covered in shame behind her glasses. "You need to stop this, bitch."

Danielle grabbed the piece of paper and looked at it. She knew Jordan was the guest appearance on The Marked Day Show. She didn't care to read about someone's gossip, but she was interested in what The Marked Queen figured out about Jordan.

Sorry, I was away. Sometimes you have to recharge from a long week of scandals and sluts. Don't worry boys and girls, I wasn't going to throw in the towel just yet. I heard some delicious gossip as I was shopping this weekend. Who knew that Jordan enjoyed some time with the football team? If you thought she was the Queen of the party, you have no idea how far she'll go to entertain her guests. Maybe this Queen should learn the value of a locked door. Too bad for her, the morals and dignity she tries to project were tarnished after the second-string quarterback had his own turn playing with her end zone. Don't worry about it, Jordan. We know how much you love chasing pills with booze. This time the pill will just start with the letter b. -The Marked Queen.

Danielle laughed when she stopped. "I told you to stop having sessions with the football team during your fucking parties. You knew damn well The Marked Queen was going to find out."

Jordan crossed her arms. “I’m not going to be slut-shamed because I love having a good time. Besides, we were safe. I’m not fucking stupid. You going to do anything about this?”

“I can’t. She’s got shit on me, and you know it. We’re all fucking puppets.”

Jordan laughed. “I never thought I’d see the day when Danielle Tyler would be scared of a bitch.”

“I’m not scared of her. I’m scared of the shit she has on me.”

Jordan raised an eyebrow. “I’m curious what those secrets are.”

Danielle knew Jordan was all bark, no bite. She will be over this once she has her next scrimmage with the football team later. She might even get another team to sponsor her next. “Aren’t we all.” Danielle felt her phone go off. It was a message from Dan saying he was waiting for her at the playground.

“I need to go. I have an appointment that I can’t miss. Good luck with all the drama.” She walked away from Jordan, because she had nothing else to talk to her about.

****

“You’re oddly quiet over there,” Dan said, as they were sitting on the swings together. Dan was your fly-under-the-radar, attractive. He had a buzzcut, strong bone structure, freckles, and hazel eyes that changed from blue to green from time to time.

Danielle turned and smiled at Dan. “Sorry, I just have a lot on my mind. The Marked Queen struck again, and I can’t get her out of my head.”

Dan nodded. “You don’t want her to find out about us.”

“Because I don’t want the fucking world to judge us.”

"Judge us or you?" Dan asked. Dan had always questioned their relationship. They started dating a couple of months back when he moved to the neighborhood. He knew she was still in high school, and he was a sophomore in college. She told him that she came from wealth, but they lost it once her parents decided to divorce.

She didn't look at him because she would begin to cry. "I've always hated that we were poor. I lived a life filled with the choices of whatever I wanted for myself. My mom chose her happiness over options. I never could understand that."

"What about me?" Dan asked.

She finally looked over at him. "You're the only thing in this world that makes me feel rich and comfortable. I never want to lose you in my life. You're this incredible, attractive, and sweet guy that fell for me. I can't be more grateful than right now."

He got up and leaned down in front of her. He captured her lips with his, and they felt the magic in this kiss. Danielle forgot all about her poverty, The Marked Queen, and her parent's divorce. In this kiss, she only cared about Dan, and she could live with her struggles for a couple more minutes.

"Did that help?" he asked.

"Yes, it did."

"See, you don't need money to be happy," Dan said. He came from a big family, and he grew accustomed to having no money. He had to work since he was fifteen to get anything he wanted, and he wanted Danielle to understand that she didn't need wealth to find joy in life.

You couldn't make this shit up. Dan, are you seriously that stupid? This was New York City, and she was the social Queen of Johnson Prep. Of course, she needed money to find joy in her life. She couldn't control her peasants, if she actually was one.

Danielle, you should have found someone a bit smarter than the jester.

Chapter 15

"You're so fucking worthless," George said, as he slapped Jasmine across the face. "If your mother was here, she would be ashamed of you." George was disgusted that Jasmine was his daughter. His ex-wife, Kelly, was beautiful, smart, and ambitious. He saw none of those traits in Jasmine.

Jasmine grabbed her face. "What do you want from me? I'm keeping up my grades. I've tried to stay as thin as I could, and I'm trying to make you love me like you loved mom."

George was fed up with his daughter's failed ambition. He slapped her again. "You'll never be her."

"But you want me to be. She left us, dad."

George shook his head. "No, she left you," George raged. He turned to walk out of the room. He didn't care that it was eight in the morning. He was going to take the day off and have himself a scotch.

Jasmine had been dealing with her father's grief since her mother walked out of the door two and a half years ago. She had enough of this life with her father, and she needed space. She was currently in Europe living her best life. She sent Jasmine postcards all of the time, and she knew once she graduated, she would join her mother in Europe.

Jasmine walked over to the mirror. Her face was red, and she applied make-up. She was hoping the swelling would go away by the time she got to school. She put on a happy smile, because she wouldn't let her enemies see her like this.

Did Jasmine really think people would love a child abuse case? Kids at Johnson Prep wanted a bitch, not a sob story. You could apply all the make-up you wanted, but we all knew the truth. You were nothing more than a punching bag. It was tragic when the weak tried to be the Queen. Why didn't you sit down for this one, Jasmine? We only wanted tears from your enemies, not yourself.

Jasmine walked into the school with glasses on, and she tried to keep her composure with her best resting bitch face she could create. She saw Susan walk up to her. "Calvin and Danielle are talking. You might want to get in there," Susan said.

Jasmine took off her glasses and smiled. "We know they're friends. I have nothing to worry about."

Susan looked at Jasmine like she doubted her. "I don't know. They seem cozy."

Jasmine looked at her dumbass of a minion. "Are you trying to piss me off today?"

Susan shook her head. "No, I'm just trying to keep you aware."

Jasmine grabbed Susan's hand and squeezed it as hard as she could. It was a move she learned from her father. "Don't you dare think I have any competition." Jasmine raised an eyebrow. "Do you understand?"

Susan felt the pain in her arm, and she wanted Jasmine to let go. "Yes."

Jasmine smiled. "Good." She didn't wait for Susan. She walked past her toward Calvin and Danielle.

"Calvin, you look cute as ever today," Jasmine said, with a smile.

Before Calvin could respond, Danielle jumped in, deciding to have a little fun. Danielle crossed her arms, "Don't you have some other boy to harass?"

Jasmine turned to Danielle. "Shouldn't you fix your make-up?"

Danielle smiled. "I don't know, but I do know how to blend, though."

Calvin raised his hand. He knew Danielle and Jasmine were having a pissing contest, but he didn't want there to be a fight. "Thank you, Jasmine. I like that dress on you."

Jasmine smiled. "You should see what's underneath." She winked.

Calvin felt uncomfortable, and he didn't know how to respond. He was grateful Danielle was laughing. "I can't with this conversation." She grabbed Calvin's hand. "Let's leave before her thirsty ass tries to dry hump you here," Danielle snarled as she and Calvin walked away.

Jasmine smiled. She saw the sheer horror on Calvin's face, and she knew it was because she wasn't as beautiful as her mother. She turned to see Susan standing there. "I'm so sorry," Susan said.

Jasmine kept her emotions in check. "I'm fine. I just need to use the bathroom." She wouldn't let lower-class Susan see her cry. She walked into the bathroom and saw that no one was in there. She went into one of the stalls where she bent in front of the toilet, and put two fingers in her mouth. She needed a release, and this was the only way she could make herself feel better.

She puked as much as she could get out. She knew once she lost the weight, then she would get Calvin and her father to love her. She walked out of the bathroom and made sure she cleaned up after herself. She wanted no one to know her extracurricular activity.

She walked over to her locker and opened it to see a note that she wished she could have skipped. She saw the red handwriting, and it was from the one bitch they all feared. She opened the note and read it.

I'm worried about you. I saw a little throw up on your skirt the other day. I get it. When your muffin top is showing, you need to get rid of it. Poor you, maybe trying to be the bitch of the school has you eating your guilt? Don't worry, your secret is safe with me. I would have given you a cupcake with this note to make me look less heartless, but I thought your fat ass might have enjoyed it too much. – The Marked Queen.

Jasmine crumbled up the note and threw it in her locker. She wouldn't let this bitch get the best of her. She would be pretty, and she would be loved. She wouldn't fucking let anyone take this away from her.

Jasmine, we knew you were going to be the Queen of the cafeteria. We heard you do love yourself some cupcakes, so why not try focusing your energy on something you were good at? We get the appeal of being pretty and popular, but that was not in the cards for you. What we meant was, you have the gene to be fat and a loser, it was why your father beat you, and your mother left.

Chapter 16

Andrew was looking around in Aman's room while Aman was setting up his webcam, so they could start their interview. Aman needed a good video, because his father was getting concerned with his lack of views. He was getting some sponsors, but he wasn't making enough from YouTube. He needed a viral video, or even one that was trending. He was hoping this would give him the step in the right direction. He knew everyone at Johnson Prep was curious about Andrew, and he would milk it.

"You seem close to Calvin," Andrew said. He saw a bunch of pictures of them together.

Aman got nervous for a second. He didn't look at Andrew. "He's my best friend."

Andrew nodded. "You went to the Streamy's?" He was surprised that he knew someone that went to an award show.

"Yeah, they invited me because I've been gaining attention on my videos." The truth was, his father pulled strings to get him there. He thought he could network with other stars, but none of them wanted to work with Aman. Must be hard to find friends when you ripped off a lot of their ideas.

"The camera is ready, if you still wanted to do this," Aman said.

Andrew took a seat in front of Aman. "And your parents are okay with this?" he asked.

Aman looked at him weirdly. "What do you mean?"

"With you trying to be an Internet celebrity."

"What's with all the questions about my life?" Aman asked, growing frustrated.

Andrew shrugged. "I don't know a lot of people here, and I'm trying to make friends. I only have Tucker and Bethany. You're about to dive into my personal life. I can't dive into yours?"

Aman smiled. "You should learn that at Johnson Prep, there is a small amount of privacy. You don't expose all your demons for the world to see."

Andrew was the one that looked at him weirdly. "Why not?"

"No one likes when you're vulnerable here." Aman turned and pressed record. "Hey, everyone. I hope you're having a great week so far. I wanted to do something different this week around," he began to say. "I had the idea that I would interview interesting people in my life, and the new people that entered my orbit." He turned to Andrew. "I'm here with Andrew Daniels. He is the newest member of our school, and I thought it would be cool to see what he's all about." Aman got this idea from Shannon David. She had a whole segment about getting random strangers off the street and interviewing them. She believed that everyone influences your life, and it was perceived extremely well.

Aman pulled up the same questions that Shannon asked the random strangers, but twisted them so they weren't exactly the same as hers. "How are you liking Johnson Prep so far?" Aman asked.

Andrew felt weird being in front of a camera. He didn't know if he should look at Aman or the camera. He felt like this was instantly a huge mistake, and he wanted to stop it. He closed his eyes and took a breath. He knew that he wanted to do this for people to get to know him. He liked Tucker and Bethany, but he wanted more friends.

"It's interesting, to say the least. People are friendly, but they seem to always be bitching each other out, or arguing and competing to see who can do it best."

Aman laughed. "We're known for starting wars. Everyone wants to be on top."

Andrew smiled. "I guess being part of Johnson Prep royalty has its perks. I see these beautiful people walk up and down these halls, and it's something magnificent."

"You didn't have these back in Maryland?" Aman asked. He did some digging on Andrew before their interview.

Andrew shook his head. "I come from wealth because of my father, but we tried to keep it modest. I envy everyone here, because they're proud to show off their money. They aren't ashamed of people judging them. It seems everyone here has a fuck-it attitude, and I can respect that."

"So, what brought you to New York City?" Aman asked.

Andrew knew this question was coming. "My father got a new job here, and he wanted me to get a taste of the city life. He didn't want me to be sheltered," Andrew laughed, as she spoke the last part.

"You haven't talked to me about your mom a lot. Where is she?" he asked.

He thought about what Aman said. He didn't want the whole world to know the story about his mother. "She travels a lot for work, so it's pretty much just my dad and I. We skype my mom all the time, but it's hard with the time differences," Andrew said.

Andrew, this was where it all went downhill for you. We understood the appeal to be liked by your classmates, but would you love your reflection?

They continued their conversation about activities Andrew was into, and how he actually loved photography, and was hoping to be a National Geographic photographer one day. Aman thought it was cool, and people would eat it up. "Guys, I hate to cut this interview short, but that's all the time we have today. Andrew, thank you so much for being here."

"Thank you for having me."

Aman turned to look at the camera. "If you liked this video, hit the thumbs up button and subscribe to my channel. I'll see you all for another day in my life." Aman waved before he cut the record button. Aman turned to Andrew. "That was actually pretty impressive."

Andrew smiled. "I guess I'm a natural in front of the camera."

"You got weirded out by the mom question, though." Aman looked at Andrew. He felt like there was more to the story.

"You got weirded out by the Calvin question," Andrew shot back.

"There's nothing to tell with Calvin," Aman said. He knew that Andrew didn't buy it, and he prayed their secret wasn't blown.

"Same with my mom."

Aman nodded. He stood up. "Thanks again for doing the video. I should have it up by tomorrow. I don't have much homework, and my parents have a business dinner." He wanted to spend tonight with Calvin, but he was at an away game. Aman's parents hated the idea of him going out of the city without them, so he was stuck on what he called, "house arrest."

"I can't wait to see it."

"Remember people will now know your name," Aman said.

That was what Andrew was hoping for. "Can't wait," Andrew said, walking toward the door. Andrew, you should be scared about the attention you were going to receive. You might think all your secrets were going to stay in the closet, but you were wrong. You better make sure that closet is double bolted, because we have a feeling everyone would be dying to break in.

Chapter 17

It looked like Johnson Prep had a new king in town. People flocked to Aman's new video, curious about who Andrew was. Andrew walked into school, and he was bombarded by stares, whispers, and the lovely fuck-me glances. Andrew hadn't had this much attention since he got his DUI-- but he liked these stares better.

He saw Aman talking to Calvin, and he was still curious about how close they were. He had friends back in Maryland, but he didn't plaster photos of them all over his wall. He didn't want to think too much into it, because he was busy joining the royal court.

He walked into the photography room to see how his photos from yesterday had turned out. It was his one place of peace, because he knew that he once he was on the radar, it wasn't going to be the same. He saw Bethany and Tucker looking at something on Tucker's phone. He could hear his voice, and he assumed they were watching his interview.

Tucker looked up and seemed upset. "Why would you do an interview with Aman?"

Andrew shrugged. "He asked me, and I didn't see the harm in it. What's the big deal?"

Bethany rolled her eyes. "The big deal is, now you're going to be popular and leave us behind."

Andrew was hurt by this. He wasn't planning to leave Tucker or Bethany in the dust. Yes, he indulged in the fact that people were talking about him, but these were his two friends. Oh, Andrew, you wanted to be loved by the masses. You had better dump the dead wallflowers, or your fifteen minutes of fame would end real quick.

He crossed his arms. "I'm glad you guys think so highly of me."

"You kept your life private from us, but you spill it out for the world to see," Tucker said.

Andrew was getting frustrated. He didn't see what the big deal was. All he did was answer a few questions for a stupid interview. "I lied in that interview. My mom isn't away on business. She's dead," he rushed out.

Bethany looked at him with sorrowful eyes. "Why lie?"

"Because I want to keep some things in my life private. Are you two open about everything in yours?" he asked, eyeing them both carefully.

They looked at each other, then back at him. "Yes, because I have nothing to hide," Tucker said.

"It must be nice to not worry about your skeletons," Andrew said sarcastically.

"They wouldn't be skeletons if you were open and honest about them," Bethany argued.

"I don't want to be known as the kid with the dead mom." Andrew was getting tired of this back and forth. He wanted nothing more than to forget about this whole damn thing. He was happy with the interview, and he wanted people to get to know the person he was trying to perceive. We were proud of Andrew. In two weeks, he had learned to create a character everyone would enjoy. No one liked the real you, because this school only felt betrayal, lust, and the need to backstab.

Bethany shook her head. "Who cares what people think of you? It's what I hate about this school. People are so busy worrying about their fucking image. I know people don't like me, and I love it," she exclaimed as she grabbed her stuff. "I have a prom committee meeting I need to get to."

"Are you seriously judging me because I decided to give an interview, and kept some things a secret?" Andrew asked.

Bethany turned. "Yes."

"Then you're no better than the people you hate. I have received nothing but kindness from them, while you're sitting here attacking me. Maybe you're worse than them."

"No one is worse than the people you idolize. Haven't you seen what The Marked Queen has posted about them? They think they're better than all of us, but we get to see their true colors," Bethany said.

"And you're relishing it?" Andrew asked. He was starting to see a side of Bethany that he didn't like.

"Someone's got to show them for who they are. I would be careful, because you don't want to get on her bad side," Tucker said, and walked toward Bethany.

"Whose?"

"The Marked Queen," they both said.

"I'm not scared of her. She won't find out my secrets, and I'm not planning to spill them out," Andrew said. He knew to keep it simple, and he wasn't trying to piss anyone off.

They didn't say anything as they walked out the door. Andrew, you were so naïve, that it was adorable. How many warnings did you need, before you realized you were playing right into The Marked Queen's hands? You had better enjoy this moment on the top, because we were all rooting for the rock bottom. The game had just gotten more interesting with the new kid entering the ring. The only remaining question we had was, who would he backstab to keep his secrets safe?

Chapter 18

"Your new video is doing well. It has over one hundred thousand views," Calvin said, as he lay in Aman's bed.

"It's not that impressive for two days. I need to think of a new angle for the next video. I have to make sure my next video is good, or my dad's going to stop helping me out," Aman said.

"Really?" Calvin asked. He turned to look at his boyfriend. "You will always have me as your number one fan."

Aman rolled his eyes. He leaned forward and kissed him quickly on the lips. Calvin wrapped his hands around Aman and Aman grabbed his hands. "Calvin, we can't."

Calvin groaned. "We could have gone to my house. My parents aren't home."

"Well, my parents didn't want me to go out. They're picking up food, because some of my dad's friends are coming over for dinner."

"You always have to be the good son, don't you?" Calvin asked.

Aman gave him a weak smile. "I have to do what they want me to do. I don't get a say in my life. I was lucky that my dad let me do my YouTube channel."

"But that's not a life to live," Calvin said. "You should be able to do whatever you want. You guys came here from India to give you a better life. Don't they get that?"

Aman laughed. "You truly think that I get the same luxuries as you in this world? Calvin, I'm not lucky like you. I know damn well my parents will never accept me being in love with another man. I won't be able to have the whole world of options like you."

"My dad wants me to be a baseball player," Andrew tried to argue.

"He wants you to do it until you find out what you want to do with your life. It's your safety net. Your dad is being realistic. My dad wants me to follow him in business. It's not my safety net, it's my prison sentence."

Calvin got up and pulled Aman into a hug. He knew Aman hated when they were intimate like this, but he wanted to hug his boyfriend. He didn't give a damn if it was risky. "You know that I'll never stop loving you."

Aman looked up. "I know that, but sometimes it isn't enough."

"So, what are we doing here?" Calvin asked. "We plan to be together. We wanted kids and a future. We're we just playing house then?" Calvin wanted to make sure that they weren't wasting each other's time. Yes, they were in high school, but Calvin wanted to end his life with Aman.

Aman sighed. "I can't promise you a timeline. Yes, I want those things, but I want them eventually. It kills me being with you, because I can't give you everything you want. This isn't a normal relationship, and I don't know if it will ever be."

Calvin leaned forward and kissed him on the lips. Aman broke it up quickly, but they had a moment to truly cherish it. "I don't want you to believe that I expect normal with you. I'm with you because I love you. If I wanted easy, then I would be with a girl. You know that it's hard sneaking around with you."

"But we both have to keep our image intact." Aman walked over and started looking at other videos for inspiration.

Calvin sighed as he sat down on Aman's bed. He started texting Danielle about feeling lost, he was so over having to hide who he was. He got that he was the big baseball star, and that he couldn't be gay. He wanted to scream and get out of this cage. He was tired of people hitting on him. He wanted to wrap his arms around Aman, and tell everyone that he was in love.

Aman turned and looked at Calvin. He saw that he was in his rabbit hole. It killed him that he couldn't be as strong as Calvin. He knew that Calvin saw the beauty in the world, but Aman was being realistic. His parents didn't support homosexuality, and he would be disgracing his family.

Aman got up and kissed Calvin on the lips. He kneeled down in front of him. He knew that he needed to bring Calvin back to reality. "We will run away from New York. We can go wherever you want. We will have the life that we planned to have together."

"I don't know if I want to run away," Calvin said. They would still be putting up a charade in a different city. He just wanted them to be honest with themselves and each other.

"It's the best we will have as a couple," Aman said.

Calvin grabbed Aman's hand. He intertwined their fingers. "I want you to come out, but I'll never force you to. I just want you to realize what we could have."

"And I need you to realize that I'm not as strong, or as a lucky as you are. This be an issue in our relationship. You truly need to accept me for all of this, or we won't work together."

Calvin didn't want to lose Aman, so he kept his mouth shut. He just nodded. "Okay."

"I love you," Aman said.

"I love you, too." Calvin didn't have the same emotion in his voice as Aman did. Calvin, we understood why you were upset about the fact that you needed to hide your relationship. It looked like you were the only one that wanted your secrets to be spilled for the whole world to see. Calvin, you should have been careful about what you desired. It could all blow up in your face, and The Marked Queen didn't do heartfelt. Calvin, you had better enjoy all those sweet moments, because we had a feeling it was about to turn sour.

Chapter 19

Delilah was currently in the dining room going over the final revisions of her new short story when her mother, Erika, walked in. She saw her daughter looking over her story. She worried that Delilah would be nothing more than an insipid girl, and she was proud she found something to be passionate about. Erika, you should have thought again. We heard your daughter enjoyed being in a scandal as much as writing one.

"How's the story coming along?" Erika asked, grabbing a cup of coffee while sitting next to her.

Delilah sighed and ran her fingers through her hair. "I just don't know if the ending is going to work. I know that it flows, but maybe I should rearrange it."

Erika reached across the table and squeezed her hand. "You know we have editors in the publishing world. Why don't we send it to them?"

Delilah shook her head. "Mom, I want to do this on my own. I get you and dad are writers, but this is something I want to do for myself."

Erika shook her head. "We're giving you a way to be successful."

"Don't you believe that I can do this on my own?" Delilah asked. Her parents were thrilled when she wrote her first story. Her brother decided he would be a doctor, and he was off in medical school.

"I don't want you to have heartbreak. Your father and I have made a name for ourselves, and we can use that power to help you."

Delilah shook her head. "You don't think I'm good enough. Why should I be surprised?" Delilah stood up.

Erika took a sip of her coffee. "You should leave the dramatics for your work. I'm being honest with you."

"Do you think that I can't make it on my own?" Delilah asked again.

"We don't think you can handle rejection," Erika said. They had read some of Delilah's work, and they were impressed. They thought she had the potential to be an excellent writer, but she needed time to get there.

"I have a thick skin."

"It's not about having a thick skin. It's realizing when your time will come. You've always tried to prove your worth since you were a little girl."

"Because I'm not some idiotic girl," Delilah said. She knew she was just the pretty daughter growing up. She wanted to play sports and read books, but she was forced to do pageants. She knew her parents were more focused on her looks than her smarts.

"No one said that," her mom argued.

"But, you were worried when I decided to be a writer."

"We were thrilled you became a writer. We were surprised. We won't lie. We honestly thought it would have been Ethan, but he decided to become a doctor."

"Because you think he's smarter and has the potential," Delilah said. She knew her mother was trying to sugar coat the truth right now, and she was sick of it.

"Delilah, your grades aren't the best in the world. You're going to be barely graduating from high school. We had to pull strings to get your application selected at Columbia. Why not let us pull strings again?"

Delilah laughed. "I thought this would have been the one thing you guys would be proud of me for. I thought you guys would see me as something, other than some moronic child."

"We just don't think your book smart."

Delilah slammed the papers down. "I don't need to be book smart to write. You both had a tough time getting things published. You've made a name for yourselves. I want to do that myself. I don't want to use you guys to get there."

"You're not being smart. Use what you have around you."

"Because, god forbid, I have to do something the hard way." She felt her phone go off. It was Flynn asking if they wanted to meet before class. "I need to get to school."

Delilah tried to walk past her mother, but her mom grabbed her wrist. "We love you so damn much. We want nothing more than for you to succeed. I pray you to remember that."

Delilah didn't say anything. She walked upstairs and closed the door. She walked into the bathroom and locked that door, too. She took in a deep breath. She felt a lot of emotions coursing through her right now, and she needed to get it out somehow.

She opened the drawer to her sink. She lifted up her make-up bag to reveal a blade. She took in a deep breath, before dragging the blade across her skin with some pressure. She felt the pain and saw the blood pour out. She felt the release in that second. She felt the thoughts of a worthlessness escape.

She grabbed a tissue paper and started to apply pressure to make the bleeding stop. She fixed her hair and grabbed a bracelet to cover up the cut. She looked herself in the mirror. She wanted to feel like she could be more than a dumb whore.

Delilah, we didn't want you to cut yourself or even have thoughts of suicide. Well then again, we didn't think you were smart enough to pull it off. We did pray that you understood that it was okay to be the brainless bitch that no one valued. It was what you were the Queen of. Please, we hoped you took this small piece of advice to heart, you were going to be nothing more than a Stepford Wife. We heard you were good on your knees, now we just needed you to learn how to bake an apple pie.

Chapter 20

"Can I grab you something to eat?" Danielle asked, looking at the guy sitting in the booth. She couldn't tell who it was, because he had the menu hiding his face.

Andrew put the menu down and looked at Danielle. "Danielle? What are you doing here?" he asked.

Danielle's heart dropped. She hadn't expected to see anyone from school here. It's why she worked in the Bronx. She knew she could make more money on The Upper East Side, but she knew people would catch her.

Danielle, it was New York City after all. This might have had seemed like a big city, but it was more of a small town when you tried to hide. You kept your dirty little secret out in the open, and now you were caught. The only question we're going to ask is, how you planned to get out of this one?

"I work here from time to time. My dad thinks it's good for me to work, so that it humbles me," she paused. "What are you doing here?" she asked.

"I just wanted to come to a different part of the city." Andrew had just gotten out of another AA meeting, and he was starving. It was late at night, and this was the only place that he could find to come to eat.

She raised an eyebrow and took a seat across from him. "So, you come to the Bronx?" She leaned forward. "I'm going to call bullshit."

He smirked and leaned forward himself. "I'll tell the truth, if you tell the truth."

She leaned back and crossed her arms. "Exposing each other's secrets. Do you think that's smart?"

"If you expose me, then I expose you. I know how much everyone likes to put on a happy front. We've all got skeletons in the closet that we're trying to hide."

"I thought you were so open in your interview with Aman," she said.

"And I thought you were a rich girl. I guess we both were lying," he said.

She laughed. "It looks like the new kid learned his way around the school."

He took a sip of his coffee. "Or, I come from a small town, and I figured out pretty quickly how to make my front porch look nice, while my backyard is a mess."

She nodded. She didn't know Andrew, but she felt drawn to him. She didn't find any romantic feelings for him, but she wanted another friend she could trust. Calvin and she grew up together, and knew everything about each other. She wouldn't mind having someone else in her corner if the times got tough.

She looked down at her fingers. "My mom left my dad a few years back. She was tired in the marriage, because he was violent and always cheated on her. He also had the money in the family, while my mom was a housewife. In their prenup, it said if she left, then she wouldn't get anything except a small fraction for expenses."

"And, I'm assuming it wasn't much."

Danielle laughed. "It was a hundred thousand dollars. He still pays for my schooling and gives me an allowance, but it isn't much."

"So, why work here?" Andrew asked.

"I have to keep up appearances. I buy fabric to make all my clothes and buy thrifted purses. People think I'm some rich girl, but I'm probably the poorest," she laughed. "I have to keep my grades up, so my dad keeps paying my tuition."

He nodded. "Not some spoiled rich girl that the school thinks you are." Andrew was impressed that Danielle could have kept this secret up for this long. It made him see her in a different light. He thought that people at Johnson Prep didn't go through struggles, and it was nice that he was wrong.

"So, what about you?" she asked, smirking.

"I came here for AA," Andrew said. He knew that he was nervous to tell her the truth, but she spilled her secrets, so he could do the same.

"You're an alcoholic? What? Community service?"

Andrew laughed. "I wish I could say that it's community service, but my mom died over a year ago. She was an alcoholic herself, and she was diagnosed with liver cancer. She continued to drink until it took over, and I never could get over it." Andrew felt the emotions building up.

Danielle reached across the table and squeezed his hand. "It must have been hard, and I'm not going to sit here and act like I know what you're going through."

Andrew was grateful for that. He was tired of people trying to connect with his pain. He knew no one could understand what he had been through, except maybe for Demi. He was grateful for her in his life, and she was becoming his rock.

"I drank to see what the magic of alcohol was, and then I drank to forget. I wasn't the best person, and my father was destroyed when he saw me get my stomach pumped numerous times." He looked down at his coffee. "I wish I had been stronger. I wish I didn't indulge."

"You learned your lesson, and you're stronger for it now. You can't fault yourself for the past mistakes."

He nodded. "Let's hope that this city doesn't turn me into someone I won't like."

"Stick around good people, and you won't." Danielle knew that it was her mission to bring Andrew into the fold. She wanted to protect him, and she was praying that he would let her.

Andrew and Danielle got along so well. Too bad Andrew, we wanted you to turn into someone you didn't like. This was Johnson Prep, and god, did the people from the audience love a good shit show. You might have wanted to act like you were strong enough, but we had a feeling you were going to hit rock bottom soon enough. Danielle, you could be the best friend all you wanted, but what would happen if The Marked Queen found out? What was more important to you; image or friendship?

Chapter 21

Jasmine had her headphones in as she ran across the track. She knew her father would be home soon, and she wasn't ready to deal with his violent tendencies just yet. She felt free with the music blasting in her ears. She didn't have anyone calling her fat, pathetic, a reject, or worthless. Those were the best compliments she had ever received.

She didn't notice that someone had been running next to her. She turned to see this Hispanic guy, with facial hair, brown eyes, and shaggy black hair running next to her. She stopped, and he copied. She took off her headphones. "Can I help you?"

He smiled. "I thought I would run with you. You're pretty fast, and I need to get ready for my match."

She looked at him strangely. "Who are you?" she asked. She tried to remember if she had seen him in the hallways of the school before.

"I'm Carter. We have biology together."

She tried to go through who was in her biology class, but she knew Calvin was in that class. She sat behind him, and she tried every class to find a way to talk to him. "I'm sorry that I haven't noticed you."

He laughed, and she liked his laugh, oddly enough. "I sit in the back of the class. I usually keep to myself, because I don't know a lot of people here."

"Did you transfer in?"

He shrugged. "Coming from a family that isn't extremely wealthy, I'm not on anyone's radar."

"How can you afford Johnson Prep?" she asked. "Are you here on a scholarship?"

"My parents live a comfortable life. We just live in Brooklyn, and we don't flaunt the money we have. Yes, I was offered a scholarship to be on the track team here, though."

"Do you come to any of the parties?" Jasmine asked. She thought that Carter was attractive, but she was worried his social standing wouldn't help her. She was trying to be the Queen of the school. She needed a prince on her arm, not a toad.

"I've never been invited to any of them. It's fine, though. I get that I don't fit in with a lot of these social settings. I watch all the popular kids have the thrill of high school," he said, with such disdain. He believed that all the superrich kids thought they were better than everyone else.

She crossed her arms. "I'm friends with a lot of those popular kids. It sounds like you look down on us."

"I only look down, because you guys do the same to me."

She shook her head. "Trust me, I'm not as shallow as they are." Really, Jasmine? You weren't shallow? Aren't you at the track right now because you were trying to lose your gluttony gut? You should have been proud of your curves, maybe then, someone would have overlooked your shitty personality.

"You didn't know who I was. I see you in biology all over Calvin. He's the hot, wealthy, and popular guy in school. Isn't it all social standing with you guys? You're just trying to be the ruler of this school."

"There's nothing wrong with power. Maybe you should try it sometime," Jasmine said. She shouldn't be bashed for wanting to make it in this world.

"You do know that this all will fade once school is over. People won't care down the road."

She gave him a weak smile. "These are traits that you can take into the real world. Do you think the nice kids of the school got anywhere in life? Once you leave these halls, it doesn't get better. You need to have thick skin, determination, and have the ability to backstab when necessary."

Carter raised an eyebrow. "Sounds like you have a cynical view of the world."

"More like a realistic one. I'm not going to be ashamed of the world that I try to thrive in. I want to go out into the world and be a badass bitch." You were going to need to stop being the sob story, to be the badass bitch. It was just a slight suggestion, Pathetic Queen.

"What do you want to do with your life?" Carter now was interested in her. He thought she was beautiful, but he didn't know about her personality. Now, he wanted to know more about this spitfire.

"A lawyer. My father is one." She remembered growing up and going into his office looking over cases. He would bring her to court, and she was in awe when she watched him perform. She knew it was what she wanted to do with her life. It was the only thing she and her father connected on.

"We all need a good lawyer."

"And you?" she asked.

"IT or software," he said. He stepped closer to her. They were in each other's bubbles. "Now that we know what we want for the future, how about we get dinner and talk about the present?"

Jasmine felt flattered that a guy was interested in her, and she didn't need to plead with him. She saw the enjoyment in his eyes, and she's never seen that before. She's only received disgust and pity. "Fine."

"Good. I'll see you around." He began to run.

"How will I know when we are going on our date?" she asked.

"I've waited for you, now you can wait for me." He winked, before he ran away from her.

Jasmine, you should get used to the sight of men running away from you. You might have thought this guy was interested in you, but you had another thing coming. He would soon realize how bat shit crazy you were. You were right, that the social order prepared you for the outside world, but all we could see it was teaching you, was how to be the bottom of the barrel. This would be the first and last man to ever find you attractive, but we weren't surprised. Hot guys don't go for the fat wannabes.

Chapter 22

"Alright, class. I wanted to talk to you all about the One Teen Story contest. You know that our school has entered this contest every year, and I think one of you could actually win the contest this year," Mr. Rozengota said, passing out the flyers to his creative writing class. "You've submitted pieces this whole year, and I want you to pick the best one. That will be your final for this class. You can choose the piece you're currently working on, or an old piece with my guidance."

Flynn leaned over to Delilah. "Are you going to submit something?" he asked. He was thinking of doing a piece he wrote a couple of months ago, about a teenager going through a divorce.

She looked at her story of the student who had no self-worth and felt lost in the world. "I don't know." She knew that it was too personal of a piece, and she was afraid people would hate it.

"Why not? You're a good writer," Flynn said.

"I would have to agree with Flynn, Delilah." Mr. Rozengota walked up to them. "Delilah, I think your body of work has been the best of any student this year, and I know anything you submit, would give you a winning shot."

Flynn's face faltered a little bit. He wanted those praises for his own work. "What about me, Mr. Rozengota?"

He gave Flynn a weak smile. "I think with more growth, then you'll find your writing voice." He grabbed the story off Delilah's desk. "This is the story you should submit. It's raw, dangerous, and it tells the story that a lot of teens are truly facing. People will connect with it."

Delilah grabbed the story back. She folded it up and put it under her book. "I just don't know if I have the confidence that you think I have. I don't know if I'm that strong of a writer."

He laughed. "People shouldn't always have confidence with their writing. We spend our whole lives lying to ourselves, and it's freeing when you can admit you aren't perfect," Mr. Rozengota said.

"But shouldn't we be proud of our work and stand beside it?" Flynn asked. He felt a sense of accomplishment from everything he's written, and he didn't want to feel ashamed for it.

"Maybe that's why your writing sometimes feels a little fake." He nodded to Flynn and turned to Delilah. "You have the talent, and I don't want you to ever forget that." He turned and walked away.

"I can't believe he would say that my writing is fake." Flynn felt a little hurt by Mr. Rozengota's assessment of him. Maybe you needed to be brought down a couple of pegs, Flynn. We got that you thought you were the next big writer, but maybe you were just supposed to be the arrogant prick after all.

"Maybe, he has a point." Delilah always thought there was something holding Flynn back in his writing. She never wanted to admit it to him, because she's always had a crush on him, but it was out in the open.

He crossed his arms. "I think you're both wrong. I know my writing will inspire the masses."

"I know it will, and I can't wait to read it." She smiled.

"Maybe it will be too late. You're going to see my name on the New York Times bestseller list and realize what mistakes you've made." Flynn would show all of them that he was someone real, and he would be legendary in his own way.

"Delilah, will you come here for a second?" Mr. Rozengota asked.

"Sure." She got up and walked to his desk. Flynn turned to see the short story that she thought about submitting under the desk. He wanted to know what was so special about this short story. He looked to see that she was distracted. He never saw her as competition until now, and he was curious about what got Mr. Rozengota so impressed.

He grabbed the story and quickly put it in his bag. Flynn, you might have looked like the innocent book nerd, but you were just like every other bitchy girl in this school. You wanted to be on top of the book world, and you found your competition. We never thought you would be worried about the dumb whore of the school, but we enjoyed the idea of you breaking her heart in this form. We hoped Delilah understood, and learned the hard lesson that you never trusted anyone, when it came to a contest.

"I wanted to give you this," Mr. Rozengota said, handing Delilah his recommendation letter.

She looked at it and started reading over his view of her. "What is this?" she asked.

"Congrats on your acceptance to Columbia, and I know that your application to their writing program is due in the next couple of weeks. I wanted you to have a recommendation letter from me. I will never understand why you don't have confidence in your writing. It's really good, and I see so much potential in you."

She smiled while still reading his kind words. "I just never thought I was good enough. I look at my parents, or even Flynn's writing, and I felt like I wasn't up to par."

"The difference between you and Flynn is humility. He has a lot to learn," he said.

She nodded. "Thank you for this."

"I really do hope you submit for this contest," he said.

She turned and walked to her desk. "What did he want?" Flynn asked.

She looked at his letter again. "Nothing." She turned and smiled at him.

He didn't believe her, but the bell went off. He got up and ran out of the class. She packed up her things, and didn't notice her short story was missing. She thanked Mr. Rozengota as she walked out of the room. She should have been more aware of her surroundings. Maybe then, she would have realized the boy she was crushing on, only wanted to destroy her. High school was a series of wars, and love was the perfect tool to manipulate with. Delilah, we prayed you learned this lesson the hard way, because we loved a Titanic ending, not a High School Musical one.

Chapter 23

Aman and Calvin were walking hand-in-hand as they looked at the different art pieces in the LGBT exhibit they were attending in Harlem. "This is beautiful," Aman said, looking at the watercolor painting of two men dancing together.

"See, I told you this was a good date idea," Calvin said. They hadn't had a lot of alone time together, and he wanted to make sure they regrouped as a couple. He felt that they were starting to drift, and he knew a huge part of it was Aman's parents. He was tired of feeling like the mistress. Calvin, you were the mistress, and the biggest problem with the side bitches was when they thought they meant more.

Aman rolled his eyes. He started looking around and listening to what the other gay couples were saying to each other. He started thinking of a new video idea then, but he would keep it to himself. "I don't get why we needed to come to Harlem," Aman said.

"Because this is where the exhibit is."

Aman looked at him. "Did it have to be an LGBT exhibit? I get the whole idea of showing that we are proud of being gay, but do we really need to consume our lives into it?"

"Well, since we're both in-the-closet gays, it might give us the courage to come out."

Aman laughed. "Yes, because all of these paintings, art pieces, and simulations are going to make me feel comfortable in the fact that I love cock," Aman said with a laugh. He thought it was rather stupid of people to assume being around acceptance would give that person self-acceptance.

"What's that supposed to mean?" Calvin asked. "There are different races, cultures, and viewpoints in these pieces. There is something for everyone."

"Except my culture," Aman said, looking around. "I don't see one piece on Indians or even Muslims coming out. Where are those pieces?" he asked.

Calvin looked around, and he couldn't find any at first glance. "I don't know."

"Exactly. We don't have any. We don't get to be proud when we were raised that homosexuality is an abomination. I don't get to love myself, because it's in my DNA to hate a part of me."

Calvin tried to squeeze Aman's hand, but he rebuffed Calvin. "I love you. Isn't that enough?"

"Not in my society," Aman said. He turned to walk away from Calvin.

"Just walk away from me. It's easy for you to do that. You don't care about this relationship. I put everything into us, and I feel like you've checked out," Calvin yelled out.

"You think that it's easy for me to love you? You don't think I want to be out and proud of you? I want my family to know you as my boyfriend, not my best friend. It kills me seeing you get hit on by girls. I want nothing more than to be with you, asshole," Aman cried out.

Calvin stepped forward. "That's all I want to hear from you." Calvin grabbed the front of his shirt and crushed his lips on Aman's. It was a kiss filled with passion, love, and yearning. They've been insatiable for physical contact from each other. "Do you want to go back to my place?" Calvin asked.

Aman was about to say yes, but he was getting a phone call from his mother. "I've got to take this," Aman said. Calvin nodded as Aman walked outside to talk to his mother. He wandered around looking at the pieces. He saw the couples so open, and he couldn't wait till they were at that level.

Aman came back inside with a grim look on his face. "I can't come over. My mom wants me home right now," he said.

Calvin was frustrated because this constantly happened to them. Their dates would always be cut short, because his parents wanted him home for some stupid reason. "Really? You couldn't tell them that you were busy?"

Aman shrugged. "They're my parents, what do you want me to do?"

"Stand up to them," Calvin said.

"I can't."

"Why not? Is it your religion? Is it money? Is it that you're scared? Why can't you tell them you're busy, and you're going to be home later?" Calvin asked. He didn't get why he couldn't try to be independent without them.

Aman felt conflicted. He wanted to tell Calvin that he was terrified to stand up to his parents. He liked his world staying the same, and he didn't want it to ever change. "I can't explain it to you," he said, sounding defeated.

"Or, you don't want to. You've kept me in the closet for so long, and I feel like I don't even know who you are."

"You knew who you were dating when we started this relationship," Aman reminded him.

Calvin shook his head. "So, I just need to accept it the way it is then?" Calvin asked. Calvin thought Aman's reasoning was bullshit, and he couldn't stand it.

"Yeah, you need to. I'm tired of you trying to force us out in the open. We have a good relationship now, and I don't want to change it. Once we're out in the open, then we can never go back in."

"But aren't you ready to stop being fearful?"

"You don't get it," Aman said. He felt his phone going off. It was his mother again. "I need to go." He leaned forward and gave Calvin a chaste kiss. "I love you. I'll text you later." He turned and walked out of the exhibit, leaving Calvin alone.

Poor Calvin. We wished you learned your lesson about being someone's dirty little secret. You thought you were both in the closet together. It seemed this closet had a secret room, and that was where Aman kept you. Aman, you should have been careful about tossing Calvin to the side. You wanted to keep your secret safe, but we had a feeling Calvin was about to drop the truth bomb. We hoped you were in your safe space to handle the blast.

Chapter 24

"What scares you the most?" Demi asked, as she took a sip of her coffee. She was sitting with Andrew at a local coffee shop talking. She was worried when he didn't talk much during the meeting, and she wanted to make sure that everything was okay with him.

"I'm just worried that I'll relapse. I'm surrounded by the temptations at my school. We have another party coming up, and I don't know if I'll be as strong."

She leaned back and crossed her arms. "Why go?"

He looked at her. "Because, I want to make friends."

She nodded. "You want to be welcomed in by society. You want your peers to validate you, but what's the point? It's all bullshit if you ask me."

"You're not in high school anymore. I'm stuck trying to regroup myself, when I don't even know who I am anymore."

"Because of your mother?" Demi asked. She knew little of Andrew's past. He has only given her piece by piece of what happened.

He looked down at his drink. "She loved me, but near the end, she would kiss my dad, and then she would turn a blind eye to me. I don't even remember a moment when she was sweet to me," Andrew said. He felt embarrassed talking about it, but he needed to get this out of his system.

"Was it because of the alcohol?" Demi asked.

"It doesn't matter." He looked at her. "I found out that it was the alcohol that caused her to shun me, but it doesn't mean that the damage isn't already done. In the end, I still felt like I wasn't wanted by my own mother," Andrew said. He felt his blood boiling, and he tried his hardest to keep it in check.

"But you know that it's a disease," Demi reminded him.

He slammed the table, rattling their drinks. "It doesn't matter what it is. I still showed affection to my fucking father when I was drunk off my ass. Shit, I still showed remorse and sadness for my mother. She acted like I was a stranger. I was her fucking son," Andrew yelled, as he looked right at Demi.

She knew he had a lot of damage, and it was becoming very apparent that it was still heavily affecting him. "Is that why you did what you did?" she asked.

He leaned back and crossed his arms. "She deserved it at the time. She doesn't get to keep a legacy with me. She wanted to act like I didn't exist, and I want her to feel the same."

"But you got sober after it."

He looked out toward the cars driving by. "Because I knew how much it destroyed my father. I woke up in the hospital after they pumped my stomach. It was the same expression my father had when my mother passed. I couldn't hurt him like that."

"And, you still haven't forgiven her?"

"What's the point of forgiveness?" he asked. He didn't get why he needed to forgive someone that had destroyed him. She was the villain, and he would show her no kindness.

"My ex was the reason I got into drugs and alcohol. He told me time and time again that it's fun. You'll have a great time. He peer pressured me," Demi shared.

"Didn't they warn you about those people in high school?" Andrew asked, as a joke.

Demi laughed. "Yes, you would think we would have learned that lesson." She paused. "I did it because I loved him.

I got so consumed in that world. I would go days without knowing where I was, and my parents were so worried. I eventually flunked out of college, and I didn't care." Demi looked back on her life, and she felt like such an idiot for letting this guy influence her that much.

"Why didn't you leave him?"

"Because I was so in love with him, and he was my access to drugs. He cheated on me and abused me. I didn't care, because I used everything to numb it all."

"What caused you to stop using?" Andrew asked. Demi doesn't really talk about her story in the meetings. She let others have the floor, and he was curious about it.

"We were driving somewhere, and we were both fucked up. We ended up hitting a car. We survived, but the other person didn't." Demi shook her head. She tried to keep it together. "He didn't care that he killed someone. He was upset that he had to be sober. He valued drugs and alcohol more than life. It hit me that I couldn't be in this situation anymore. I needed to walk away."

"But you forgave him?" Andrew asked. He didn't get how she could forgive someone after a story like that.

"Because I knew if I didn't, that he was still in control." She leaned forward. "You need to forgive, or you're going to be controlled by your mother."

Andrew played her story again in his head. He still couldn't comprehend that she could forgive a monster. He didn't know if he had the strength to show that kind of forgiveness. "Maybe, I'll try."

Andrew, we all knew you weren't going to try. You were a momma's boy at heart. You were still pleading for her approval, even though she chose alcohol over you. How did it feel knowing you were nothing more than a regret, unlike her addiction? We couldn't wait to ask you the same, once you destroyed your life and everyone else's around you.

Chapter 25

"Babe, dinner is almost ready," Dan said, walking into Danielle's room. Danielle's mom went off to work, and they had the house to themselves. Danielle looked up at Dan and smiled. She was working on her prom dress still.

"I'm almost done. I just want to fix the corset," she said. She wanted to make sure it was tight on top and flowy on the bottom. It was a Tiffany blue, and she was really looking forward to wearing this at prom. She had put a lot of work into the dress, and she would be the talk of the school. Danielle, we believed there were going to be other reasons you were going to be the talk of the town, but those were soon to be found out.

Dan walked over and kissed her on the lips. "I love when you're working on a new dress," he said. He could never comprehend how she could be this talented. He thought she was some spoiled kid when she first met him, but he has been happily surprised ever since.

She looked at him and smiled. "You look like a creeper right now," she said.

"I can't admire a pretty girl?"

She leaned back and crossed her arms. "I'm just a pretty girl to you?"

"Beautiful woman?" He thought that might have been the right response.

She got up and kissed him on the lips. "I think that's a better answer." She paused and sniffed. "I think something's burning."

"Oh shit!" He remembered he forgot to stir the pasta sauce. He ran out of the room.

She laughed and walked out of her bedroom. She took a seat at the dinner table, as he prepared the chicken alfredo. He walked over with the meal and placed one in front of her. "Thank you for cooking," she said. It was a rare occurrence that Danielle could actually just breathe. It must be exhausting being a bitch and living a double life.

He shrugged. "You decided to date me, so I can at least make you dinner."

"I'm dating you because you're sweet. Why can't you see that?" She knew Dan had a huge worry that she was ashamed of him. Wouldn't you be ashamed of him? He lived in the Bronx, and you went to one of the most elite schools on the Upper East Side. He wasn't stupid about being insecure.

"Because I can't give you what those other guys can give you. I want to believe that you love me for me, but I have a worry in the back of my mind," he admitted.

"And what's that?" she asked.

"That you're going to ditch me once something better comes around."

Danielle got up from her seat. She leaned forward and cupped Dan's face in her hands. "I'm with you because I love you. You make me pasta, you support my designs, and you're okay with me being a giant bitch sometimes."

"Why can't I meet your friends, yet?" he asked.

"Because I want to keep that world and this world separate. I don't want to have my fake life intrude in my real one. You're something incredible, and I never want our bubble to burst. Can you accept that?" she asked. She prayed that he would understand where she was coming from.

He nodded. "I guess I'm just being paranoid."

She took her seat again. "Yes, you are."

"I love you," he said. He felt confident in their relationship--for right now.

"I love you, too." They enjoyed their night together, because tomorrow their bubble was about to pop. She thought that she could keep her worlds separate, but The Marked Queen had different plans for you. You might want to give him more confidence, because you were about to go to war, Danielle. We hoped he survived when the dust settled.

Chapter 26

For every girl's big day, they say 'something old, something new, something borrowed, and something blue.' At Johnson Prep, a girl's big day was something sinister, something designer, something sexy, and something red. It was the day you were marked by The Marked Queen. A package was delivered to your house, and you were supposed to be a good servant as you were a messenger of the Queen now.

Jasmine opened her package that morning, and squealed for joy because she had been dreaming of this day. She had always wondered when she would be marked by the Queen, and when her day to stroll down the hallway in a red leather dress would come true. She pulled out the dress, and saw her black devil pin was under it.

Jasmine, you've been marked. We know how you've waited for your day to wear the prized red dress. I did make it a little loose for you, because no one wants to see your back rolls. You better wear the dress with pride, or you will go downhill. Have a fun day being my bitch. We know how much you love being in the spotlight. -The Marked Queen.

She looked at the note that she was supposed to spread, and she couldn't have been happier. She was marked, and she got to take down her least favorite person in the world. It was a day she would never forget. Yes, most girls would think their wedding day was their biggest moment, but for Jasmine, it was when she was marked.

She opened the doors to Johnson Prep, and people stopped to stare at her. She saw people whispering about her, and she basked in the glory that was her fame now. She continued to walk, until she saw Danielle and Delilah talking.

Danielle turned to see Jasmine walking up to her. "She finally picked you. I guess she was running out of people to torture," Danielle said.

Jasmine crossed her arms. "You're just jealous that I wear red better than you." Jasmine ran her fingers down the dress.

Danielle rolled her eyes. "You do know that I didn't wear that stupid thing or the pin."

Jasmine shrugged. "I guess that's going to bite you in the ass."

Danielle raised an eyebrow. "What's that supposed to mean?" Danielle exposed the scandal like she was supposed to. She just decided not to wear the stupid costume. She thought she was safe now.

"You're about to find out." Jasmine walked past her and went to put up the post. People watched as Jasmine pinned up the note. She turned to see everyone have their eyes on her. She felt like she was a celebrity, and she savored every moment. "Enjoy." She winked and walked away as she left them with the news.

Danielle pushed everyone out of the way to see what Jasmine posted. Her heart dropped, because the blast was about her. People stepped back and looked at Danielle with judgment. Danielle read it to herself.

It looks like this Queen has been slumming it in the Bronx. Danielle, we were told to never get with the stable boy, but you didn't even have the class or grace for that. We shouldn't have been surprised that you're too busy kissing filthy toads. Maybe this Queen's standards are low because everyone's had enough of you. Enjoy your last days on top, because I have a feeling you were about to be in the swamp with your new boyfriend. -The Marked Queen.

She looked at the picture above, and it was of her and Dan kissing. She grabbed the paper and crumbled it up. "I don't care what this bitch has to say." She turned and stormed off. Delilah followed her.

"Danielle, wait up."

Danielle turned. "What?"

"Who cares if you're dating someone from the Bronx," Delilah said. She wanted her best friend to be happy. She was a little hurt that Danielle kept this a secret. "Why didn't you tell me?"

She knew if she told Delilah about Dan, she would have to tell Delilah about the fact that she was poor. "I want to keep somethings to myself. I didn't think it would get out." She threw the blast in the trash. "I fucking hate this bitch." She lost her composure, and people were staring at her. She didn't care at the moment.

"What are you going to do?" Delilah asked.

Danielle crossed her arms. "I don't fucking know, but she needs to be taken down. I don't need this bitch going around spreading any more secrets," Danielle cried out.

"It doesn't feel good, does it?" Jordan asked, walking up to her.

Danielle turned to look at Jordan. She rolled her eyes. "You just switched to the lacrosse team, instead of the football team. No one cares about lacrosse here."

Jordan gave her a death glare. "This girl needs to be stopped. Why does she feel like she gets to be on her high-horse? So what if we love sex, keeping up appearances, and having fun? It doesn't mean she gets to call us out on it."

"You're right, but we need to make sure that this bitch doesn't find out any more of our secrets. We keep it together, and she loses her power."

"How do we do that?" Jordan asked. "We can't expect everyone to have a moral high ground and keep it to themselves."

Danielle played with Jordan's hair. "Prom is right around the corner, then it's graduation. If we can keep our secrets safe, then we survive this bitch."

"Do you believe she'll stop after high school?" Jordan asked.

Danielle shrugged. "I don't know, nor do I care." She looked at the time. "I have to get to class and deal with the fact that people found out about my boyfriend." She stormed past Jordan and Delilah. She was more hurt once she got to her locker, because she wanted Dan to stay out of this. The Marked Queen had no right to attack him like that. He was a wonderful man, and he didn't deserve to be judged the way he was.

She opened her locker to see a note from The Marked Queen. She opened it to see a hundred-dollar bill fall out.

Here's a hundred dollars for your next date with Dan. You can count it as my tip for the shitty service you gave me the other night. Aw, you thought that I would forget that you're trailer-park-trash poor? Well, think again, bitch. I'll never let that go. Besides, I have bigger plans for your real scandal. Hopefully, then, you'll be rich again. Who are we kidding? Your beautiful carriage turned back into a rotted pumpkin, and that's just me commenting on your body. Have fun below the poverty line, peasant. -The Marked Queen.

Danielle crumbled up the note, and she tried to keep her emotions in check. She wanted nothing more than to take this bitch down, but she worried about her truth coming out. It looked like this Queen realized she had lost her kingdom. She was just a place holder, and The Marked Queen was really ruling this throne. We hoped you loved a gun to your back, Danielle. You had better keep playing her game, or death would look better for you once the scandals came out.

Chapter 27

"Why couldn't you have stayed with him?" Danielle asked, when she saw her mom.

Lily had just worked three doubles in a row, and she wanted to sleep. "Danielle, can we talk about this later?"

"No, you're going to explain to me why you couldn't have sucked it up and stayed with dad."

"Did you want me unhappy?" Lily asked. "Did you want me to be some ridiculous housewife?"

"You didn't have a problem with it for twenty years," Danielle said. She thought her parents had the perfect marriage. She knew her father wasn't the kindest man in the world, but Danielle assumed her mother was okay with it.

"I only stayed with him because of the money."

"Now look at us." She grabbed her purse and turned to leave.

"What kind of example would that have set for you?" Lily asked.

Danielle turned back to look at her mom. "What does any of this have to do with me?"

Lily walked toward her daughter. "I wanted to make you proud. I knew that if I stayed, then you might find someone just as equally as bad."

"I wouldn't marry a man for his money."

"But you're coming into this house, yelling because you wanted me to stay. You grew up in a world with everything at your fingertips. You grew up to be a spoiled brat. I woke up one morning, and I had enough of it. Do you think any of my friends have my back now that we live in the Bronx?" Lily asked.

Danielle knew that her mother's friends had all walked away from her once the divorce was finalized. None of them truly cared about Lily's fate, because she was dead to them. Upper East Side cast people away once you became poor. It was the land of the rich, not an episode of Barney. "Because you turned your back on them."

"Or, they didn't care about what happened to me. I don't want you to turn out like them."

"But I still go to school with half those kids."

Lily nodded. "Do you feel like you have friends?"

"I have Calvin," Danielle said. "And Delilah."

Lily smiled. "I'm happy you have friendships, because I didn't." She removed the smile. "I also want you to know that this city is toxic. You might think that people have your back, but they could stab you in it at any time. You have to be strong and stand your ground."

"Because you don't want me to marry a guy like my dad," Danielle sighed.

"He cheated on me countless times, he hit me, and he treated me like trash. I got drunk at every party, just to be able to sleep in the same bed as him," she said. "There were so many times that I cried in the closet, because I was miserable. I couldn't do it anymore."

"But you're okay living in this filth of an apartment? You're okay stressed about paying our bills?"

Lily walked over and touched both sides of Danielle's face. "Yes, because I'm truly alive now. I want you to see that no matter what, you can get out of a situation. You're strong enough on your own."

Danielle rolled her eyes. "Spare me the feminist speech."

Lily laughed. "You'll eventually understand what I mean. Money and power don't mean anything, if you lose yourself in them."

"Maybe you should have realized where we lived. You're no one without money or power."

"Then I failed you as a parent."

Danielle shrugged. "Or, maybe you should have realized that lesson before you walked away from dad. Now I'm stuck keeping my social standing intact. Thank you for finding yourself, while destroying me in the process," Danielle cried, as she walked away from her mother.

She walked into her room and took a seat in front of her vanity. It was one of the few pieces of furniture she got to take when she and her mother left her father's house. She looked in the mirror, and all she saw was a girl trying to keep her rich mask on. She was worried it would eventually fall off, and everyone would look at her like she was poor little, Annie. She wanted people's respect, not pity.

Danielle, no one was going to respect you once they realized you were lying to them this whole time. We wouldn't worry about it, because you have all your so-called, "friends" to give you some moral support. The only problem was, they weren't going to be friends with you once you betrayed them to keep your secret safe. The Marked Queen didn't like friendship; she loved a scorned one.

Chapter 28

"Thank you so much for your time," Delilah said, as she got up from meeting with Mr. Rozengota. She wanted to ask him about edits for the story she was going to use as her final.

Mr. Rozengota looked at Delilah, and he was worried. He saw the sheer fear on her face. "Is everything okay?" he asked.

She nodded. "Yes, I just have a lot of ideas, and I want to go write them down before I forget."

"You don't have to worry. You're a very talented writer."

She smiled. "Thank you." She knew he said that to all of his students. She didn't think her writing was anything special. She knew it meant nothing, because why would it? She wasn't going to be some writer that inspired the world. She was meant more to be known as the student who slept with the principal.

She walked down the hall when she saw Principal Grand walking out of a classroom. He smiled. "Ms. White, I haven't seen you in a couple of weeks. I do hope all is well in your classes."

Delilah nodded. "Yes, I've been busy focusing on studying and keeping my grades up." She tried to walk past him.

He grabbed her by the arm. "I think you need to come to see me privately."

She looked around to make sure no one saw them. "I think we're done. I don't want us to keep going on. It was fun for a while, but you have an ex-wife and kids." She also knew her feelings for Flynn were real. Delilah, you might have thought Flynn had feelings for you, but he only had a boner for stealing your work.

"I can make it where you fail, do you want me to do that?" he asked.

"I could come out and say we had sex."

He laughed and crossed his arms. "No one's going to believe you."

"I bet I'm not the only student you've fucked," she said, with a sly smile forming.

"But you're the dumbest," he said. His feelings were hurt, and he was going to make sure she knew he wasn't someone she should mess with.

Delilah looked down for a moment. She didn't need him telling her things that she already knew. She sucked it up and looked at him. "You're the one that decided to sleep with a student, not me. I think that makes you the dumb one." She wanted to get out of this conversation. She felt like the walls were closing in, and she didn't know how to feel open anymore.

"I'm scheduling a one-on-one meeting with your principal for next week. I wouldn't miss it if I were you," he said. He turned and walked away. This was the problem with high school girls. They started getting confidence and wanted to be independent. He needed to break them down again.

Principal Grand, are you going to teach your daughters the same lesson? We hoped they turned out to be feminists, just to piss you off. We also would like you to know that there were many problems with dating a high school girl. One would be the fact that you were her principal, but we could see where you might have missed that one. You were too busy enjoying her lips around your small cock.

Delilah rushed to the bathroom. She closed the stall and pulled out the razor blade from her purse. She only carried it for emergencies, and she felt like this was a huge one. She applied the same pressure to her right arm, and felt the pain course through her body. It felt good to get some of the emotions out.

She began to cry, and she felt relieved for a moment. She felt like she had some control in her life. She took in a heavy sigh and then pulled out a bracelet from her purse and put it over the cut. She hoped the toilet paper would stop the bleeding. She fixed her make-up and walked outside.

She bumped into Tucker while he was going to photograph a landscape. "Sorry," Delilah said.

Tucker smiled. "It's fine. I wasn't looking where I was going." He saw that she had recently been crying. He also noticed the blood coming from her wrist. "Is everything okay?" he asked, concern etched on his face.

She crossed her arms. "Why wouldn't they be?" she asked, trying to hide her anger.

"You looked like you were crying, and you're bleeding." He pointed to her wrist.

She crossed her arms. She channeled her inner-Danielle. "If you have to know. My bracelet snagged onto my skin, and it ripped a part of it off. It's why I was crying, because it hurt like a bitch. Don't you have a life of your own to focus on?"

He put his hands in the air. "I was just making sure you were okay. You don't need to be a bitch about it."

She smiled. "I don't care if I'm being a bitch or not. Your kind doesn't really matter." She turned to walk away. She needed to get out of the school before she lost it. She didn't need anyone finding out she was cutting herself. She wished she had waited till she got home, but she couldn't keep the emotions in anymore.

Tucker saw the blood still dripping down her wrist. He turned to take a picture of it. He thought Delilah was the sweet one, but apparently, she was as evil as all of them. He didn't know what her problem was, but he wasn't going to let her be a bitch to him. It was time he sent some information to The Marked Queen.

Delilah, you thought your secret was safe, but you being a bitch just bit you in the ass. We hoped you were ready for your moment in the red dress. You didn't have to worry about the blood anymore. It would match perfectly now. Go home and cry your tears over self-doubt and perverted principals, because tomorrow you were going to cry about pity looks and outed secrets.

Chapter 29

Jasmine walked into school feeling like she was on cloud nine. She had a cute boy that hit on her. Her father was actually being nice to her this morning. He said that her outfit was cute. We all had to admit that a nice yellow, flowing dress did hid your obese body.

Jasmine saw Carter and wanted to talk to him. She was stopped, because some blonde girl was talking to him at his locker. She was annoyed because they seemed to be having a friendly conversation. She felt like her heart dropped to her stomach. He seemed interested in her, but was he a player? Jasmine, he wasn't a player, he just decided to go for someone who didn't have constant camel toe.

Jasmine shrugged it off. He was a confidence builder, but he had no social standing. She didn't even know the tramp that he was talking to. She wasn't worried about it. She turned to see that Calvin was all alone so she began walking toward him, as he was putting books in his bag.

Calvin just wanted to be left alone today. He couldn't get ahold of Aman because he was working on a new video. He knew that things were awkward after Aman left him in Harlem.

Jasmine walked up to Calvin and placed a hand on his arm. "It's so good to see you, Calvin."

Calvin turned to see Jasmine. He groaned mentally, because he didn't have time to deal with her right now. "How are you, Jasmine?"

She shrugged. "I'm good. I've missed you, though. I feel like we haven't gotten any alone time together."

He smiled. "I've been busy with college recruitments, baseball, and life."

"Plus, prom is right around the corner, and everyone's still looking for dates." She leaned against the lockers. "It's pathetic if you ask me. It smells like desperation." We all could laugh at this stupid bitch. Jasmine, you were the Queen of desperation. You were throwing yourself at a gay guy. We understood that every fat girl needed a gay best friend, but did you honestly have to try to suck his dick, too?

He shrugged. He knew what she was trying to imply, and he wanted nothing to do with it. He knew that he couldn't go to prom with his real date, and it made him want to skip out on the whole event. "I guess, but you could always go with a group of friends."

She didn't want to go with a group of friends. She wanted to go with him. "We could get a limo for the whole prom court. We are all princes and princesses after all."

He nodded. He forgot he had prom committee tomorrow because he was nominated. "We have that stupid rehearsal tomorrow, too."

She touched his arm. "I totally forgot about that. I guess we should go together, make things less awkward?"

Calvin saw Aman walking while looking at his phone. "Sorry, I have to go. I'll see you tomorrow." He ran off to talk to him.

Jasmine was ditched by Calvin, and she felt a blow to her ego. She leaned against the locker and sighed. She tried to get the bile of rejection out of her throat. She ran to the bathroom and went for the stall. She closed the door and leaned against the toilet.

She heard a knock on the door. "Someone is in here."

"Are you okay, Jasmine?" Susan asked.

Jasmine rolled her eyes. The one person she didn't want to see her like this. "Susan, I'm fine. I had something bad to eat this morning."

"Are you sure? I've seen you throw up in the bathroom a couple of times now," Susan said. She was worried about her friend. She didn't want her to have an eating disorder. Susan, an eating disorder was supposed to work. Jasmine still had enough rolls to make her own bakery. You shouldn't worry about her too much. She would be getting full off her deserts soon enough.

Jasmine got up and wiped her mouth. She composed herself and went to open the stall. "Are you implying that I have an eating disorder?"

Susan raised her hands. "I'm just worried about you, that's all."

Jasmine smiled. "I think it's quite cute you think that I feel bad about myself. Have you seen me? I'm fucking hot. Any guy in this god damn school would want me."

"Except for Calvin," Susan mumbled.

Jasmine learned one thing from her father's abuse. If someone disrespected you, then you put them in their place. She slapped Susan across the face. "I have men flocking to me, you useless bitch. I don't see men lining up to have their dicks sucked by you. I'm fucking nominated for prom Queen, were you?"

She looked down like a kicked puppy. "No, I'm not."

"Exactly. Why don't you go back to the hole you crawled out of, and we will make sure to forget this." Jasmine fixed Susan's shirt. "I love you. I never want anything bad to happen to you."

Susan looked up. "Are you threatening me?"

Jasmine smiled. "I never threaten anyone." Jasmine pulled her in for a hug. "I'll talk to you soon." She winked and walked out of the bathroom. She needed to get to class, and she wasn't going to let the help get to her.

She opened her locker and saw a red envelope. She knew damn well who this was going to be from. She opened the envelope to see a letter from the bitch herself.

My little piggy Queen. You weren't fooling anyone with your new diet. I think it's actually having the opposite effect on you. I shouldn't have marked you, because the bitch is supposed to make the red dress sexy, not kill the boners of the American boy. Don't worry my fatty Jazzy, I'll make sure you gain the weight you were desperately trying to get rid of. Maybe then, someone might actually notice you. It won't work out for you, though, because I hear cats are in your future, but this Queen always needs a good sob story to laugh at. -The Marked Queen.

Jasmine crumbled up the letter and tried to keep the tears back. She wouldn't let The Marked Queen get to her. Jasmine, you already let her get inside your head. How did you think you acquired this new hobby of yours? You thought the girls looking for dates were desperate, but what about the girl trying to be head bitch? We hoped you kept believing in your confidence, because it was going to be so delicious to see it all burndown.

Chapter 30

Knock, Knock. Whose there? Danielle opened the door to see her prayers have been answered by Satan himself. Hello daddy, it has been a while. Danielle's father, Ethan, stood there looking at her. She raised an eyebrow, because she wasn't expecting to ever see him--especially in the Bronx. "Dad, what are you doing here?" she asked.

He smiled. "Can I come in?" he asked.

She stepped to the side, and he walked in. "Is your mother home?"

She crossed her arms. "She's no longer a housewife, so she actually has a job."

Ethan turned to look at Danielle. "I see someone's attitude hasn't changed one bit."

"And I see someone's still a prick." Danielle had nothing but hatred for her father. She wanted to believe that he was a good man, but he put her in this mess.

He chuckled. "You're still my little spitfire."

"What are you doing here?" she asked. She didn't have time for his bullshit. She was planning to meet up with Dan in an hour.

"Always to the point."

"My father taught me to see right through bullshit." Danielle knew damn well this trip was something for him to gain.

"I need you back in my life," Ethan said.

She raised an eyebrow. "Why would you need me? I haven't heard from you in over a year, and now you've had a change of heart."

"Your mother ran out of those doors with only a note. You could have stayed with me if you wanted." Ethan had been on a business trip when he came home to a note from his wife, saying she and Danielle were leaving.

"You could have come back for us, but you just like using your checkbook. It's gotten you this far in life."

"I don't remember you complaining about all the shopping sprees."

She ignored the comment. "What are you doing here?" she asked again.

He pulled out a credit card from his pocket and handed it to her. "Here's access back to all my money."

She was hesitant to take it. "Why are you giving me this?"

"Let's say, quid pro quo."

She didn't take the card. "And what do you want in return?"

"I'm trying to gain a new client that could be worth potentially hundreds of millions for the company. The only problem is, he knows that I'm not close to my family, especially my daughter."

"And?"

"And he's an asshole with a heart."

Danielle laughed. "I know how hard that must be to actually care."

He rolled his eyes. "I need you to come with me to a couple of events, and act like I'm the perfect dad. In exchange, you can have access to all the money you had before."

Danielle thought about it, and she knew this would be a perfect way to shut The Marked Queen up. "And I want access to the house to throw parties."

"I don't want you to destroy the house, and Cheryl might not like having kids around."

"Of course, the fucking whore lives with you," Danielle said. She shouldn't have been surprised that the business trip he was taking, was to bang his side bitch. Danielle thought she was cheap and stupid, but that was her dad's type.

"She's been good to me, and we have a beautiful relationship."

"What blowjobs in the morning and fucking at night?"

"You will respect her," Ethan said.

"Please, there's no respect. It seems you're backed into a corner. You could let me have access to the money and house, or you're screwed." Danielle knew that money and business meant the world to her father.

Ethan had to give Danielle everything she wanted. He would just take Cheryl on a fancy vacation when Danielle had a house party. "Fine, you can have both."

Danielle squealed. She grabbed the card and hugged her dad. "I love you."

"Just do that in public," Ethan said, not really hugging her back.

Looked like daddy came back to save all of Danielle's issues. Too bad for her, the past wasn't going to be forgotten that easily. We hope you're relishing in this newly found money, because we had a feeling it was going to be counterfeit. We enjoyed you having a moment back in the royal court, because every Queen needed the perfect gown before she was guillotined.

Chapter 31

Welcome to the world of trending videos, Aman. It looked like your new video got the views that you were so desperately trying to get. Too bad for you, there were a lot of dislikes on that video, and the comments weren't glowing reviews. What do you expect when you make fun of a culture that you were desperately trying to hide from?

Aman walked to his locker as people were high fiving him. His newest video was a satire on gay culture. If you didn't believe me, that was perfectly fine. The title was, "Shit Gay People Say and Do." It wouldn't have been an issue, if Aman wasn't proud to have a cock in him.

Aman felt the wave of excitement having people enjoy his video. He looked at the trending video, and he was at number seven. Even his father texted him to congratulate him on the success of his video. The shocking thing was, his father didn't have to pay anyone for ads to help his son out anymore. What could we say? People loved bashing minorities.

Aman got to his locker and was putting his video camera and books away, when Calvin walked up to him. Calvin had spent all night watching Aman's video. He felt more and more betrayed by the man that he loved. "What the fuck?" Calvin said.

Aman looked at his boyfriend. He had ignored Calvin's calls, because he knew this conversation was going to happen. "It's all in good fun," he said.

"It's only in good fun if you were out. You're clearly bashing a fucking group of people." Calvin leaned closer. "Our people," he whispered.

Aman rolled his eyes. "It's a joke, and people shouldn't take it so seriously. Calvin, I was just having fun. I see these types of videos all the time on the internet. You can't be angry with me because I decided to jump on the bandwagon."

Calvin laughed. "Maybe they were right about you. You couldn't come up with original material if it saved your life."

Aman crossed his arms. Calvin knew that was the one comment that would piss Aman off. "Fuck off. You're just upset that I've been ignoring you lately. I got a video trending on YouTube. I would think you would be proud of me."

Calvin shrugged. "It's like a fart joke. They're good for a laugh, but they don't have much originality."

"Someone's being very sassy today," Aman said.

"Maybe because I'm a faggot," Calvin said. He didn't give a shit if anyone heard him. Too bad people were focusing on themselves, instead of these Queens having a go at each other. Aman, you really were losing yourself to the trolls behind the keyboards.

"Calvin, you can't sit here and be upset with me. I'm doing what I thought was funny. I don't see any malice in it."

"Don't worry, Aman. I guess I'm just a sensitive snowflake, and you're the insensitive asshole. Have fun with your new fame. It looks terrible on you. Calvin grabbed his baseball gear and walked away.

Aman had to ignore Calvin and his feelings. He was getting his subscribers, and his views were up. Aman knew Calvin loved baseball, and he wanted to prove himself if he ever came out. Aman was doing the same damn thing. They worked hard to be accepted by a sea of assholes who wouldn't see past them being gay.

Aman smiled when he saw his video hit two million views. He scrolled down and saw a comment that he wasn't too thrilled about.

Congrats on your new video trending at number seven. Quick question, how much did that cost you? Oh, Aman, we know your daddy is paying for these views and subscribers. It's rather pathetic since you're doing it for his love and admiration. We hear that the camera adds ten pounds of bullshit to your personality. We know you love to fake it like you have happiness in your life. – The Marked Queen.

Aman locked his phone and threw it in the locker. This was supposed to be his moment, but the bitch was taking it away from him. He also knew a part of him hated that he was fighting with Calvin. The one person that he wanted to share this with, he couldn't. He wanted to believe that Calvin had the strength for both of them, but he wasn't sure their foundation was strong enough right now.

Aman, maybe you shouldn't be pushing away the man that loves you, but you learned that trait from your father. You wanted to be the biggest YouTube sensation, but you needed to accept the truth. Your videos are fake, and you're just another bullshit actor. The only problem was, what would happen to you once you were pulled off the stage? We thought tomatoes were more your style than roses. After all, your performance has been less than subpar at best.

Chapter 32

Bethany sighed when she had to stand in front of the royal court. She loved planning the perfect prom, but she didn't like the tradition that the royal court had to help with the planning. Aw, Bethany were you sad that the only reason you were there was because you were president of the prom committee? We knew when the school voted for King and Queen, the only person that voted for you was that loser boyfriend of yours.

"The plan is to have all six of you on the stage. Once the announcer says your name, there will be a video montage of all your accomplishments and photos of you around the school," Bethany said, looking down at her notes for the meeting.

Danielle smiled. She crossed her arms and leaned back. "At least there will be good looking people on the stage, while you're behind the scenes. We don't want the ugly on display."

Bethany rolled her eyes. "At least my boyfriend comes from wealth."

Danielle felt her anger bubble over. She had enough of the comments this week about Dan. No one knew him like she did. She leaned forward. "At least people are talking about my boyfriend, you boring bitch."

Bethany smirked. "I didn't think anything could ever get under your cold, dead skin."

Danielle was about to say something, before Calvin grabbed her hand. "Danielle, we aren't here to start shit with Bethany. Let's get this meeting over with, and we can leave."

Danielle nodded. "Fine." She looked back at Bethany. "Continue with your useless instructions. I know this is all you have to live for, but the rest of us have outside lives."

Bethany ignored the comment as she went on to tell each person who they were paired with. Danielle and Calvin were paired, Delilah and Eddie, and Jasmine and Aman. Aman leaned over to whisper in Calvin's ear. "Thank you from stopping that fight."

Calvin turned to Aman. "Why? Are you too busy to make fun of another group? I saw your video was going down the list of trending videos."

Aman felt a little annoyed that Calvin couldn't let it go. "I'm sorry that it upset you."

Calvin crossed his arms. "Whatever. I have baseball practice after this, so I don't need you distracting me." Calvin didn't look at Aman anymore.

Aman felt guilty, but he had to do it to get his views up. Yes, why didn't you admit that it was only professional? The only problem was, there would be tears from someone, and we bet it was you. We hoped you turned that crying session into a video.

Jasmine raised her hand to stop Bethany from talking. "Why am I stuck walking with Aman? I get he's cute and a vlogger, but I feel like I should go with either Eddie or Calvin."

"Why?" Danielle asked. "They're both athletes. Don't you think it's a bit ironic if a big girl is paired with the baseball or football star?" She paused. "I guess you could go with Eddie, he's used to touching pigskin."

People started to laugh, and Jasmine wasn't going to let Danielle get to her. "You can call me fat, but at least I'm not a useless bitch. You might want to blend more on the make-up, it's coming off too harsh."

Eddie laughed. Eddie wasn't anyone special or meaningful for this story. He was just the quarterback of the football team.

You could look up any cliché comment about a football star, and he would be right there. "I love when you two go off on each other."

"Yes, because feminism was meant for bitches to go off on each other for the enjoyment of the male species," Bethany said interrupting. "Can we please get back to this meeting?" She looked around.

Delilah raised her hand. "What accomplishments are you going to show?" Delilah asked. She didn't feel like she had anything to talk about, and she was worried.

Bethany looked down at her clipboard, and she still had a giant question mark next to Delilah's name. "Aren't you in a creative writing class?" Bethany asked.

"Yes."

"Maybe we could bring that up?" Bethany suggested. Bethany, we thought you should show a picture of her going down on Principal Grand. That would be more of an accomplishment, instead of her getting her feelings out on paper.

Delilah felt nervous about her writing being exposed to her classmates, but she needed something to be proud of. "I guess that works."

Bethany nodded. That was one crisis she didn't need to worry about anymore. "The theme of this prom is royalty. We want to make it luxurious, glamorous, and sophisticated. There will be no slutty dresses allowed. We want to show the world that Johnson Prep prom is above the rest."

"Oh look, a prude prom headed by the most stuck up bitch in the room," Danielle said. She stood up. "I'll wear whatever I want. People elected me to the royal court because of my style. You won't stop me from impressing my people. We get that no one cares what you wear, because you're as entertaining as beige paint." She turned to Calvin. "Shall we leave?"

Calvin nodded. He didn't even look at Aman as he got up to walk away. The rest of the group followed, leaving Bethany by herself. "Fucking bitches," she said. She wanted nothing more than for The Marked Queen to ruin all these cunt's night. Bethany, you were going to get your wish. You just had to be patient, because we had a feeling the only thing getting lost on this prom night was their reputation.

Chapter 33

Jasmine walked out of the school. She tried to ignore Danielle's comments, but they continued to play in her head on repeat. It wasn't fair that bitch got to be escorted by Calvin. That should have been her.

Carter was waiting outside for her. "Jasmine." He waved toward her.

She looked at him and smiled. She needed someone to distract her, and she was hoping Carter would get her out of this state of mind. He might not have had the social standing, but at least he was hot. "How are you?" she asked.

"Good. Do you want to go on that date?" he asked. He had been thinking about her the past couple of days since they met on the track.

Jasmine wanted to say yes, but she remembered the blonde bitch he was talking to. "Don't you already have a girlfriend?"

Carter raised an eyebrow. "What? I'm single."

She rolled her eyes. "I saw you talking to some blonde the other day."

Carter had to think for a minute. "Do you mean, Claire? She's also on the track team. She was asking if we had practice."

"And there's nothing going on between you two?" Jasmine asked. She didn't want to be the second choice again.

Carter laughed. "She's a lesbian. I'm pretty sure I'm not her type." Carter thought it was kind of cute when Jasmine got jealous. Carter, if you thought her being jealous was cute, then you should have seen her throw herself at a guy. It was downright adorable.

Jasmine looked away from him. "Now, I feel like an idiot."

Carter grabbed her hand. "It's fine. I'm single. I don't play games, and I'm very honest with people."

She smiled. "That's refreshing. I feel like everyone's playing games, and I don't know who to trust anymore." Jasmine, you were a fucking bitch. Why would people want to be in your corner? They would rather watch you burn at the stake. We had our lighters ready for the day you go on trial.

Carter grabbed her hand. "Come with me." He took her hand, and they started walking a couple of blocks. They both felt comfortable in the silence. Jasmine enjoyed having her fingers intertwined with Carter's. Jasmine, you only enjoyed it because a guy was touching you and not throwing up after the interaction.

They ended up at a hot dog stand. Carter ordered a couple of hot dogs for them. He paid cash and handed one to Jasmine. They walked to sit in front of a fountain. Carter started eating his, and Jasmine stared at it. She didn't want to eat, because she kept thinking about the comments from Danielle.

Carter turned to look at Jasmine. "Do you not like hot dogs?" Carter was worried, because he never actually asked if she liked them.

She shrugged. "Sorry, I'm not really hungry." She placed it down. She wrapped her arms around her knees.

He scooted over to have their bodies touching. "Is there something wrong?" he asked.

She looked at him, and she didn't want to tell him the truth. She felt embarrassed by it. "No, I just…" She let the thought go away.

He placed a hand on her knee. "Tell me."

"Do you think I'm attractive?" she asked, looking at him.

"Yeah?" He was nervous about his answer. He didn't know where she was going with this line of questioning.

"Do you think I'm fat?"

"Is that why you're not eating?" he asked.

"Answer the question." She wanted to know his opinion. She hated this about herself. She knew she cared about what people thought, and she wished she didn't give a damn. This was why you were the Pathetic Queen, Jasmine. A real Queen didn't give a damn what her subjects thought.

"I do see you're thicker than other girls."

"I fucking knew it." She stood up. "I'm just some charity case. I bet all your friends are having a good laugh."

He stood up with her and grabbed her hand. "I wouldn't call you fat. I like thicker girls. You're sexy to me, and that's why I wanted to talk to you."

Jasmine blushed. "Thank you for that." She sat down and opened the wrapper to her hotdog.

"You going to explain why you were asking me that?" Carter wanted to know the backstory. He wanted to know everything about her.

She shook her head. "No, I'll keep that to myself."

He took a seat next to her. "I can't wait to know more about you."

The lovely new couple sat on the steps, eating their meals, watching the fountain, and enjoying each other. They might have thought this was the beginning of a beautiful relationship, but we were ready for another tragedy. Carter, you should have enjoyed your time with Jasmine, because she truly cared about her social standing unlike you. She wanted a prince, not a gardener. Young love in a battle for power. We loved casualties;

too bad it was the hot runner that was about to learn to never give your heart out so easily.

Chapter 34

Calvin continued to hit the baseball as hard as he could. He wanted to forget about everything that was involved with Aman. He couldn't get the video out of his mind. He started missing the ball, and he continued to strike out. He screamed after the fifth one, and he threw the bat across the field.

He could tell that his teammates were starting to look at him with worry. He waved them off, and he went toward the locker room to cool off. He went to his locker and grabbed his towel, and as he did, his wallet fell out. He bent down to pick it up, and he opened it to a photo of him and Aman. They looked so fucking happy, and in love. He wondered where they went wrong.

Coach Soto walked into the locker room to check on Calvin. "Someone has a lot of stress to get off his chest today."

Calvin nodded, grabbing his water bottle. "I don't really want to talk about it right now."

Coach Soto leaned against the lockers. "I don't need one of my players to be going through shit, especially, when states are right around the corner."

Calvin sighed. "I thought things would be better by now. You think someone is going to fight for you, but you're stuck fighting for the relationship."

Coach Soto nodded. "Girl trouble?"

Calvin turned to glare at him. "You know damn well that it's not a girl." Calvin had told coach last year when he caught him and Aman in the locker room together. Coach Soto didn't see Aman, because Aman ran out of the locker room before Soto could get a glimpse of him.

"You know it's my joke for it."

Calvin rolled his eyes. "God forbid I'm gay. God forbid that I can't be with the person that I love. It's all fucking bullshit! We're trapped like animals for what? Because someone doesn't agree with our views? We can fucking love whomever we want!" Calvin screamed.

Coach Soto leaned over and put a hand on Calvin's shoulder to calm him down. "I see that you're worked up about something. You can let it out." He paused. "Just not on the baseball equipment."

He shook his head and looked down. "I really believed we had something special. I thought he loved me, but he just wants us to stay in the closet."

"But you agreed to be in the closet because of baseball," said Coach Soto. Calvin made it clear that he would stay in the closet. He wanted to go off to the majors, and he understood the consequences of being gay.

"But, what if I don't want to be some big baseball star?" Calvin asked. "I don't want to have to hide myself."

"People were doing it for years." He paused. "People are still doing it. You got lucky to have a family that loves you, friends, that accept you, and a coach who encourages you. Not many people get that."

"You don't think I know that?" Calvin asked. He knew he could be like Aman's family, with the threat of being tossed on the street as a real fear. "I know damn well I got the jackpot in a lot of ways, but I can't fully be me. I look out at people being their true selves, and I am stuck feeling like an actor in my own life. I feel like I get pulled back into being the straight baseball star."

"You need to realize that no one acts like themselves. We all keep things close to our chest. We let a select few in the world see our true colors."

"And that's a tragedy. I want people to see me for who I am."

"So, you want to be defined by your sexuality?" Coach Soto asked.

"No, but I'm being held back because of it. I feel like I have a rainbow flag pin on my shirt, and I hide it every day because it won't be easy for me."

"It's never easy for anyone."

Calvin laughed. "Coming from the straight white male."

Coach Soto nodded. "I guess you have a point." He didn't know what it was like to struggle with the color of his skin, his sexual orientation, or feeling less than. He lived a good life, and he prayed his students had the same luxury.

Calvin closed his locker. He just wanted to take a shower and forget about all of this. "I'm going to snap. I'm going to break this cage open, and I'll be out. I can't wait until I'm pushed to the limit." He walked toward the shower.

"You need to be careful. You have no clue who you might hurt in the blast." Coach Soto didn't want him to do anything reckless. He prayed that Calvin found clarity, and he made the smart move here.

Calvin shrugged. "Why should I worry about other's feelings? They didn't give two shits about mine." He turned and walked away from him.

Be careful about breaking those walls down, Calvin. You weren't in that prison alone, and we had a feeling your cellmate wouldn't like the sense of freedom like you. You believed the truth would give you all the answers you had been seeking, but what happened when you realized it was all bullshit? We truly rooted for your happiness, but it seemed you were ready to pull someone from the shadows to the spotlight. Would that make you better than the rest of these bitches? Keep being a baseball star, not a whistleblower.

Chapter 35

Delilah had her eyes closed as she embraced the spring sun. She wanted to forget about all the problems in her life. She tried to write something new, but she couldn't stop looking at the blank page.

She couldn't get the feeling of Principal Grand off her mind. She didn't want to remember his lips on her neck, or his fingers on her thighs. She wanted to push him away, but she desired the feeling. She felt like she had no value, but he was the first person to see her. Delilah, he only saw you as a cum dumpster. We wouldn't call it a grand romance.

She felt someone's fingertips on her arm. She opened her eyes and turned to see Flynn. He had a smile on his face. "You look so beautiful right now," he said.

She rolled her eyes. "I probably look like shit."

Flynn shook his head. "I would never think of you as anything but gorgeous."

She blushed. She was called hot or sexy from guys, but gorgeous implied beauty from the inside. "It's refreshing to have someone say that to me."

"No one's told you that before?" Flynn asked. He thought Delilah was one of the most interesting people in the world. He didn't get why she had so much doubt in her heart. She had the talent that he could only dream to possess, though he would never admit that out loud.

"My father calls me his special star. He's always believed in me and my writing." She stopped to smile. "He's always traveling, because he continues to come out with bestsellers." She slid up. "My mom's books do well, but she's not on high demand. She sticks to her romance novels, and there's no need for book tours."

"And your mom doesn't want you to be a writer?" Flynn asked.

She shook her head. "My parents were thrilled when I started writing. They were more ecstatic than when I walked." She paused. "They don't want me to fail."

"They don't believe in you?"

"They want to give me all the tools to succeed. They want to use their influence to get me into the best colleges, get the best agent, and to get my book published." Delilah had a conversation with her mother last night about having friends on the board at NYU, and how she could always transfer to a better program there. She ignored her mother, because she had applied for the colleges she wanted, and she didn't want her mom using her influence.

"I think that's rather stupid," Flynn said.

Delilah looked at him. "How so?"

"I would use any tool I could to get ahead. My parents always raised me to take advantage of what people can bring to the table for you. If my parents were in publishing, I would use them to get my book out there."

"But wouldn't you feel incomplete, because you didn't do it yourself. Wouldn't you feel like it was all just a bunch of bullshit?" Delilah asked.

He shrugged. "I would know that I used my smarts to get ahead. Writing isn't just about creating a captivating story. It's about using your resources to get that book out to the masses."

She shook her head. "I want to believe that my body of work could inspire the world."

"Do you think it can now?" Flynn asked.

She shook her head. "I don't know what to believe anymore. I look at my writing, and I think that I've written a masterpiece. I go back and read it, and all I see is the mistakes, all the false hope, and the bullshit that people won't connect with."

"Do you think you're an imposter?" Flynn asked.

"Yes, I think I'm a little kid playing dress up. I try to believe that I could amount to something, but it's all a lie. I won't be anything except for a failed human being."

Flynn got closer to Delilah. He grabbed the bottom of her chin. "I would never consider you a failed human being."

"You're biased." She didn't believe a word that he said. She believed that there was lust in his eyes, and he couldn't see the broken human being standing in front of him.

He shook his head. "No, I'll always be honest with you. I think you're one of the most interesting people I know. You look like a stuck-up bitch, but you have a heart with such inspiring voices. You'll become someone unstoppable once you get your confidence up. I believe in you."

She looked in his eyes, and she could see he really meant it. She leaned forward and captured his lips with hers. She felt the spark of romance and the addiction to trust in this kiss. She had never felt like someone truly got her, until this moment. She could fall for Flynn, and she knew that he would be there to catch her. She wouldn't have to go through this world alone.

He broke the kiss and pushed her hair behind her ear. "Know that you can always send me your work, and I'll give you my honest feedback. I'll be your biggest cheerleader."

She nodded. "Thank you, and the same goes for you."

"We all need someone to trust in the writing world."

"Agreed." She leaned forward and kissed him again.

Delilah, you had no clue that you kissed the man that would break you the most. He had already stolen from you, and we weren't talking about your heart. You might have thought he was building up your confidence, but he was just trying to get access to that naïve brain of yours. Flynn brought up a valid point about using the resources around him. He found a stupid slut with self-doubt, but a talent for words. Who wouldn't manipulate to get the writing gold from you? You had better enjoy the moment in the sun, Delilah, because we had a feeling a Hurricane was coming, and you weren't going to have rainbow skies once it was done with you.

Chapter 36

Andrew walked into the pool hall in Williamsburg. Danielle had enough of Andrew hanging out with Bethany and Tucker. She invited him to come and play pool with her and some friends. She didn't like the idea of Bethany talking shit to Andrew about her, and her friends. She wanted to show him that they were a good group of people.

He looked around, and he couldn't find Danielle. He felt his phone go off and pulled it out to see Danielle had texted him.

Danielle: *Sorry, I can't make it tonight. My mom asked me to work her shift tonight. She's not feeling well.*

Andrew groaned before texting out his response.

Andrew: *I thought you didn't need to work anymore because of your dad.*

Danielle had told him about her and her dad's agreement earlier.

Danielle: *My mom doesn't know about the agreement, so I have to keep up the charade.*

His phone chimed again and it was Danielle.

He didn't know why she had still had to keep it a secret, but he wasn't going to ask questions.

Andrew: *Have fun. Jordan should be there with our other friend Emily.*

Andrew barely remembered what Jordan looked like, and he felt awkward going up to her. He thought about going home, but he had come out to meet new friends. He really enjoyed Tucker and Bethany, but they were asking a lot of questions about his past.

He walked around until he saw Jordan talking to a couple of guys at the pool table. He walked up nervously. He could tell that she was flirting with these guys, and he didn't want to get in the way. "Hey, Jordan."

Jordan had her hand on the taller, dark-haired guy when Andrew interrupted her. Jordan turned to look at Andrew. It took a minute for her to recognize him. "Andrew, right?"

He nodded. "Yeah."

She got off the pool table. "Danielle told me you were coming. Happy to see you're hanging with the cool kids and not the lame ones." She looked around, until she saw Emily talking to some girls. "Emily, come here."

Emily had jet black hair, a nose ring, hazel eyes, and part of the side of her hair was a buzz cut. She walked over to Jordan and Andrew wearing tight skinny jeans, a white t-shirt, and a black leather jacket. "What do you need, Jordan?" She looked at all the guys. "I know you can handle yourself with four men."

Jordan rolled her eyes. "Fuck off." She pointed to Andrew. "This is Danielle's friend. She couldn't make it for some stupid reason, but I'm busy."

Emily crossed her arms and looked him up and down. "You're the new kid from that small town?" she asked.

Andrew nodded. "Yeah, I just moved here a couple of weeks ago."

She smiled, and he could see her dimples. Andrew hadn't been attracted to anyone in New York until Emily came around. She looked like no one else at Johnson Prep. She didn't have this preppy, good act going. She looked like she could kick your ass in a bar fight, and she had some scars on her heart. "Welcome to Pocket." She walked over and pulled him away from Jordan.

Andrew waved to Jordan as they walked away. Emily escorted him to the bar. She got behind the bar and grabbed a bottle of whiskey. "Can you do that?" he asked.

Emily laughed. "I guess you haven't gotten used to the lifestyle of New York." She grabbed two shot glasses. "My father owns this place and a series of bars and restaurants." She poured two shots. "Unlike our classmates, my dad's money isn't from business. We are considered the scum because of it."

He chuckled. "You'd think that even with money, you wouldn't have a class system."

She looked at him. "Please, there's always a hierarchy in this world. It doesn't matter where you go. There's always the concept of being on top. Why do you think there's always someone backstabbing someone at our school?" she asked.

"I thought it was because that's what they do in high school," he said.

She grabbed her shot and threw it back. She looked at him. "What? You going to tell me that you're a good guy, and you don't drink?" She leaned against the bar. "Someone like you being so innocent in this world seems crazy."

He looked at the shot. He remembered the moments that he was at his lowest. "I wouldn't consider myself innocent."

She raised an eyebrow. "You have my interest. What demons do you have in your life?" she asked, pouring herself another shot.

"I just met you. I think somethings should be left for mystery, don't you?" Andrew prayed that would keep her off his back for more answers.

"I agree to the mystery, but I also agree to the fun. Either you tell me your past, or you drink. There's nothing wrong with a couple of shots, right?" Emily asked. She was interested in him. Sure, he looked like the quiet, shy kid that kept to himself, but she felt there was a dark side in there.

He looked at the shot and then Emily. He came to this city to get away from his past. He thought maybe it was just a moment that he went off the handle. Maybe he had grown since then. He didn't think one shot could hurt him. He grabbed the shot and took it. "See, I'm not so innocent."

They continued to talk and take shots, but it wasn't like they were spilling their secrets to each other. We assumed this was the part of our golden boy's story about dabbling into his dark past. We enjoyed a good train wreck, because where was the fun in people keeping their shit together? We hoped you enjoyed your true love, Andrew, because we couldn't wait to see you fall from grace. Maybe this time, you could end it all.

Chapter 37

Andrew woke up the next morning with a raging headache. He didn't know what time he got home from the bar, but he knew the sun was slowly coming up. He heard his phone go off. He turned to see that it was Tucker calling him. He picked it up. "Hello?" He knew his voice sounded groggy.

"Hey, I thought we were still meeting up to take photos for our project."

Andrew let it slip his mind. He forgot that he and Tucker were skipping the first three periods to go take photos for their portfolio. "Yeah, I remember. I guess I slept through my alarm. I'll be there soon." He got out of bed and walked into his bathroom to see that he looked like a complete mess. He quickly took a shower, and powered through the urge to throw up.

He walked downstairs to see his dad in the kitchen. Mark looked up from his paper. He was meeting with a new client in the afternoon, so he took the morning to get acquainted with the gentleman he would be defending. "Someone had a long night."

Andrew walked over and grabbed a to-go cup. He poured himself some coffee and put the lid on top. "Yeah, I was out with some friends, and we lost track of time."

"I hope there was no drinking involved."

Andrew turned to see the worry on his father's face. Andrew smiled. "Dad, I'm not going down that path again. We came to this city for a new start, and I plan to keep it that way. You need to trust me."

Mark smiled. "I know, but this is a hard time for you. Your mother's anniversary is coming up. I don't want you to do anything reckless."

Andrew knew subconsciously that his mother's anniversary was right around the corner. It will be two years since she was diagnosed, and he didn't want to think about it. "I'm going to be late for this project with Tucker."

"I love you," Mark said. He wanted to say it as many times as he could to Andrew. He remembered seeing him almost dead on the bathroom floor, and he would appreciate every second he had with him moving forward.

"I love you, too." Andrew walked out of his apartment and toward the elevator. He felt his phone go off. He saw it was a text from Emily saying she had a good time last night. Andrew vaguely remembered last night, and he loved every second of it. He wasn't the boy that lost his mother. He wasn't the train wreck, and he could restart here. He could escape from the problems, and he felt like people cared about him. Andrew, we were going to warn you once, you could never reinvent yourself because your demons didn't like the idea of change. You were running, but soon enough, they would catch up to you.

****

"Sorry, I'm late." Andrew ran up to Tucker and Bethany. They were meeting at Botanical Gardens in the Bronx.

Bethany was looking at her checklist for the day. Prom was only two weeks away, and she had to make sure everything was perfect. She had spent way over budget on the decorations, but she was hoping the ticket sales would balance it out. Worse case, she would write a check for the remaining balance. It wasn't like she was poor.

Tucker had been setting up his camera and tripod. "It's perfectly fine. We just got here twenty minutes ago."

Bethany locked her phone and walked over to Andrew. She looked at him with a once over. "You were out drinking last night, weren't you?"

Andrew raised an eyebrow. "Why would you think that?" he asked.

She crossed her arms. "You have bags under your eyes, and your breath reeks of alcohol," she laughed. "I knew Danielle and her friends would corrupt you."

Andrew got a little upset. "They've been nothing but nice to me. I don't get why you're so critical of them."

"Because they've reminded me since we were little that I'm nothing but a quiet loser. I spent my time in the library, not getting drunk at some bitch's house. I'm trying to achieve my dreams, not destroy them."

Andrew thought about Danielle and her goal to be a fashion designer. He heard Danielle talk about Delilah's aspirations of being a writer. Aman wanted to go into film, and Calvin wanted to be a baseball player. "I think you've spent too much time judging them. They have dreams and goals just like you. They also want to enjoy the high school experience."

"And you think I don't?" Bethany asked.

"Maybe you're too focused on hating them, and your studies, that you've lost focus of having memories for yourself."

She enjoyed her high school experience and had memories for herself. Yes, Bethany, we were sure you had a lot of fond memories of high school. Our favorite was when Eddie rejected you in front of the whole school, and Danielle filmed it. Our other favorite was when you told Tucker you loved him for the first time, and Jasmine decided to kiss him right in front of you without, Tucker knowing. Yes, you were our favorite wallflower because it was so easy picking on the scum.

"You don't know these people like we do," Bethany said.

"Jasmine tried to make it seem like I was cheating on Bethany. Jasmine barely talked to me, and then one day, Jasmine all of a sudden kissed me in front of Bethany," Tucker said. He couldn't believe Jasmine was kissing him, and he pushed her off instantly, because he would never hurt Bethany like that.

"They're a bunch of cunts. I figured you would realize that after The Marked Queen has been exposing their bullshit for the entire school to see."

Andrew shrugged. "I've been focusing on getting to know them without all of that mess. People can spread any rumor they want, and I'd rather hear the real story from that person."

Bethany laughed. "You'll never hear the real story from anyone." Bethany felt her phone go off. She saw it was an email from her OBGYN. She read the email to herself.

Bethany, we know you were in a rush last time, and we didn't get a chance to give you your results back. We need to schedule another appointment, since it's urgent.

Bethany deleted the email instantly.

"What was that?" Tucker asked. He saw that Bethany seemed a bit spooked.

Bethany smiled. "Nothing. It was my mom sending me prom dress options." Bethany couldn't get the email out of her mind, but that would be her secret. Tucker and Andrew went on to do their project, and Bethany helped when she could.

Secrets, lies, and cover-ups. This school should have made that their slogan. Bethany, what test results were you keeping from the world? You finally got our attention, because the only thing semi-interesting about you, was how you and the mouth breather fucked. We were positive that your scandal would get lost in the shuffle, after all, you were just the Queen of the library. The Marked Queen wanted to take down a kingdom, not a measly village.

Chapter 38

"Aman, we are proud of you and your success these past couple of weeks," Taj said, raising a glass to his son.

Aman smiled. This was the first time, in a long time, that his father had been proud of him. "Thank you so much."

"Now, we need to discuss the future."

"Future?" Aman asked. "I thought you said I could continue to do my YouTube channel. It's helping me with training for when I go to film school."

Taj waved off his son. He didn't mind his son going into movies. He thought there was good money in production, directing, and behind the scenes. "I know you still have your aspirations, and I have no problems with that. I wish you were going into business, but you're proving your worth with this channel finally." He paused. "This has to do with your love life."

"My love life?" Aman was a bit taken aback. His parents had never mentioned that he should be with anyone. His parents had always told him to focus on his studies, because girls were a distraction.

"Do you have a girlfriend?" Taj asked.

Aman shook his head. "No girlfriend." Why didn't your father ask if you enjoyed sucking cock? We had a feeling your answer would be something different. Although, you and Calvin haven't seen much of each other lately. Trouble in paradise, but who wouldn't be mad at you for making fun of them?

Taj smiled. "That's what I like to hear. I've taught you well." He paused. "My new business partner has a daughter, Sana.

She's beautiful and a year younger than you. She's been homeschooled her whole life, but they are moving here from London. I want you to show her around Johnson Prep."

Aman raised an eyebrow. "Why did you ask me about my dating life then?" He didn't get where the correlation came from. He didn't mind showing someone around the school. He knew he could make it another video. He had some success with Andrew's video.

Amara leaned over and grabbed her son's hand. "We want you to date her."

Aman turned to his mother. "What?" He stood up. "You can't force me to date, someone."

Taj stood up. "You will date her. I don't care if you're opposed to it. I pay for everything in your life, including that hobby of yours. You will do what you're told, and I don't want to hear it."

Aman looked at his father. "So, I date this girl, or you're going to take my YouTube channel away from me?" he asked, shock and anger ringing from his voice.

"Yes."

Aman threw his napkin on his plate. "I need some air." He walked toward the front door.

"It's past your curfew," Taj said.

Amara got up. She walked over to her husband. "Let him get some air. I think that will do us all some good."

Aman turned to look at his father. "I'm obviously going to agree to date this girl. It's not like I have a choice. Thank you for creating a life for me, where I don't get to choose what to do in it."

"You chose your YouTube channel, and I allowed it."

"Except now you're using it as a bargaining chip." Aman walked into the elevator and let the door close on him. His mind was swirling all over the place, and it killed him to know the one place he would end up; he was not allowed.

****

"I don't get why you're here, don't you have other friends you should talk to?" Calvin asked. They were sitting on Calvin's front steps. Calvin wanted to slam the door in Aman's face, but he still loved him too much.

"I can only come to you, Calvin." Aman turned to look at him. "I shouldn't have posted that video, and I'm sorry. I just don't want to lose this channel. It's everything to me, and I hate that my father uses it to control my life."

Calvin had always seen Aman struggle with the fact that his father wanted to mold Aman into the son he wanted. Aman was into the arts, and he was gay. Those were two things his father would never accept. "I love you."

Aman looked up and smiled. "I love you, too. I've missed you so much lately, and I feel like I'm starting to unravel."

"Why not give up your channel for a little bit?" Calvin could tell the pressure was getting to him.

Aman shook his head. "I can't. It's the only thing I have right now."

"You have me, babe." Calvin leaned forward and kissed Aman on the lips. It was a kiss filled with reunion and love.

Aman needed this kiss to feel grounded, and it gave him a wave of calmness. Aman broke the kiss. "Calvin, you have baseball. I have my channel. Would you give up baseball?"

"In a heartbeat. I don't need it as my security blanket."

Aman smiled weakly. "I guess that's where we disagree." Aman stood up. "I want to believe that my family would love the real me. They enjoy this persona I've created, and I'm thinking that's the persona I should be."

Calvin shook his head. "Your family will love the real you. I love the real you. You need to give them a chance to get to know you. You're becoming exhausted, because you have to keep playing this charade. Take the walls down, and you can be with me."

Aman shook his head. "Calvin, I wish I could be with you more than you know, but I can't."

"Why can't you be with me?" Calvin asked.

Aman wanted to tell him about Sana, but he couldn't. He would lose Calvin, and he didn't want that to happen. "I can't tell you."

Calvin was done with all these secrets and lies. He wanted to know the truth. "Tell me the truth," he demanded.

Aman leaned forward and gave Calvin a chaste kiss. "I wish I could tell you, but I can't." Aman got up and walked away from Calvin. Calvin was stuck wondering where their relationship went wrong, but it kept coming back to Aman's family.

Aman, you kept running away from your secrets, but they were going to catch up to you. You should have listened to Calvin about taking your walls down, but it was too late now. We could see the cracks in the foundation. Your house was starting to fall apart, and The Marked Queen was coming for you, piggy. You better watch out, she loved to huff and puff.

Chapter 39

Jasmine looked at the recent postcard from her mother. She read about how her mother was having the best time in Barcelona, and she wanted nothing more than to escape this city and be with her.

She inhaled a shaky breath. She pulled open her nightstand drawer and pulled out the letter from her mom from when she decided to leave for Europe. It talked about how she was unhappy, and she wanted nothing to do with her or her father. She wanted to believe her mother would come back for her, but she wasn't so sure.

She needed to hear her mother's voice. She called her mother, hoping she would pick up. Kelly picked up on the second ring. "Jasmine, how are you?"

Jasmine smiled at her mother's voice. "It's so good to hear your voice. I've missed you so much."

Kelly smiled. "I know, honey. I miss you terribly, too."

"Why not come back?" Jasmine asked. "I would love to see you, even if it's for a weekend." Jasmine just needed a hug from her mother, and she wouldn't feel so defeated right now.

Kelly sighed. "You know that I can't come back to New York. Your father would instantly find out. I want to wait until the divorce is finalized before I come back to the city."

"But what about me?" Jasmine asked. "Don't you miss your daughter?"

"Jasmine, don't you dare think that I don't want to see you," she paused for a moment. "I have to protect myself right now."

Jasmine looked at the letter. "Because you had to find your own happiness."

"Yes, I told you this. I was so miserable there. I couldn't do it anymore."

Jasmine thought for a moment. "Why don't I come to you?" she asked. "I could get my GED. We could be together."

Kelly thought about that so many times. She couldn't ask for anything better. She lay in bed at night worried her daughter wasn't okay. She could even hear it in her voice right now. "Your father wouldn't approve of it."

"Fuck, dad."

"Jasmine, he's still your father."

Jasmine didn't feel the need to show her father respect after everything he's done to her. He deserved to be abandoned. "No, I won't. You have no clue what kind of monster he's been since you've left."

"I can only imagine," Kelly said.

"Then let me come."

Kelly sighed. "I can't."

"Fine. You enjoy fucking leave me in the dust. Did I mean anything to you?" Jasmine asked. "Do you care that you left your daughter?"

"I will always regret leaving you behind, but I wasn't strong enough for the both of us."

"Excuses, if you ask me. Forget it. I meant nothing to you, and I shouldn't have bothered calling you." She hung up on her mom. She wanted her to be the answers to all her issues. She believed if she got up and ran out of this town, that maybe things would get better. Jasmine, just because you were in a different city, didn't mean you would get a clean slate. You were still fat and desperate for attention. Those qualities don't magically go away.

She grabbed the letter and crumbled it up. She didn't need to read her mother's words about how much she hated living in the city. She didn't need to be reminded of how she wasn't good enough for her parents. She walked down the stairs into the kitchen. She walked into the pantry and grabbed all the junk food she could find.

She sat at the kitchen counter in an abandoned house. She was truly alone in the world, except for the food she was shoving down her throat. No one cared for her, unless it was to break her heart or bones. She didn't understand why she was everyone's rag doll. Why couldn't anyone love her? She consumed the food hoping the pain in her heart would eventually go numb. Fatty Jazzy, you had better keep on eating. We wanted you good and plump for the pig roast The Marked Queen was hosting in your honor.

Chapter 40

"Get off me," Delilah said, pushing Principal Grand away. She had just sucked him off, and he craved more.

"You don't get to push me away like that." He placed his hands on her hips. "After everything that I've done for you. It's the least you can do for me in return."

She pushed him again. "I blew you off. I've been very accommodating. You can fuck off." She walked toward the door.

"You think you're something because you can write? You would just be some bimbo bitch if I wasn't getting your grades up. You're nothing without me."

She turned to look at him. "My writing has nothing to do with you. I've done that all on my own. I just know that I want to be with someone that doesn't look at me like I'm some slam piece." She thought of how sweet Flynn has been to her. "I want to be with someone that doesn't use me."

Principal Grand laughed. "Everyone is using someone for something. You think people always have sweet intentions, don't you?"

"Or maybe, I'm done dealing with low lives like you."

"At least I'm honest about my intentions. You knew damn well you were using me to get your grades up. We were both in this for something. You want out because you act like you got a moral compass all of a sudden."

She looked at the door. She didn't want to look at him anymore. "I'm not sleeping with a teenager." She opened the door before he could respond. She walked away from him, knowing she left him with blue balls. Delilah, we were proud you stood your ground, but he would get off somehow. We had a feeling you weren't going to be fond of it.

She began to feel disgusted with herself, and she wanted to breakdown in tears. She wasn't looking where she was going, when she ran into Flynn. Flynn was leaving the library trying to think of a short story to write. He wanted to use a lot of Delilah's work, but he knew he couldn't outright steal the material. She had turned this in, and he was stuck with writer's block.

"Delilah, what's wrong?" he asked, noticing she was distraught.

She shook her head. "Nothing, I just have a lot on my mind."

"Do you want to talk about it?" he asked.

She looked at him, and she wanted to tell him everything. She wanted to open up to him about Principal Grand, her doubts, and her writing. She knew she couldn't because he would run away from her. "I can't right now. I just feel like I'm caged up, and I want to scream."

He towed her to the library. They sat down at a table and he pulled out his laptop and slid it in front of her. "Here."

"What's your laptop going to do?" she asked.

"Why not write? Why not get it out on paper? You said you feel like you want to scream. You're talented, Delilah. Why not get it out this way?"

Delilah looked at him. She thought he was crazy, but he had a point. She began to write her frustrations about Principal Grand. She turned it into a story about a girl continuing to drink because of a boyfriend. She knew it was cliché, but she continued to drink, even though it was killing her. She would rather be dead and liked, than alive and alone. She didn't know where the story was going, but she continued to write anyway.

She felt engaged in the story, until it got to the point of the main character sleeping with the villain. She felt repulsed because she could feel Principal Grand's breath on her skin. His lips on her boobs, and his fingers in her hair as she was blowing him. She felt herself about to vomit. "I need a minute." She got up and ran to the bathroom. She walked toward the stall and began to throw up. What was with you girls throwing up during school hours? Didn't you know to keep that shit at home privately?

She took a moment to breathe, and leaned her head against the cool tile. She felt a bit free getting those emotions out on paper. She didn't believe that everyone was using everyone for something. She looked at Flynn, and he was trying to help her.

Once again Delilah, we just wanted you to be a slut, not a dumb whore. As you were puking out the vile of blowing a middle-aged man's cock, your boyfriend was stealing your story. You needed to learn that the only thing he was using you for, was your creative brain. We get that was a shock, because most men used you for your talented tongue and open-leg policy. We hoped you kept thinking Flynn was your knight in shining armor, because we couldn't wait for you to go in for your true love's kiss, to discover your Prince Eric was nothing more, than Ursula with a dick.

Chapter 41

"Your dad's place is really nice," Dan said, looking around. He had heard about nice apartments on the Upper East Side, but he had never actually seen one. Aw, poverty Dan, you should have soaked it in as much as you could. She said she was a girl with a heart of gold, but she got a taste of diamonds again; too bad for you all you could give her is a case of bed bugs.

Danielle was fixing her hair. She turned to look at him. She smiled and got up. She walked over and kissed him on the lips. "Let's not act like this is all new to you, when we go downstairs."

"Why not?"

"Dan, the kids I go to school with have lavish apartments, townhouse, and condos like this one already. This is the Upper East Side. Everyone's rich."

"But we live in the Bronx."

Danielle placed a hand on his lips. "No one knows that about me." She fixed her dress. "Except for one fucking person, but I'm going to prove her wrong tonight." Danielle, didn't you know that The Marked Queen saw through the bullshit. You had better fix that dress, because the next time you wear one, it was going to be ruined by the stains of your secrets coming out.

Dan rolled his eyes. "Why do you care about what people think? There's nothing wrong with being poor."

"And there's nothing wrong with trying to get through high school. I have a month left before I walk out of those halls. Prom is in less than two weeks. Can't you give me this?"

Dan sighed. He knew that his girlfriend cared what other's thought, and he didn't understand it. He rolled his eyes, but he leaned forward and kissed her on the lips. "I just don't want you to go down a dark path."

She smiled. "I'll be perfectly fine."

"I don't date phony people." Then why the fuck were you dating Danielle? Did she have you tricked into thinking she was a better human being? We had proof she was nothing more than a cunt.

She rolled her eyes this time. "Have I shown you that I'm phony?" she asked.

He shook his head. "No."

"Let's go have some fun," she said. They left the guest room and walked down the stairs, to see everyone was mingling in the living room and into the balcony. People looked up at her as she descended the stairs. She stopped for a moment and smiled. "Welcome to my home. I'm happy everyone's here tonight. I expect everyone to have a great time and make sure that you never forget tonight." People cheered and went back to their conversations.

"Do you mind if I go be a wallflower?" Dan asked. He kept trying to fix his tie, and he felt extremely uncomfortable in this social setting.

Danielle sighed. She knew that he liked his peace and quiet. "Maybe it's perfect this way."

"And why's that?" he asked.

"So, I don't have to introduce you to people," she said. She was hoping this party would make people forget about The Marked Queen post on Dan.

He put on a brave smile. He always knew that she was ashamed of him, but it was her night. He had to act like it didn't phase him. "No problem."

"Thanks for coming. I know it isn't really your scene," Danielle said.

"No, but you are." He walked away with a wink.

She laughed and rolled her eyes. She looked around at people talking and mingling. She saw Jordan talking to some guys, and she had to say, she was impressed with the junior. She had taken Jordan under her wing two years ago, and the girl hasn't disappointed. She looked and saw Andrew and Emily getting comfortable. She knew that was bad news because Emily didn't have an off switch. She got even more worried, because she saw them taking shots. She didn't want to be the cause of Andrew's relapse.

She was about to stop, him when Bethany walked up to her. "Thank you for inviting me."

Danielle turned her attention to Bethany. "I invited everyone tonight, because I know one of you bitches is The Marked Queen."

"You threw a big party for her?" Bethany looked at her weird. "What's the point?"

Danielle was about to explain why, but she realized that no one knew she was poor. "Because she wants to spread something that's false about me, but I had to prove her wrong."

"I think you're proving her right," Bethany said.

Danielle crossed her arms. "In what way?"

"You're throwing a party with alcohol and food. People are getting drunk, and we're underage. It's proving to her that you and your friends are just a bunch of insecure alcoholics lacking any substance."

Danielle leaned over and saw Bethany was sipping champagne. "But you come into my home to insult me, but drink my champagne? That's classy of you."

Bethany laughed and rolled her eyes. "I didn't say a glass of bubbly was in the wrong. She turned to see Andrew and Emily together. "You know she's going to eat him alive."

Danielle saw them take another shot. "Yeah, I don't want that for him."

"Why? Isn't that what your group of friends like to do? You destroy the innocence in everyone because you are all dark inside."

"Why do you hate us so much? Yes, we've been cruel to you, but we haven't been that vicious. I need to stop Andrew before he makes a mistake."

"Because everything you touch goes to shit. You believe you're the royals of this school, and you're invincible. You act like you're above consequences. Look at Andrew, he didn't act this way until you became friends with him." She shrugged. "Maybe he needs to be the cautionary tale for all of you."

"In what regards?" Danielle asked.

"That someday, all of this will come biting you in the ass. I hope you're prepared, because I have the popcorn ready for it."

"You act like we are going to be burned at the stake," Danielle said.

"Isn't that what The Marked Queen is trying to do?"

"You know so much about her," Danielle said. She noticed a glimmer in Bethany's eyes when she talked about The Marked Queen.

Bethany smiled. "Please, I don't give a fuck about your pathetic lives. I have a future I'm working on." She walked past Danielle, but she stopped and turned around. "I do love watching you squirm, though," she whispered. She went to talk to Tucker about leaving.

Danielle ignored Bethany because she was wrong. She knew her actions had consequences, and she feared that Andrew wasn't going to realize his mistakes. She looked for him, but she couldn't find him.

She felt her phone go off, and she saw it was a text from an unknown number.

You might have thought throwing this lavish party means I forgot the days of you living like trash. You can bask in this moment, but soon we will learn you're just a knock-off spoiled girl. You're my favorite Queen, and it's because you believe your disciples actually worship you. Don't you remember a wholesome story called Judas? Look around, Danielle. They might be drinking your champagne, but they're toasting to the day the knife in your heart turns fatal.

She turned to see who could have sent the text. She saw that Bethany was having a conversation with Tucker, and she didn't even see her phone. She was convinced that Bethany was The Marked Queen, but now she wasn't sure.

Danielle, you should stop trying to figure out who The Marked Queen really is. You should have enjoyed your last couple of days in bliss. The Marked Queen's day of judgment was right around the corner. She was about to change the game, and you were all going to be on trial. Take a sip of champagne with your friends now, because tomorrow they were going to be your biggest enemies.

Chapter 42

"Is this as awkward for you as it is for me?" Sana asked. Sana was a beautiful Indian girl. She had long, black hair, a petite figure, and big brown eyes that were warm upon looking at. She took a sip of her coffee and smiled.

Aman smiled. "It's good to know that I'm not the only one feeling like this is uncomfortable." Aman looked down at his cup. His parents had arranged this, and he had to go with the motions now.

"My father has set me up with a series of his business partner's son. At least you're the best looking of the group." She winked.

He laughed. "How do you do it?" he asked. "How do you sacrifice your goals for your families?"

She shrugged. "Because this is how I was raised. Yes, I wish I had the chance to make my own choices, but what's the point? You know it's our culture to abide by our family."

Aman shook his head. "I don't want to believe that my destiny in life is to make my parents proud."

She laughed. "You're so Americanized. You might believe that you have a choice, but you don't. We are still rooted in the culture, and you better accept that you don't get to live the life you fully want to."

Aman thought of Calvin. He thought about the life they dreamed of, and he thought maybe one day, they could have that together. "What if I run away from it?" Aman asked.

She took a sip of her coffee again. "Run away from comfort, wealth, and power? No foolish man would do that."

"What if it's for love?"

"I've learned that love isn't guaranteed. I'm seventeen-years-old and being pimped out by my father. Normally, that would be disgusting, but it's part of the game. You have to accept that you can't be anything other than who your father has decided you to be."

"But he lets me have my YouTube channel."

She nodded. "I've seen it, and I'm impressed."

"Really?"

"I've had to do my research on you," she laughed. "That's my job in life, to make sure my boyfriends are happy."

"What are your dreams?" he asked. He could tell that she had been brainwashed by her family, and he wanted to know the real her.

"I've always wanted to be a dancer. I know it's silly to see an Indian girl as a hip-hop dancer, but I went to Los Angeles two years ago, and I saw a performance. I fell instantly in love with it."

"Why didn't you pursue it?"

"My mother found out. She says my place is in the kitchen and household. I must make sure that I'm a suitable catch for any man that might come my way. I can't be distracted by the arts," Sana said. She hated the day her mother threw out all her hip-hop magazines. She wanted to run away right then, but she knew there was nowhere to go. She couldn't disown her family and disgrace them in that way.

"I'm sorry to hear that."

She smiled. "It's fine, really. I've come to accept that this is my reality. We all have to accept it, eventually. You need to be the perfect son for your family, or you will live a miserable life."

"What if I can't?" Aman asked. He didn't know if he wanted to accept that he didn't have any control in his life.

She nodded. "Then you're going to make it worse for yourself. Eventually, you become the son they want you to be."

"And I have to give up my love life?"

"There's no such thing as love, when it comes to our lives. We're all pawns, and we're trying to get ahead. The sooner you accept that, then you might actually like the person you become." Sana saw so much hope in Aman, and it killed her to see him breaking inside. She wished she had someone to give her that advice, because the heartbreak nearly killed her.

Aman thought of Calvin, and he didn't know if he could say goodbye to him. He knew that he was already pushing him away, but once he found out about Sana, it would be the final nail in the coffin. He didn't know if he could say goodbye to his old family for this new one. Aman, you didn't have a choice about any of this. The only thing you controlled was when your video was published. You were just a handsome puppet, and you were about to have a battle between your masters. We hoped for your sake you liked the winner.

Chapter 43

"I wanted to talk to you," Demi said. She had noticed that Andrew was checked out of the meeting, and she was worried.

Andrew just wanted to get out of this meeting. He had spent the whole morning trying to prove to his dad that he didn't drink the night before. He was hungover and exhausted. He didn't know Emily could be this much of a party animal.

"I have a lot of homework to get to. How about I text you tomorrow when I have the chance?" he asked as he walked toward the door.

"Or, when you have the chance to sober up?" she asked.

He turned to look at her. "I don't know what you're talking about."

She raised an eyebrow. "So, you're telling me that you aren't hungover right now?" she asked.

He shook his head. "I don't get why you think that I would relapse." He tried to make sure he was confident in his answer. "I would never give up what I've worked for."

"I doubt that. I think everyone finds the real reason they escape with alcohol. I think you're finally figuring it out." Demi used alcohol because of loneliness. She feared if she didn't with her boyfriend, she would be stuck in that quiet apartment every night.

"I was grieving my mother's death."

Demi nodded. "Are you still grieving?"

"I don't think you could ever stop." Andrew woke up every morning wondering what it would be like to have his mother there. He would then think about the times he would have to clean her up. He would remember the times he had to fight her to take her medicine and reward her with a shot. His father never had to see any of it. He was too busy at work.

"Why are you drinking again?" she asked, arms folded across her chest.

He ran his fingers through his hair. "I don't get why you're assuming I fucking drank. I've been sober. I'm becoming a better person. I'm becoming someone she would have been proud of." The truth was, he was turning into someone his mother would be proud of. It was sad his mother wanted a drinking partner, instead of a proper member of the community.

Demi walked over and placed a hand on his shoulder. "I wish I could believe you. I want nothing more, than to say that my suspicions were wrong."

He pushed her hand off his shoulder. "Maybe I am sober. I'm not like you."

"What's that supposed to mean?"

He laughed. "You believe you're curing people in this room. It's all a bunch of bullshit. We could never be cured. We must live with our stigmas for the rest of our lives. I don't want to be known as an alcoholic."

"Accept it, Andrew. There's nothing you can do about it. No one wants to be labeled one, but here we are. Do you think we enjoy having that stigma attached to our name? Do you think we love going to a fucking party and knowing we can't partake, because we can't control ourselves? Believe me, there have been so many times that I've wanted to run away from the stigma."

"Why don't we run away?" he asked. "Why can't we be freed of it?" He wanted to be a high school student. He didn't want to have any cares in the world. He wasn't ready to grow up.

"Because, that's not the path that was meant for us. You should know that by now. We don't get that luxury."

"Bullshit. That's a quitter's mentality. We can do whatever the fuck we want." He turned to see that Emily had walked into the room.

She thought she was picking him up from a group study session. "You ready to go?"

He turned to look at Demi. "I have never wanted to leave more than right now." He walked toward her and put his arm around her, and they walked out the door.

"Did I miss something?" Emily asked. She felt like she walked into an intense moment.

He shrugged. "I was just disagreeing with her about the theory of my paper. I'm going to go with it anyway. I feel confident in it."

"Remember, you can't walk away from your label," Demi screamed, trying to get their attention.

Andrew turned around and looked at her. "But I can walk away like a thief stealing back my identity." He walked out the door feeling invincible. He wasn't going to let anyone judge him, or tell him how to live his life.

They say at some point, you would go on trial for your actions. Andrew, we understood that you wanted to plead not guilty, but we had a feeling you might have wanted to take a deal. You continued to believe you were dancing along the line of self-control and indulging in fun. Too bad for you, your judge was one cold-hearted bitch. She believed you deserved to be sentenced to a town hanging. You believed your ally was Emily, but she was the one you were going to be hung next to. You should believe in what we said; take a sip because it was time we had a real tragedy, not a bitchy commentary.

Chapter 44

"Selena, please be careful when you go down on that slide," Carter screamed, to his seven-year old sister. Jasmine and Carter were babysitting her after school. Carter could have just left her with a baby sitter, but he wanted Jasmine to meet her.

"Cart, I'm fine," Selena screamed, before going down the slide.

"Cart?" Jasmine turned to look at Carter.

He rolled his eyes. "My sister couldn't say Carter when she was little, but she could say cart, so that's my nickname."

She chuckled. "I think it's really cute."

He poked her in the side, which made her jump. "Are you ticklish? That's so cute." He went to tickle her again.

"No, you get away from me." She ran away from him.

"You can't get away from me that fast." He grabbed her, wrapping his hands around her. We were surprised you could with how big she was.

"I hate you," she said, but she could get used to being in his arms. She wouldn't admit how nice it felt. Jasmine, it was probably because this was the first time someone thought you were semi-attractive.

He turned her around. "I don't think you hate me at all. I think you enjoy me."

She shrugged. "I wouldn't say you were the worst person in the world."

"Good." They looked at each other in the eyes for a moment, before Carter leaned forward and kissed her. We assumed the kiss tasted like hamburgers and tears, but it was a sweet moment. Jasmine never thought she would have met someone like Carter. He made her feel like she wasn't this ugly fat girl, even though she was. He made her believe in herself, even though she shouldn't.

He heard the ice cream truck bell. He turned. "Do you want some ice cream?" he asked. Carter, that was a stupid question. How did you think she spent her Saturday nights after she had been beaten by her father?

She nodded. He turned to see Selena coming up to them. "You want some ice cream?" he asked.

She shrugged. "Sure."

He walked away leaving Selena and Jasmine alone. "You like my brother, don't you?" she asked. "Like have a crush on him."

Jasmine turned and smiled. "Yes, I like him a lot."

Selena smiled. "Good."

He walked back with three ice cream cones. He gave Jasmine her treat, and she began to enjoy it. We wanted you to eat up, Fatty Jazzy. He then handed Selena her cone. Carter went to enjoy his. Selena looked at the ice cream cone for a moment, before she crushed it with her hands. The ice cream fell to the ground and all over her. Jasmine noticed the moment, but she didn't say anything.

Carter looked down to see ice cream all over her. "Selena, you're such a slob. Let me get you some napkins." He walked away.

Jasmine bent down in front of Selena. "Why did you crush your ice cream cone?" she asked.

"It was an accident," Selena said.

"I know it was on purpose. Did you not like it?" Jasmine asked. Selena shook her head and stayed silent. "Did you not want it?"

"It would make me fat," Selena said.

"Why are you worried about getting fat?" Jasmine asked.

"Because kids at school call me fat," Selena said, holding back tears. She wasn't a big girl, but she had a belly. Kids in her school called her a piggy, fat, and a loser. She would sometimes go into a slide and cry.

Jasmine placed her ice cream cone down and pulled Selena into a hug. She didn't care if she got messy. She could relate from the years of torment. "You are nowhere near being fat. You're a beautiful girl, and you should tell them all to piss off. You have to be confident in your skin."

"Are you?" Selena asked.

Jasmine was hesitant at first, but she couldn't break this little girl's dream. "Of course, I am. You have to be proud of your curves and ignore the people that are twigs." Jasmine, we made fun of you because you thought you were hot shit. We had to knock you down a couple of pegs.

Carter came back and cleaned Selena's hands. "Did you two have a good chat?" he asked.

"Yup," they both said in unison.

"Good. Race you to the monkey bars," he said, running with their ice cream cones.

Selena and Jasmine ran after him, and they played the rest of the afternoon. Jasmine felt free with Carter, and it was nice to relax, because she hasn't done it in so damn long. She forgot her parents, high school, and became delusional that someone could love her.

It was good to see someone looking up to you as a role model, Jasmine. Too bad no one was going to like your future actions. Maybe you should have been honest with Selena. You weren't confident, nor were you gorgeous. Fatty Jazzy, you were running away from the reflection in the mirror and self-doubt in your mind. Well, you weren't running clearly based on your body. If you were proud of the pathetic person you were, then maybe things with Carter would have worked out better. Oh well, this wasn't a romance, unless you counted our obsession with The Marked Queen making you her bitch puppet.

Chapter 45

"Could you at least look happy to be here?" Ethan said. Danielle was in the corner during a gala, while texting Dan about how stupid the party was.

"I'm surprised that you can see me since you've been shoved so far up Crystal's ass." Danielle couldn't stand her father's new wife. She was a young, mid-thirties whore in her eyes. She was a gold digger like there was any other. Danielle saw through her fake smiles. Danielle, you should have realized that if you continued on this path, you would end up like Crystal. You would be nothing more than beauty with no substance.

Ethan glared at his daughter. He wished she would have kept her attitude in check. He knew that he raised a firecracker, and was proud of who she was becoming, but he needed her to be the best daughter right now. Ethan, if you wanted the best daughter, you shouldn't have tossed her out like leftovers. "She's trying to be nice to you."

Danielle took a sip of her champagne. "Asking about school isn't cutting it."

"I paid for that gorgeous dress you have on. It was over two thousand dollars."

Danielle looked at her father. "But you're getting fifty million from your new client. Ethan Tyler, family man, how ironic?" Danielle turned to walk away.

Ethan grabbed her arm in frustration. "We had an agreement, and you're going to keep up with it. Deal?"

She ripped her hand out of his. She knew what she would lose if she bailed, and she couldn't do that. She might have had one party, but she still had people circling. She needed to get through prom, and then things would have be better. "Fine."

"Good." Ethan saw Christian walking by. Christian was his business partner's son. "I want you to meet Christian." Ethan grabbed Christian's hand. Christian was a tall drink of water. He had dark features, a full beard, slicked-back dark hair, and blue eyes like the ocean. He was a walking wet dream. Boys and girls alike went home to jerk off thinking about those broad shoulders, and strong arms choking them out while being pounded by him.

Christian put out his hand for Danielle to shake. "It's nice to meet you."

Danielle smiled. "Same to you."

"I feel the chemistry now. I'll leave you two, to it." Ethan walked away.

Danielle rolled her eyes. "Does your dad bluntly set you up on dates?" Danielle asked. She wished she could tell her father about Dan, but she knew her father would ruin it. He would see beneath him.

Christian smiled. "I think every girl I've ever dated has been because of my father thinking we could work out together."

Danielle smiled. "I should let you know that I have a boyfriend."

He shrugged. "No problem. I'm fucking a model right now anyway."

"And she didn't come with you?" Danielle asked. She shouldn't be surprised this guy was dating a model.

"Well, he's a he."

"Oh, you're gay?"

Christian shook his head. "I bang whatever comes my way. I enjoy sex, but my dad thinks that it will be bad for his reputation. He's trying to come off as a wholesome businessman. He can't have his son being a coke whore."

She took a sip of her champagne. "The irony isn't lost on me. My mom and I are actually poor."

"But your father isn't?"

"My mom left him, and he didn't give us anything. He thought it was his way of teaching us a lesson." She rolled her eyes. She looked over at her father and Crystal. "He then decides he wants to marry that trash, and I have to be the loving daughter."

"What we do for money," Christian said. He had to go to rehab, and act like he was an upstanding citizen. He was in business school because of his father. He wanted to be a world's traveler. He wanted to meet interesting people and write a book about it. His father thought it was a pointless dream, and he needed to be practical.

"Are you happy then?" Danielle asked. "Do you feel you've lost yourself for it?"

"We all agree to the arrangements by our parents for some reason. Yes, I love coke and sleeping around, but I get to go on trips and still travel when I can. I get the half-life that I've always wanted."

"But doesn't that make you want the full life?"

Christian grabbed the glass of champagne. He took a sip. "But why would I want to be poor?" he asked.

"Not in this city." Danielle knew The Marked Queen held her poverty over her head. "But sometimes having money doesn't make you happy."

Christian laughed. "Don't be a cliché. Of course, money makes you happy. You compromise yourself a little to make your life better. No one can have it all. I'm assuming your boyfriend isn't from a family of wealth."

"No."

"And soon you'll realize that you can't have both. Enjoy both parties because eventually, you'll have to pick one."

"Did you?" she asked.

"That's why he's just a plaything. You don't get attached, because then they won't get broken." Christian saw a girl winking at him. He thought she was cute, and he wouldn't mind seeing her out of that blue dress. "I have someone wanting my attention. All I'm saying is that you wanted this world for a reason. You'll have to give up something to keep it." He walked away leaving her deep in thought.

Danielle saw her father and stepmother. She wanted nothing more than to feel like she belonged, but she feared she was just another object tossed to the side. She didn't feel welcomed in this world anymore, even though she would do anything to keep up the appearance. She saw she had a text from Dan telling her that he loved her. She felt the most like herself when she was with him, but she worried Christian was right. She would have to give him up to keep all this.

Danielle, did you want your life to turn out like Christian's? We loved a vapid Queen, but we wished you would realize that there were other ways of being rich. Yes, we vomited in our mouth at how corny that sounded. So, would you give up your kingdom for the stable boy? Would you accept that you're nothing more than a food-from-a-garbage Queen?

Chapter 46

"You seem out of it today, Del." Matthew looked at his daughter, worried something was wrong. He had been busy promoting his new novel, and this was the first time he had seen her in nearly a month. They were seated waiting for one of their favorite authors, Ryan Hernandez, to come up to read passages of his new novel. It was a favorite pastime of theirs.

Delilah took a sip of her drink and looked forward. She felt emotionally drained lately with Principal Grand and Flynn. She felt extreme highs and lows with both. "I don't know if I want to be a writer anymore," she said. She had been thinking about it a lot lately. She didn't know if she had the chops to do it.

Matthew grabbed his daughter's hand. "Look at me." She turned to look at him in the eyes. "I've never seen your face light up more, than I have with your writing. I might be biased, but I think you're so talented. Why would you give it up?"

She shrugged. "Maybe I'm not good enough. Mom wants to use both of your connections to get me a publishing deal. She doesn't think I can do it on my own."

Matthew nodded. "That's because your mom struggled for years in her twenties, getting her first novel to be published. She felt like a complete failure. She wanted to quit writing so many times. She even tried to commit suicide."

"Really?" Delilah asked. She started to think that she was more like her mother. "How did she get through it?"

"She had me supporting her. I pulled her from a dark place more than once. I found her in the bathroom after she attempted." Matthew knew that image would be something he could never erase from his mind. He tried to write the scene in a novel, but he could never finish it.

"Dad." She grabbed his hand. "I'm so sorry."

He smiled. "But she pulled through. She used that depression and worked on her novel. She used that as inspiration. Did you know when you and your brother were born, she wanted you to stay away from the arts?"

"Really? Why?"

"Because she didn't want you to have the same experience she had. She wants to protect you from all this hardship. She believes in you and your talent."

Delilah smiled. It made her understand her mother even more. She thought that her mother thought she didn't have the talent to write, and it made things better to know that her mother was protecting her instead. We wondered if your mother went through the same phase as you, being a whore? Maybe you two could chit chat about that over a glass of champagne.

"I just feel like there's a voice in my head telling me that I'm never going to be good enough. I work my ass off on my writing, and I look at it, and think that it won't matter to anyone."

Matthew laughed. "I think every writer goes through that phase. We always doubt what we share with the world. We read it, wishing we could change everything. We seek the flaws, instead of praise the accomplishments." He paused. "Do you have someone you could lean on with your writing?"

She smiled. "Flynn. He's been incredible during this whole experience. I've been struggling with my confidence, and he's been telling me to use it as inspiration. I've been lucky to find him."

Matthew saw the same light in her eyes, as he saw in his wife's. "You really like this boy."

She nodded. "Yes. I don't think I've ever been this open with someone before. I'm so damn grateful to be with him in any form. I think I might love him." Oh, sweet Delilah, we wished you didn't drop the L-word, especially toward Flynn.

"Love can be a powerful thing, and I hope you use it in your writing. This new series I'm working on is because of you and your mother. I lost your grandmother and aunt when I was little myself. It was just my father and I growing up."

"Why do we come from tragic lives?" Delilah asked.

"Every writer lives a tragic life. It's why we become writers. We have to get out our pain somehow."

Delilah smiled. "Thank you. I needed this."

Matthew kissed her on the cheek. "Delilah, you should always believe in yourself. Your words will inspire people someday, and you should never forget that."

"I won't."

Delilah, we knew your words would inspire the world one day, but we weren't sure if you were going to be the one taking ownership of them. You might have wanted to believe you were in love with Flynn, but he was in love with your words. You had better enjoy this high of confidence, because it was about to be destroyed by the man that built you up in the first place. Maybe, you could use that pain to write something delicious for us to savor every page. We didn't want a sob story; we craved a blood bath.

Chapter 47

Aman was at a local coffee shop going through the comments of his new video. He saw another comment from The Marked Queen.

Aman, you're really impressing us with your new fame. Does this have anything to do with the new girl you're seeing? We're just wondering why you're keeping us from her? Do you have a secret lover? We wouldn't be surprised if you've kept up this charade. You do love having two faces.

Aman knew that once he posted a picture of him and Sana, that drama would ensue. His parents had asked him to post something to show that they were dating. He didn't get why he needed to show it on social media. He could tell they were happier with him, and he had to take that as a win.

He had his history textbook open, when he saw a phone plop down in front of him. It was the picture of him and Sana. "Do you want to explain to me what the fuck this is?" Calvin asked. Calvin was at baseball practice when one of his teammates asked about his best friend's new girl.

"I can explain," Aman said, looking up at Calvin. He could see the betrayal splashed across his face.

Calvin took a seat. He crossed his arms. "Explain to me why you're dating someone else? Why you're posting about it on Instagram without telling me?"

"My parents set me up with her. She's a business client's daughter. I couldn't say no to them."

Calvin laughed. "Of course, you couldn't say no! That would be insane!"

"What do you want from me?" Aman asked. He was so sick and tired of having the same damn fight with Calvin. He couldn't come out of the closet.

"I want you to stand up to your damn parents." Calvin stood up. "I want you to choose. Me or them?"

Aman laughed. "You can't be serious right now." Aman never thought this conversation would happen.

"Yes, I want you to choose either come out and be with me, or lose me."

Aman looked around, and he could tell they were making a scene. Aman packed up his things and left quietly. He would have this conversation with Calvin in a different setting. Aman walked out of the coffee shop, and he could tell that Calvin was following him. They turned into an ally to give each other some privacy.

"What's your answer?" Calvin asked.

"What happened to you never making me have to choose? You knew what you were getting into."

"Bullshit. I'm so done with your same response."

"Nothing's going to change."

Calvin laughed. "Because you don't want it to change." Calvin shook his head, and he could feel the tears starting to form. "I was so stupid to be with you. I knew damn well that this conversation was eventually going to happen. You were never going to come out."

"Eventually down the road, I was going to. We planned a future together, and I'm going to stick by that."

"When we move to Chicago?" Calvin asked. "I don't even think that's going to happen. I feel like we're going to be going around and around in circles."

"I want us to work out, Calvin." Aman knew that there were some struggles with their relationship right now. Aman, you were the one causing all the problems in the relationship. You wanted both worlds, and they were falling apart. You had to choose, and you couldn't have been surprised that he asked you to.

"Really? Then you could make this decision easier for the both of us." Calvin hoped that if he pushed Aman into a corner, then maybe he would come out. This would be his chance to fight for their relationship.

Aman knew the risks, and he wasn't willing to take them. "I'm sorry, but I can't."

Calvin nodded his head. "I was so fucking stupid to believe that you would choose me."

"So, this is it for us?" Aman asked. "I don't want us to be over."

"And I don't want to be the second choice!" Calvin screamed. "I have compromised so many fucking times in this relationship. When we got together, I wasn't ready for the world to know that I was gay. I stayed there, because I wanted to play professional baseball."

"And that's not my fault you decided to switch up career paths."

"You can't be mad at me for wanting to not be in the closet," Calvin said.

"And you can't hold it against me that I'm not ready to be out like you," Aman said. He wanted nothing in the world more than to be on the same level as Calvin.

"Do you like her?" Calvin asked.

Aman shrugged. "We are starting to get to know each other. It's all still brand new, and I'm enjoying my time. It's nice also not worrying about being caught. I can keep my secret of being gay and being with you."

Calvin shook his head. "I'd rather you be single. I don't think I can handle you showing off someone that isn't me. I won't be your dirty secret anymore."

"Calvin, I love you, and I really wish you would see my side of things. I don't want us to keep fighting because it's not healthy," Aman said. He wanted them to get back on the same page. He was hoping that Calvin would see him dating Sana as a good thing.

"I need to go. Call me when you realize that the life you're living is all bullshit," Calvin yelled, as he walked away feeling broken hearted. Aman, you really knew how to toy with a guy's emotions. You made him believe that you were struggling with your decision, but we had a feeling this is the one you wanted to make all along. We prayed you enjoyed this moment of feeling like you got away with it. Too bad for you, that enough loose ends could come back and could cause your demise. Hope you didn't choke too easy from them wrapping around your neck.

Chapter 48

Danielle saw Andrew and Emily walking toward the doors of the school. "Andrew, where are you going?" she asked. She had been worried about Andrew since her party. She had tried to contact him, but he has been ignoring her texts.

Andrew turned and saw Danielle. His smile faded. He had been putting Danielle on the back burner, because he knew that she wouldn't approve. She knew everything about his past, and Emily was the opposite of his treatment. "Hey, give me a second." He kissed Emily on the cheek and walked over to her.

Danielle crossed her arms. "What are you doing?"

Andrew shrugged. "Emily wanted to go to the pool hall, and I didn't feel like being in school anymore."

"But it's only fifth period."

Andrew laughed. "Are you telling me that you've never skipped school?" Andrew thought that was hard to believe.

"I've skipped school to go on vacation, not get drunk at some dingy bar." She paused. "Especially someone like you."

"Are you referring to the fact that I'm a recovering alcoholic?"

"I wouldn't label recovering anymore. What happened to you?"

He turned to point at Emily. "You introduced me to her. You ditched me that night, and I made my own friends. You can't hold that against me, can you?"

"I wanted you to hang out with them once, not go down on this dark path." Danielle felt like she made a huge mistake ditching him that night. She should have protected him from Emily. She was the complete image of bad news. She has sent boys to hospitals for overdosing. They didn't know their limits around her, and she knew Andrew wouldn't either.

"Don't be such a wet blanket, Danielle." Emily decided to come join the conversation. "I know how much you love a good line or two."

Danielle crossed her arms and raised an eyebrow. "I only enjoy it on occasion. You don't see me skipping class to go fucking do it." She turned to Andrew. "Don't go with her. She will destroy your life."

"I have done no such thing," Emily said, as she flashed a wicked grin.

"Really? What about Matthew Ryan?" Danielle asked.

Emily's smile went away. "You don't get to bring him up. I had nothing to do with that night. He did it all on his own. I was just along for the ride."

Danielle chuckled. "You mean along for the ride, until you left him dead in his room while you fled away."

"I stayed with him."

"That's not what Page Six reported," Danielle said.

"Fuck you." Emily went to slap Danielle.

Danielle grabbed her hand. She turned to Andrew. "See, this is someone you don't want to get caught up with. She was a freshman and Mathew Ryan was a Sophomore. He would have been a star on the football team, but he got caught up with her."

"Then why do you hang out with her, if she's bad news?" Andrew asked.

"I don't hang out with her. Jordan does. I have nothing to do with her. I was friends with Matt, and she killed him."

"But you wanted to introduce me to her. It seems like you made the mistake, because we're all having fun here. Why don't you go back to your fake life, and I'll keep living in mine?" Andrew didn't want to hold that against Danielle, but it was desperate measures.

Danielle smiled. "So, it seems this school has really done a number on you already. What happened to the guy that I met at the diner?" she asked.

Andrew shrugged. "He learned to be fake like everyone else in this school. You think people are themselves here. I figured out why my father brought me here. I could be whomever I wanted to be. I didn't have to act like myself. It's all just a bullshit production here."

"You can find good people to connect with. I thought we had that ourselves."

"We did, but now I want to connect with someone else." He turned to Emily. He leaned forward, and they started kissing. It wasn't romantic, nor filled with love. There was lust for the drugs and alcohol they were about to have coursing through their bodies. It was like a train wreck before their eyes.

Danielle separated them. "Let's keep this disgusting mess for the outside world."

"Have fun in your lie, while I have fun in mine." He grabbed Emily's hand, and they walked toward the door.

"What's her lie?" Emily asked. She was curious what the perfect Danielle was hiding, that Andrew seemed to be holding over her head.

Andrew turned to Danielle before turning back to Emily. "Nothing that really matters." He might not have cared for Danielle giving him shit for the people he was hanging out with, but he wouldn't expose her like that. He had some morals, for now. He also didn't know how to be a backstabbing cunt. He would have to be sober to accomplish that.

Danielle watched them walk out of the doors, and she got concerned. She pulled out her phone and looked up the AA meetings around her dinner. She vaguely remembered the place he went to that night. She called the number and asked to speak to the sponsor of the meeting.

"Hello?" Demi picked up the phone.

"My name's Danielle, and I think there's a person in your group, Andrew Reynolds."

"I don't know who this is, but our meetings are anonymous."

She rolled her eyes. "Fine, if this is his sponsor, you might want to know that he's fallen off the wagon, and he might not survive with the girl he's hanging out with." She didn't give her a chance to respond before hanging up.

Andrew, you had better watch your back, because your past was about to be revealed. You wanted to live in a world where you could be free, but you didn't get that luxury. People truly cared for you here, but you would never see that. We didn't want you to turn out like Mathew Ryan, or did we?

Chapter 49

"Dad, are you okay?" Jasmine asked, walking into the living room.

George turned to look at his daughter. He smiled. "Why did she have to leave?" he asked. He took another sip of his whiskey, while looking at the photo taken before she left for Europe.

Jasmine walked over and sat down across from her father. She had seen him like this so many times. It has always scared her, because he usually becomes violent after these moments. "Why are you looking at that photo?"

He smiled. "Because it was the last time we were all so happy. You were thin, your mother and I were in love, and we were a family."

Jasmine took the photo from her father. She looked at it, and she had agreed. She felt like she was invincible back then. She laughed because she used to be a nice girl. She shook her head. "I thought that I had friends I truly could count on. Two years seems like a lifetime ago."

"I don't understand what I did to cause her to walk out that door."

"Maybe because she wasn't happy here, dad."

He slammed his glass on the table. She was startled for a moment. "I made her happy. I gave her everything she wanted." He stood up for a moment. He began to sway, and he took a seat again. "I would have given her the world. I bought her all the things she wanted, took her on all the fancy trips, and I made her believe that she was good enough."

Jasmine would never admit to her father that he was violent when he was drunk. He was an extremely jealous human being. She was controlled by him, and she saw a lot of that happening toward her mother. "Maybe she felt she needed out."

George turned to his daughter. "Why do you defend her?" He grabbed the letter she wrote to them. "She left you, too."

Jasmine didn't need to read it. She had the fucking letter memorized. She tossed it to the side. "We've let our lives fall apart a little bit."

He turned to look at her. "You let yourself go." We couldn't agree with you more, George.

Jasmine swallowed the insult. "We have each other. Isn't that all the matters? We can be a family without her." Jasmine knew she was lying to herself. She wanted to get out of this hell hole, but she was scared she couldn't. Her mom was so hesitant about her going off to Europe with her, she had read the letter enough times to know that.

George laughed. "What family?" He stood up again with more strength this time. "Your mother took all the light out of this home, and you know it."

"I don't want to believe we're supposed to just accept being miserable."

"Do you feel loved?" George asked.

She knew the truth, and it killed her. "No, I don't." She hadn't felt like someone had accepted her since she started gaining weight. She became a bitch, and she thought people would flock to her. She realized that it was all bullshit. No one would or could love her.

"Exactly. We aren't lovable creatures. We go into the world thinking that people are going to accept us for the people we are, but they won't. We are scum to them all."

Jasmine shook her head. "I don't want to accept that this is the end. We have to be the bottom of the barrel for that to happen."

"I never said I was the bottom of the barrel." He leaned down to look at his daughter. "You are because you let your body image go." He stood up. "I have wealth and looks. What do you have?"

"Heart," she said.

He laughed. "No one gives a shit when you're fat. Your mother wouldn't have let this happen." He shrugged. "What's the point anymore? She's not coming back, and I have a fat daughter. Life is a fucking bitch." He walked away leaving her.

Jasmine felt a wave of anger and emotion. She grabbed the letter and went into her room. She grabbed her laptop and began to write her mother a letter herself.

Dear Mom,

I'll never understand why you decided to leave us. I don't know what I caused in your life to make you think it was okay abandoning me with this monster. He abuses me physically and emotionally. I feel like I'm complete scum, and you did this all yourself. You made me feel like I wasn't good enough. I gained weight because I felt like I needed to fill this part of my life. Ugly girls don't have pretty lives. You wrote that I wasn't good enough in that fucking letter, but you tell me you miss me? I can't get it out of my head. I get why leaving dad was the best decision, but what about me?

Jasmine

Jasmine closed her laptop and threw it across the room. She grabbed her knees and pulled them close to her chin. She began to cry because she didn't know what else to do. She thought about how much Carter made her escape. She never wanted that feeling to go, but she also wanted to feel loved by the masses. Jasmine would never understand the saying, "I'd rather have four quarters than one hundred pennies." That would be her downfall, and she wouldn't have a single cent to her name after it was all said and done.

Chapter 50

"Do you mind watching my laptop while I go to the bathroom?" Flynn asked. Delilah and Flynn were in the library during their free period.

Delilah smiled. "No problem."

He got up and walked out of the library. They had been working on their new short stories for the past couple of days, and she was curious about what he had been working out. He had asked her all about her short story, but had kept quiet on his.

She grabbed his laptop and turned it around. She began to read some of his short stories. She had a smile on her face because she was always impressed with his creativity. She loved how he could flow words together. She continued to read, until she read a passage that was extremely familiar to the story that she wrote about Principal Grand.

She opened the short story on her laptop and read them side by side. It was the exact same, and she felt her heart drop. She saw Flynn walking back from the bathroom. He stopped in his tracks, because he could see that she had read the story he had been working on.

She looked up to see that he had come back. He walked over to her slowly. She stood up and turned both of their laptops around. "What the fuck is this?" she asked.

"What?"

"Are you actually copying my work?"

Flynn laughed. "Delilah, why would I steal your work? I'm trying to get published, not get an easy A in the class."

"You wrote some of your passages word for word to mine."

He smiled. "Once again. Yes, you have good moments in your short story that are interesting, but overall, you aren't that talented."

Delilah let the insult dodge her for now. "Have you been using me?" she asked. "I thought you liked me."

Flynn leaned down and looked at her. "It goes back to what I said. You need to use your resources to get ahead. You've been too stupid to see that. I don't have parents to give me access to the publishing world."

"But your parents are in real estate. Don't they have clients?"

He laughed. "They have no clue what this world is. I want to be famous, and they can't help." They supported Flynn, but they wouldn't agree to him being an asshole.

"That doesn't mean you get to steal my work."

"No one's going to believe that you have the talent to write any of this. Delilah, people look at you as the dumb bitch." Flynn had always seen Delilah as beneath him. He only became interested in her once she started getting praises in creative writing. You could never trust the nerds, because they were bigger douchebags than the jocks.

That was the comment that sent her over the edge. "I guess I'm just the dumb bitch you tried to steal from." She shook her head. "I thought you actually cared for me. I believed you were good, but I'm nothing to you."

"Once again. It's the publishing world. You backstab everyone in your way."

She grabbed her laptop. "Have fun trying to steal my work now." She stormed out of the library. She truly felt like she loved him, and he was using her. She went into the bathroom, and she felt like her whole world was crumbling. She didn't think she had enough control anymore.

She went into the stall and closed the door. She began to cry, and she couldn't keep it in anymore. She pulled out a razor blade. She cut herself on her wrist and inner thigh. She tried to get the emotions out in the cuts, but they weren't working. She couldn't keep it in, and she was scared this would be her constant state of emotion.

She heard the door open, and she saw someone walking up to her stall. "Someone is in here."

"I don't care if you're shitting, Delilah. I know damn well you stormed in here a fucking mess," Danielle said. She had spent her free period talking to Demi about Andrew.

Delilah grabbed some paper towels, and she was hoping she could cover up the blood. "One second." She cleaned herself up and opened the door.

Danielle looked around and saw blood and a razor blade. She saw some other girls trying to walk in. "Use the other bathroom. Now!" Danielle screamed.

The girls were freshman, and were extremely terrified of Danielle. They ran out of the door without questioning her demand. Danielle turned to Delilah. "What the fuck is going on?"

"My period."

"Don't bullshit me right now." She pointed to the razor blade and the bloody toilet paper. "You're fucking cutting yourself?" She crossed her arms and stared down at Delilah.

Delilah knew she couldn't lie to Danielle, and she honestly was tired of keeping it all in. She felt like she could get it out in her writing, but it seemed that wasn't a safe place anymore.

"Yes," she said, and it felt so good to finally release that to the world. She felt a wave of emotions come over, and she cried.

"Why?" Danielle said. She kneeled down in front of Delilah. "What's going on?" She had been distracted with her own life, but she thought Delilah would have come to her if she needed something.

"Because my life's a fucking mess. Flynn has been using me to copy my writing. I've been sleeping with Principal Grand. I feel like I'm not good enough, and I don't know what to do with my life, Danielle."

Danielle had a lot of comments on the fact that Flynn was a douche bag, and that she was fucking the principal. She knew those comments would be for another day. Danielle grabbed Delilah's face. "Delilah, you are so fucking beautiful. You should never let some nerd tell you otherwise. You have so much value in this world. You should have more self-respect, than sleeping with Principal Grand. You are incredible and one of a kind. Remember that and stop being a fucking sob story in the bathroom."

Delilah laughed and hugged Danielle. "Thank you. I needed that."

She smiled. "I'm here for you any time." Danielle helped clean Delilah up, and they left the bathroom.

Aw, the sight of true friendship. Delilah, you thought you could conquer anything because your best friend was by your side. That was so sweet, but you just had broken the one cardinal rule in this school: You didn't trust anyone, especially your closest friends. You exposed all your cards to Danielle. You thought she was going to keep that close to her chest, but The Marked Queen was about to switch up the game. Now, we would find out if she was truly your sister.

Chapter 51

You were no longer a wallflower, Bethany. It was your turn in the spotlight. You wore that red dress with dignity and class. People looked at you for the first time, as you walked down the hall toward the marked board. You wore that black pin with disgust. You wanted to avoid this world, but it seemed that The Marked Queen had a different view of you. We were surprised you were the next marked girl, because let's be honest, no one gave two shits about you.

Bethany got to the board and rolled her eyes. "This is fucking stupid," she said, as she placed the note on the board.

People flocked to the new note. Danielle and Jasmine walked up to see the new marked girl was Bethany. "You've been marked?" Danielle asked. She couldn't believe the book nerd had a secret that The Marked Queen thought was worth blackmailing her for. "What secret could you have? Are you actually cheating on your tests?"

Bethany rolled her eyes. "I have nothing to hide."

Jasmine crossed her arms. "Clearly you do, if you've been marked," she laughed. "It's great to see that you're not above us."

"I don't get why I've been marked, or why I'm part of this stupid bullshit."

"Bethany, shut the fuck up. You live for this shit as much as the rest of us," Danielle said. She knew Bethany was there for every Marked Monday. "You continue to think you're above it all, but you love some good drama like the rest of us."

"What I see is a bunch of pathetic losers caring about other's lives." Bethany looked around. "You all flock to this note like it's some beacon."

Jasmine and Danielle shrugged. "Maybe it's good to know that some people aren't as perfect as they seem. Look at you, for example," Danielle said.

Bethany laughed. "Weren't the both of you marked?"

Danielle and Jasmine looked at each other. "We didn't say we were above it all," Jasmine said.

"But you try to make people think you're perfect." Bethany took off the pin and threw it to the ground. "You didn't wear the red dress, and I'm not wearing this pin. I don't get marked by anyone."

Danielle shrugged. "I would warn you that's a stupid idea, but I really want to know what you're hiding."

"I guess you'll have to wait and see," Bethany said. "I got group study to get to." She pushed past them and walked away from the group. Bethany, you really were a mysterious bitch. We wondered if the reason you were marked, had anything to do with that email you received. It looked like you had some skin in the game. We hoped you knew how to be ruthless like the rest of these bitches.

"Do you think her secret even matters?" Jasmine asked.

Danielle looked at her. "Why are we talking? Don't you have a donut to eat or something?" Danielle and Jasmine weren't friends, but they enjoyed calling Bethany on her shit.

"I thought we could be civil," Jasmine said.

Susan came up to Jasmine. "You have to read the new marked post. You won't believe it," Susan squealed.

Jasmine looked at her minion. "The fact that you're acting like a famous person just walked through these halls, shows you need a life, Susan." Jasmine pushed past her to get to the post.

Susan lowered her head. Danielle touched her shoulder. "Don't let the fat bitch get to you. We all love a good scandal. Why are you friends with her?" Danielle asked. She had seen Jasmine torture the girl, and Danielle didn't get it.

Susan looked at her. "Because she was the only person that was nice to me freshman year. I didn't have anyone, and she really was a good friend. I'm hoping she eventually gets back to there," Susan said, and she walked away.

Danielle walked away and remembered how Jasmine was freshman year. She was a delightful girl. The past two years, she got fat and became a bitch. Danielle wondered what happened in her life to cause her to be this cruel, but then again, she would have to care about Jasmine to give a shit.

Danielle walked toward the marked board. People moved to the side, and Danielle read the note. She felt her heart drop. She looked around at Delilah, Jasmine, Aman, Calvin, and Jordan. They all had the same expression of fear on their faces that Danielle had. It looked like The Marked Queen stepped up her game, and everyone needed to be afraid.

I'm having a bit of a sweet tooth lately. I'm craving some delicious desserts in the form of secrets. You have till prom to give me the dirt, or I'll expose the best scandals I've uncovered over the past months. You've all now been officially marked. May the backstabbing begin. Who can you trust and whose skeletons in the closet were about to be exposed? Good luck, bitches. -The Marked Queen.

Chapter 52

"Do you think she's really going to expose everyone's secrets?" Calvin asked. Everyone was still talking about The Marked Queen's declaration. He knew that his secret was at risk, and he had a mix of feelings about it.

Danielle turned to look at Calvin. They were at a park near her house on the swing set. She shook her head. "I don't know what that bitch is thinking, but I know it's not going to be pretty. We are all not safe at this point."

"She's going to expose Aman and me," Calvin said. He knew that he had to tell Danielle the truth. They needed to expose their secrets to each other. They could only trust each other, and that was the truth.

Danielle turned to look at Calvin. "Aman has been your secret boyfriend this whole time?" She should have seen it coming. They both were all over each other. She thought back to earlier in the day. She saw the sheer horror on his face. "Makes sense that he looked petrified today."

Calvin pulled out a note in his pocket and handed it to Danielle. "I got this a couple of days ago. I thought we were being clever."

Danielle saw the red envelope, and she knew instantly it was from The Marked Queen. She pulled the note out and read it.

Calvin, why do you have to be such a cliché? The big baseball star spends his free time in the closet. Why not be original? I guess it makes sense why you're the catcher. My only question is, who is your favorite pitcher? Don't worry about your baseball career, you could always be an icon for the thirsty boys out there. Now, remember, always use protection and make sure you watch your back in the showers. I hear you really do love a good team building exercise.

Danielle crumbled up the note. "She really knows how to be a bitch, doesn't she?"

He shrugged. "I was so worried when I got the note, but it doesn't matter anymore. My relationship with Aman is over, and I think it's better if I come out."

"Because of the new girl?"

Calvin laughed. "He doesn't see that we could be something amazing if he came out. He'd rather be safe in the closet."

Danielle looked at the sun starting to set. "Some people aren't ready to be exposed for who they truly are."

"Maybe that's why so many people are scared of The Marked Queen."

"Exactly. We can no longer pretend that our lives are what we've made people believe they've been for so long." Danielle knew that the kingdom was starting to fall. She didn't know what she was going to do if it got out where she lived. It was nice having the party, but she knew it wasn't going to be enough.

"It might be best this way. We can stop trying so hard to be someone we aren't." Calvin knew that this was the best option for him. He was so tired of acting like someone he wasn't. He knew that eventually, he would be exposed, and maybe this was the push he needed.

Danielle enjoyed Calvin's calmness to this, but she didn't have his mentality. "I can't just roll over." She stood up. "I'm going to stop this bitch."

"You don't even know who she is."

Danielle turned to look at Calvin. "I don't care. She can't come in here scaring us all, and think she can get away with it."

"Danielle, you need to accept that you don't control this school. We're just puppets to her. She's using our weakness against us."

"Maybe we get rid of our weakness." She pulled out her phone. She texted Dan.

Danielle: *We're going to a nice dinner and a shopping spree tonight.*

She knew it was the only way to keep The Marked Queen out of her hair. "She wants to believe she can have power over me, but she has another thing coming."

Calvin got up from the swing. "There's nothing wrong with being poor."

Danielle smiled. "And there's nothing wrong with being gay." She paused. "Johnson Prep isn't the outside world. We are a collection of judgmental assholes with our parents' money. You have to be the all-star baseball player, and I have to be the spoiled bitch. It's the roles we've been forced to play."

"I'm tired of playing, Danielle."

She touched his cheek. "That's sweet you think you have a choice in the matter. We are all pieces on this board. You're my king, not my pawn. I will not let you surrender to this bitch."

Calvin laughed. He pulled Danielle into a hug, and she felt comfort in this arms. She didn't realize how much she needed a hug from her friend, until right now. They could let down their walls and be themselves. It was nice and heartwarming.

"You aren't going to use me being gay to protect yourself?" Calvin asked.

Danielle rolled her eyes. "You aren't going to use me being poor to protect yourself?"

He shook his head. "I feel like you're the only one that I could actually trust."

"Same here. It might be a free for all, but I got an ally in my corner," Danielle said. She believed that she had people in her corner, but she had no clue what length she would go to make sure she ended up on top. Everyone feared what the next week held before prom, but we were going to watch with some popcorn. You had better make sure after the curtain call, you took a bow for your performance as the loyal best friend.

Chapter 53

"Is there something wrong?" Sana asked, while they were laying naked in bed together.

Aman shook his head. "No, I just need a minute." He got out of bed to grab his boxers. He couldn't get it up with Sana, and he felt like an idiot. He tried to think of anything other than having sex with her, but the reality of the situation was right in his face. Aw, was it because she didn't have a dick?

"Are you gay?" Sana asked. She didn't have a problem with him being gay. She knew that they didn't need to love each other in this situation.

He turned to look at her. "Why would you say that?"

She shrugged. "Because you can't perform. I've always sensed that you weren't really into this with me. I thought maybe it was because you didn't find me attractive, which is fine. I get that I'm not everyone's cup of tea."

He leaned forward and kissed her on the lips. He tried to give as much conviction as a closet gay could give. "I'm a virgin."

She smiled softly. "Oh, that's fine." She squeezed his hand. "So, you've never had sex with a girl before?" she asked.

"No, I haven't." He knew that was the truth, and he could spin it that way. "I don't want to look like an idiot in front of you."

She blushed. "There's nothing you could do that would make me feel like you're an idiot."

"Good. I just need a moment." He got out of bed and walked out of the room. He closed the door and walked into the kitchen. His parents were gone for the night on a romantic getaway.

He picked up his phone and called Calvin. He knew he shouldn't have, but he missed his voice. He missed being able to just laugh with him. The past month had been hard on them, and he knew that he caused a lot of the problems. He needed to apologize and get a lot of it off his chest.

"What do you want?" Calvin asked, when he answered the phone.

"I guess I shouldn't be surprised that your answer is lukewarm."

"What do you expect of me? Are you still with her?" Calvin asked. He lied awake at night thinking of how much it killed him that he was with her. He explained it to his parents, and they thought it was best for them to break up. He needed to be with someone that could be open with him.

"Yes, we are still together, but it doesn't mean we can't be."

"Aman, you can't be serious right now? We can't be together because, I'm just some skeleton in the closet."

Aman felt himself choking up. "I'm sorry for all of this. I wish that it never happened. I thought that we could make this work. I believed we were doing the right thing by keeping it secret."

"We both wanted to keep it a secret for our own reasons."

"But you've changed," Aman said. He saw how much Calvin was ready to break free from all of this. He wanted nothing more than to be able to hold hands with his significant other. "My parents are my everything, Calvin."

"But I was supposed to be your biggest supporter. I loved everything you did. I would help edit your videos." Calvin knew those were some of their best moments.

Aman laughed. "And I would help you on your swing for baseball. You've always been my best friend, and I don't want to lose you, Calvin."

Calvin felt the tears coming down his cheeks. "Would things be different if you weren't in this family?" Calvin didn't want to bring it back to his religion, but he had a feeling it would always come back to that.

"Maybe," Aman said.

"And I know that. Aman, I wish we never started."

"Don't say that," Aman said. "I know it has to end, but I truly believe we had something special. If things were different, then we could have been something more."

"But I can't be your dirty secret anymore. I can't be your second choice."

"And that's what kills me the most. I never saw you as second choice. I never want you to believe that I would pick someone else over you, Calvin. The only reason I'm with her, is because I have to be. Sana knows that this is a family agreement."

"Maybe I'm being selfish, but I wish you chose me over your family and never brought her into it. I'm done having this fight. I love you, Aman, but I need to go." He hung up on Aman before he could say anything else. Aman looked at his phone for a second. He pulled up a photo of them, and he cried for only a moment. He still had to act like he had it together.

He walked back upstairs to Sana in his room. She was on her phone and looked up when he entered the room. "Everything okay?" she asked.

He smiled. "Yeah, I needed to get some closure first."

"Ex-lover?" She didn't want there to be any issues moving forward with their relationship.

Aman smiled. "Things are all good. She didn't want it to end, but it had to." He thought of Calvin, and he felt himself getting hard. "I think we can get back to what we were doing earlier."

Sana looked down to see his boner. "I'm glad you got closure then." She pulled him in the bed, and they continued on. Aman, we knew you were thinking of Calvin as you were pounding Sana. We could have told you the best way to act "straight" was fantasying about cock during sex with a woman. We were so proud you pleased her, but would she be thrilled once it got out that you lost your virginity to the baseball star?

Chapter 54

"I thought we were going to hang out," Tucker said to Andrew, as they were at his locker.

Andrew liked Tucker, but he was getting too close. He loved his time with Emily because there were no feelings involved. Tucker wanted friendship, and Andrew needed a good time.

"I know, but I made plans with Emily. We're going to some concert tonight."

"I could come with you all," Tucker said. He felt like Andrew was the first true friend he made at this school. He had always been tossed to the side. He understood that anytime someone would be friends with Tucker, it was to get close to his brother and sister.

"Dude, it's not your scene."

Bethany was standing there, and she was getting frustrated for Tucker. She had seen this happen to her boyfriend many times. People enjoyed using him for something, and then walking away. She was tired of it. "You made plans with my boyfriend, and now you're ditching him because you made better ones?"

Andrew put his hands in the air. "I just met you guys a month ago. We like photography together, and I've always enjoyed that. You don't need to become a bitch about it."

"And you're being an asshole going back on your plans," Bethany said.

"This is why I wish I never was friends with you in the first place. I got stuck being shown the school by two wallflowers. I don't want to spend my evenings reading books or trying to connect with people. I want to go out and forget." Andrew knew it was harsh, but Tucker had wanted him to open up.

"That's fine, but you should have just told me. This is stupid. I get that I'm not the most exciting person at this school, but I thought we understood each other." Tucker shook his head and grabbed his camera bag. "I'll see you later." He turned and walked away.

"What's his deal?" Andrew asked. He didn't think it was that big of an issue to want to hang out with Emily. He thought people in this school didn't get close to anyone. He assumed they were all pawns to each other.

"Why do you care? That means you would have to get close to someone." Bethany shook her head. "Enjoy your night with your new carefree lifestyle." She turned and walked away to find Tucker.

Emily walked up to him. "Is everything all right?" she asked.

He shrugged. "People are becoming so sensitive in this school. You ready to let loose?" he asked. He wanted to put this all behind him and have some fun.

She leaned forward and kissed him on the lips. "Let's go be bad," she said. She grabbed his hand, and they walked out of the school. The only thing bad here was your outfit, Emily. You could have worn something under that short dress of yours. Andrew going down the dark path with you was a divine decision, because your rock bottom would be something we all savor.

Bethany found Tucker in the photo lab. "You want to talk about it?" she asked.

Tucker looked up. "I get that I'm not someone special. My family has always been the ones with the big personalities. I like to wait in the shadows. I understand I'm more reserved. I just thought I could have at least one friend."

Bethany smiled. "You have me and other friends, too," she said.

"Yeah, but I liked hanging out with Andrew because he wasn't here for my mental breakdown. I still see people looking at me like I'm some fucking freak." He looked at his new photo project. "I just wish people would forget about what happened that night."

She grabbed his hand. "You can't blame yourself for that car accident."

He looked at her. "Maybe I should. I was the one that fucking killed her. I only got off with a fucking warning because my family's rich." He slammed his hands on the table. "I'm still the psycho to half the fucking people in this school."

"And people will forget all about it. Prom is next week, then we have graduation. We have a little over a month left in this school. It also seems that The Marked Queen has something up her sleeve. Hopefully, people will forget about what happened months ago. You need to remember that," Bethany said.

Tucker sighed. He knew that if The Marked Queen succeeded in her mission, then people would forget all about what happened to him. He still woke up screaming at night because of the accident. "I love you so much."

She kissed him softly on the lips. "I love you, too." She hugged him, and she prayed that The Marked Queen made people look at themselves in a negative light.

It was so nice seeing these two bonding over their mutual hate for this school. Tucker, we had no clue you had such a killer instinct. We got that you love getting the perfect shot.

Maybe the reason people didn't want to be friends with you, was because they didn't know if they would live to tell the tale.

Chapter 55

"You seriously can't think this is a good idea," Danielle said, as she looked at Calvin like he was crazy.

"I want to make him jealous. I know he's going with her to prom, and I want to have someone on my side too," Calvin said. He couldn't sleep last night after his conversation with Aman, and he was hoping taking Jasmine would get Aman to feel like he was the second choice.

"Jasmine of all people. You should take me or Delilah," Danielle said.

"Delilah is hooked up on Flynn, and he knows we are best friends. It has to be Jasmine."

"She's fat and ugly. You really think a gay guy is going to get jealous of that? It's going to make him realize how lucky he is that he loves cock."

Calvin looked at Danielle. "Can you be supportive for one second?"

"I'm being your friend."

He rolled his eyes. "She isn't that bad of a person. Yes, she gets a little frisky, but she's stopped that since she started talking to Carter."

She looked at him. "Who the hell is Carter?" she asked.

"The runner?"

She shrugged. "I don't' know who he is, nor do I care. I think this plan will blow up in your face, and I'm going to be here to laugh at you."

"You're such a good friend," Calvin said.

She kissed him on the cheek. "Have fun." She looked down at the roses in his hands. "I think you should of went with donuts instead. We know that fat bitch loves her sweets." She walked away trying to ignore the fact that her best friend was making a huge mistake.

Calvin ignored her and walked over to Jasmine's locker. "Jasmine," Calvin said. He felt nervous, which he didn't understand why. It wasn't like there were going to be real feelings here. It was a move to get Aman jealous, and he hoped it worked.

Jasmine turned around to see Calvin standing there with roses. "What are you doing at my locker?" she asked.

"I was wondering if you would go to prom with me?" he asked, and he felt better getting it off his chest.

She squealed. She had been waiting for this day for months now. She always saw herself going to prom with Calvin, and she knew that Danielle would have a fit. He was the king of the school, and now, she would be his Queen. "Yes, I would love to go to prom with you."

He pulled her into a hug and kissed her on the cheek. "These are for you, and I can't wait." They stood there in silence for a moment. "I better get to baseball practice."

"Have fun. We will talk later about color coordination." She jumped up and down. She put the roses in her locker and closed it to see Carter standing there with his own set of flowers. They weren't as extravagant as the roses, but the emotions were there.

"Are you going to prom with Calvin?" Carter asked.

"He just asked me." She didn't even notice how fucked up that was.

"What about us?"

She sighed. She knew this was going to be awkward, and she didn't want it to be. "Carter, I have a great time with you, but Calvin can help me more than you can."

"How so?"

"He's popular. I want people to love and adore me after I leave these halls. Yeah, I really like you, but no one knows who you are. If I want to destroy Danielle before graduation, I have to do it with Calvin."

"You seriously care more about social standing than feelings?" Carter asked. He thought that Jasmine was above it all. He knew that she could be a bitch, but after she hung out with Selena, he thought she was different.

"Welcome to Johnson Prep. You knew these were the games being played here. You have to act like you rule it all, or you're going to be forgotten."

He dropped the flowers on the ground. "And you're going to be known to me as the shallow bitch." He shook his head. "Selena really liked you. She saw you as a role model."

"I'm playing the game. You can't fault me for that."

"Yes, I can. I don't play with people's emotions. I don't use people as pawns. I'm above all this bullshit, and I thought you were too. I get that it seems fun and exciting, but it's not going to get you anywhere. I really felt like we connected, and I had feelings for you."

"I have them for you too," Jasmine said. She couldn't deny her attraction, physically and emotionally to Carter. She also knew that she needed to do what's best for her social game. She couldn't let a romance ruin what she was trying to achieve.

"Forget it. You're just like the rest of them. Enjoy being on top. I bet it's going to be really lonely." He turned and walked away from him.

Jasmine wanted to go after him, but she knew there was no point. She bent down and picked up the flowers from the ground. They were lilies. She had mentioned to him before that they were her favorite flowers.

You stupid fat cow. Jasmine, did you realize that Carter was hot and interested in you? You thought Calvin was the answer to all your prayers, but he was gay. We understood you couldn't see that from the fucking pastries you were sticking in your damn mouth, but you fucked up royally here. You might have thought you were going to end up on the top, but there was no such thing as a fat popular girl. We really couldn't wait to see your ass sitting alone at prom, while everyone else had a good time without you.

Chapter 56

Delilah just stared at Flynn with so much disgust in her bones. She wanted nothing to do with him, and she believed he deserved horrible things. She couldn't believe the guy she was in love with would use her like that. She couldn't get the words he said out of her mind.

Flynn turned to see Delilah looking at her. He knew she was angry, but he had to do what whatever he could to get him ahead in this industry. "Why are you looking at me?"

"How can you sit there and not feel guilty for what you did?" she asked.

He shrugged. "Because it's part of this industry. You don't trust people with your work. I told you that you were stupid not using your resources. You have some talent, and I wanted to use that for my gain."

"But you had to say those hurtful things to me? What was the point in that?"

He smirked, and she thought it was adorable for the longest time, until now. "Because it's reality. No one would believe you had this talent inside of you. Delilah, you're just meant to be pretty."

"And you're meant to be an ass."

He rolled his eyes. "I'm telling you how it is. Don't you get that pretty girls have it easier sometimes? You have the power to open so many doors for yourself. You can be anything you want."

"What if I wanted to be a writer?"

He shook his head. "You don't get to be a writer. That's my thing." Flynn didn't want this girl with looks, to also have the talent. It wasn't fair. He has slaved over his work, and it seemed that everything came easier to her. He deserved something for himself.

"We don't have to compete here. We both write different styles. Why can't you see that?"

"Because it's not fair you get this. The world instantly gives you a pass. I'm not some good-looking guy. I'm not someone that people will try to do things for, to make my life easier. I have to do it all on my own. You have so much access to a better life. Why can't you see that I'm doing this to give myself those same access doors."

"You're stealing from me, and that's what makes this all bullshit."

He stood up. "Let's face it. You might as well just be someone's trophy wife. It's what we all believe is your future." He walked away.

She stood up and stormed to the front of the room with him. They both handed in their stories to Mr. Rozengota. He looked at both Delilah and Flynn. "Is there something going on here?" he asked.

Flynn crossed his arms. He was going to call Delilah on her bluff. "Is there something you wanted to say, Delilah?"

Delilah looked at Flynn, then at Mr. Rozengota. The words were on the tip of her tongue. "No, I just really am looking forward to you reading my new story."

Mr. Rozengota smiled. "I agree. I think your talent grows more and more with each piece you turn in."

Delilah smiled, but it was a broken one. "I need to go to the bathroom." She walked away from them and into the hallway. She felt the tears begin to fall, and she wanted to forget about them—needed to forget about him—just for a minute.

She walked into Principal Grand's office. He was going over some paperwork. He looked up to see Delilah standing there. He could tell that she was upset about something. She closed the door and locked it. "Is this a bad time?" she asked.

He stood up. "Yes, I'm in the middle of some time-sensitive paperwork."

She smiled. She started to unbutton her shirt. "You don't even have time for me?"

He didn't like the fact that she was practically throwing herself at him. He liked a chase more than anything. He liked when she was a bitch, and he hated when she was being needy. He wanted to make her subservient, but not clingy. "I don't have the time."

She smiled. "You always have time for me." She walked over and touched his knee. "Are you saying your ex-wife came back?"

He rolled his eyes. "Please, she didn't go down on me the last year of our marriage."

She touched his dick. "I bet I could be of service."

He looked at her puffy eyes. "Have you been crying?" he asked.

"Who cares? I'm horny, and I'm good at getting you off. Let me have some fun."

He didn't even know if he could get it up. The quickest way to kill a boner was being a hot mess. Delilah, you wanted to come off sexy, but you were coming off like a cock thirsty whore. We didn't mind the show, though.

She got down on her knees. "Let me give you a fun time."

He liked her on her knees, and he could fake it. He was already looking at sleeping with a junior, but she was playing hard to get. Delilah was becoming too old for him, and she was starting to unhinge. "Sure, a quick blow job wouldn't hurt," he said. He felt like he was doing her a favor letting her suck him off one last time.

She pulled his pants down, and she went to work. She knew the only thing she would be good at was this. Flynn was right. She was only a pretty girl, and pretty girls ended up like whores if they had no self-respect. It was a low day for Delilah, and it was going to be even worse once she found out Principal Grand found someone else to get him off. Delilah, we loved the downward spiral, and we hoped it didn't end any time soon.

Chapter 57

Danielle knew Calvin's idea was stupid, but she would help him any way she could. She saw Aman by his locker. He was probably looking up gay porn on his phone. She looked at Aman for a moment, and she shouldn't have been surprised that he was gay. She should have figured it out sooner, but she wasn't going to dwell on it.

She walked right up to him. "Hey, Aman."

Aman turned to see Danielle standing there. "Can I help you?"

"What? I can't come over here and chat with you?"

"Danielle, you've never spoken to me in your life. You want something, don't you?"

She rolled her eyes. "Your Calvin's best friend."

"So are you," Aman said. He didn't get where she was going with this conversation.

"He's being ridiculous. He asked Jasmine to prom, and I told him that's a stupid idea. I figured he talked to you about taking her."

Aman was taken aback by what Danielle said. Calvin was taking Jasmine to prom. He hated how clingy she was, and he didn't get where his sudden change of heart came from. "Yeah, he told me about it. I didn't think he actually would do it."

"He gave her roses and everything. If you ask me, I thought it was pretty pathetic. He should have asked a prettier girl, but it's his decision." She flipped her hair. "He's a big boy. I hope he knows what the hell he's doing."

Aman tried to keep his composure. "I'll talk to him myself." He closed his locker. "Thanks for telling me he ended up going through with it."

Danielle smiled. "No problem." She saw him storm off toward Calvin. She would help Calvin in any way. She didn't think Aman was a good fit for Calvin. He needed someone who would take care of him. He wanted to come out to the world, and he needed someone to be strong to handle that weight. She knew it wasn't Aman.

Aman found Calvin by his locker. He slammed Calvin's locker shut to get his attention. "You're taking Jasmine to prom?"

Calvin smirked. He was impressed with how fast it got out. "How did you find out?"

"Danielle came up to me and told me about it. She thought I knew, and she wanted me to come over here to talk you out of it."

Calvin had to buy something extravagant for Danielle. "I told Danielle that I wanted to take Jasmine to prom."

"Is this a way to get back at me?" Aman asked. He couldn't think of another logical reason he would take Jasmine. Sure, she was semi-attractive. He didn't mind the weight she had gained over the past couple of years, but she was a desperate bitch.

"Why would you think that I would do this to piss you off? It's not like you were jealous of her having her hands all over me." Calvin was playing dumb. Aman made it clear many times, that he hated how girls just threw themselves at him. Aman felt like he couldn't defend himself as Calvin's boyfriend.

"Fuck you, Calvin." Aman knew this was all a game, and it pissed him off.

"You don't get to be mad. You have a girlfriend now. You guys seem really happy together. Why are you so worried about my life?" Calvin asked.

"You don't get to be the revengeful ex. I couldn't be with you because of my family."

"No, you didn't want to stand up to your family for me. You didn't find me worthy enough."

"Is this your way of trying to get me to come out? Are you manipulating me?"

"Why do you feel like everything I do revolves around you?" Calvin asked.

"Because there's no other reason to ask Jasmine out to prom."

"Maybe I didn't want to go to prom alone?" Calvin asked. "Maybe I wanted to go with the person I love, but I was tossed to the side." Calvin shrugged. "I get that you want to protect yourself from your family, but you pushed me out. I thought we were each other's family. I keep fighting for us, and I'm so damn sick of it. You should realize that we can stop all this fighting, if you took the plunge with me."

"And I told you many times, that I couldn't do this. I'm tired of this same fight. I apologized over and over again to you. I made it clear, that I couldn't come out because of my family. I wish you were another race. I wish you didn't have fucking white privilege, because you would completely understand what it's like to be me."

Calvin threw his hands in the air. "I'm tired of you using that bullshit excuse with me. You have a family with mine. You have friends that will continue to support you. You can still live your dreams and be out and proud. Why can't you fucking see that?"

"Why can't you see that it's never going to happen this way? You need to stop pushing me toward the door. I'm tired of being played by you. This isn't a game, Calvin. This is my life. You have to stop!" Aman screamed.

"Fine. I'll stop." He turned and walked away. He didn't even look back at Aman. He thought this would work, and it killed him. He wanted nothing more than to just be free of this. He knew that it was time for him to come out alone. He didn't want to admit that he wasn't going to have Aman by his side, but he couldn't keep half of him a secret anymore.

Aman watched Calvin walk away. He punched the locker as hard as he could. He saw people looking at him, but he didn't care. They would assume that the two best friends were having a fight. No one was in hearing distance. Oh, Aman, you might have thought people thought of it as best friends fighting, but in a couple of days, they would realize it was a lovers' quarrel.

Chapter 58

"Put this on, and then we can go out to dinner," Danielle said, holding up shirts to Dan.

Dan rolled his eyes. He was over Danielle's insistent need of shopping and going out to nice restaurants. Ever since it came out that he was poor, and her father gave her money, she has taken him on shopping sprees. She has made it feel like she was been ashamed of his income.

He pushed the clothes off him. "I don't want to go to some fancy restaurant. Why can't we just stay here?" he asked. "We used to make dinner together."

She shook her head. "Now, we can go out. Imagine all the cute pictures together," she said. She knew that after the declaration from The Marked Queen, she needed to be on her game.

He walked over and touched her sewing kit. "When was the last time you used this thing?" he asked.

She smiled weakly. "I don't know. I haven't had the time for it, honestly." She paused. "Besides, I have money now. I don't need to make clothes anymore."

He laughed. "Do you really think that this is going to last? You're going to throw away all your dreams to be your dad's bitch."

She turned around and slapped him across the face. "I'm not just doing this to be my dad's bitch. I can get him to fund my own clothing line."

"Are you going to actually create it, or be a spoiled brat and get someone else to do it for you?" he asked, rubbing his face where her slap still stung.

She crossed her arms. She didn't like where this attitude was coming from. "You had no problem with all the clothes I bought you, or the parties I took you too."

Dan laughed. "Yes, I did have a problem with it. This has never been us. I have had no problem with where I've come from. I get that you lived in this world for so long, that you needed time to adjust. You were continuing to keep up the persona until you graduate. I didn't agree with it, but I understood it."

"And now?"

"I think you honestly want to go back to that world. I don't believe that you want to run away from it. I don't know which girl is the real one."

"I still am the same girl that I've always been," she said.

He picked up the dress that she was holding in her hand. "You would have made your own dress, and it wouldn't have been as tacky as this." He walked past her to see she had two prom dresses in the closet. She saw the one she made and another one with a hefty price tag. "So, you bought yourself a prom dress?"

"Yeah, I wanted to have options," she said.

He laughed. He turned to look at her. "You just didn't want to look like a peasant in your handmade dress."

"You don't need to judge me for my actions. I'm doing what I want to do. I have money again, and I wanted to give myself options."

"That's you being superficial. You weren't like this."

"Because I didn't have money!" she screamed. "I only started designing, because I wanted to keep up the appearance that I wasn't poor. Yes, I fell in love with it, but I knew what the purpose of it came from. It was all so I didn't have to tell people what was truly happening in my life.

He nodded. "I guess I should go then."

"Dan, don't be absurd. We can stay at home." She knew he was about to walk out that door, and she couldn't lose him. "I'll take it all back for you."

"No, you have never been real to me. Your true love is that credit card in your purse. I wanted to believe that I fell for a girl who loved creating, and had a heart. I just realized I was dating a poor wannabe." He walked toward the door.

Danielle grabbed his hand. She began to cry. "Dan, please don't go. I'm begging you."

He ripped his hand out of her grip. "I told you that I wouldn't date someone shallow. I knew you were going to go down this path. I should have seen it when you tossed me to the side at your party last week."

"I knew it wasn't your scene," she said.

"No, I just didn't fit in. I was someone you wanted to keep in the closet. You thought you could change me into someone you could be happy with. Danielle, I'm proud of who I am with my poor income. You aren't proud of me or yourself. Call me when the girl I fell in love with comes back," he said, and he walked out of the door.

She fell to the ground and began to cry. She wanted to believe she was doing what was best for the both of them. She wanted to believe that money would make her life better. Danielle, you really knew how to make men abandon you. How did you feel about that now? You just lost your stable boy, and you didn't have a prince waiting for you either. You were the loser Queen that no one loved.

She felt her phone go off. She pulled it out to see it was a text from The Marked Queen. "You have such wonderful timing," Danielle mumbled. She opened the text message and read it.

Marked Queen: I'm surprised you weren't the first one to give me dirt on your friends. You, are after all, are the one to lose the most. You already know what it was like to be poor. I was just wondering if you wanted to be poor in social standing too?

The text was attached to a photo of the front of her house.

She began to cry because she lost Dan, and she couldn't lose her reputation too. She thought about any dirt she had, and the only kind that came up was Delilah's. Danielle was betraying Delilah by telling The Marked Queen everything, but she had to keep her secret safe. She had to keep being the Queen of the castle, even if it was all made of paper. Danielle, you lost your boyfriend, and you were going to lose your best friend, too. You were about to be a Queen of a kingdom, but the population would just be you and the donkey.

Chapter 59

Jasmine saw her mother was calling her. She was busy picking out a prom dress that would be perfect for her skin. Jasmine, we thought you should have picked a dress that hid those back rolls, but that was just a suggestion. She didn't see the need to talk to her mother, but it seemed it was urgent, since her mom had called her three times in a row.

She picked up the phone. "I have nothing to say to you."

"That's fine, because I have a lot to say to you. He's abusing you? Why haven't you said anything? Jaz, I would have come back sooner."

Jasmine laughed. "Really? You told me in that letter of yours that you wanted nothing to do with me. Do you understand how that made me feel? I felt like you just tossed me to the side, just like Dad has been doing to me. I mean nothing to the both of you!" she screamed, and it felt good to get it out of her system.

"What letter are you talking about?" Kelly asked.

"The letter I found after you left."

"I left you a letter saying I couldn't be with your father anymore. He had become violent, and I needed to run away. I'm going to stay in Europe, as I collect myself and figure out a way to get divorced from him. I knew he would never be violent to you, and I trusted he would take care of you."

Jasmine shook her head. "That's not the letter I received." She walked over to her dresser. She pulled out the letter from the dresser. She began to read it to her mother.

"Jasmine,

If you haven't noticed yet, I'm gone. I can't stand to be around you or your father. I feel like I've failed as a person. I wanted to achieve so much in my life, and I was punished with a horrible husband and a pathetic excuse for a daughter. I dreamed of a daughter who was strong, pretty, and inspiring. I got a whiny, ugly, and useless daughter. I can't be in New York anymore because it depresses me. It's time I started my new life, and I wish you nothing but the best. Maybe when you become more lovable, I'll come back.

Your mother."

Jasmine felt the tears fall down her face, and she just wanted to burn the stupid letter right then. "Remember this?"

"Jaz, I never wrote that letter. Honey, I don't see you as any of those harsh words."

"Then why didn't you take me with you?" Jasmine couldn't see any other reason her mother would abandon her like that.

"Because I knew he would come chasing after us. I didn't want you on the run, especially while you have friends in high school. I knew it was becoming toxic, and I had to leave to make things better." Kelly felt hatred for her sadistic husband. "I'm so sorry your father wrote you a letter of lies."

Jasmine shouldn't have been surprised. Her father was notorious for destroying any kind of self-confidence she had. "Fuck him."

"Jasmine, you don't want to provoke him. He will become violent, and I fear for you."

Jasmine was filled with rage, and she was done being the weak girl her father has made her over the past couple of years. "I love you, mom. I'm sorry I've had so much hate for you for something you didn't even do."

"And, I'm sorry to make you believe that you are anything but extraordinary."

"I need to go," Jasmine said.

"Please be careful."

"Will do." Jasmine hung up the phone. She stormed down the stairs. Her father was in the living room watching TV. "Fuck you!" she screamed at him.

"Excuse me?" George asked. He was startled by his daughter's entrance. He placed his glass down.

She threw the letter at him. "You made me believe that mom left both of us. She left you, you piece of shit. I just got off the phone with her. I was so stupid to believe that you were right." She walked in front of him. "She realized how pathetic of a man you've always been, and I should have seen it sooner." Jasmine felt empowered, and she had always wanted to do this. She slapped him across the face.

George felt the rage build up in his body. He saw so much of Kelly in Jasmine. He grabbed her by the throat. He pushed her toward a wall where he slammed her against the wall. He began to squeeze, and he could hear her gasping for air. "You're just like your mother. I give you both the world, and this is how you repay me?"

He let go, and she fell to the floor. She stood up after she gained some air. "You have given us nothing but pain and misery. You've made me believe I'm not lovable."

He punched her across the face. "You've always been this way. I hoped using your mom's absence would improve you. You're a fat, ugly, and unrelatable piece of garbage. Your mother turned you against me, and I won't stand for it in this house." He grabbed his drink. "I loved you both. I've always wanted a happy family, and you both ruined it." He walked away.

She laid there on the ground crying for a moment. She needed to get out of there. She wanted to escape, and she thought about how her father would cope with this. She picked herself up and grabbed her jacket. She needed a drink, and she wanted to forget about all of the drama in her life.

She felt her phone vibrate as she left her home. She knew her father might have been passed out by now, and she was praying he was. She pulled out her phone. She felt her heart drop to her stomach. The one thing she didn't want was for this to get out, especially to The Marked Queen. Her world was crumbling, and she didn't know if she would survive.

It was a photo of her father punching her.

Unknown Number: *It explains why you're such a bitch and fat. Is this why your mother left you? She couldn't handle your dad's abuse. We should feel sympathetic, but you've been making people's lives miserable for years. I guess we can call this karma. We are waiting for your dirt, or is this boxing match with your father going to be it?*

Chapter 60

"Where are you going?" Mark asked, when Andrew came down the stairs.

"I'm going out with some friends," Andrew said. He was planning to meet Emily at The Pocket.

Mark stood up and walked over to his son. He looked him up and down. "You've been drinking again, haven't you?"

Andrew knew he wasn't being subtle with his drinking. He had been stumbling home at all hours of the night. "Maybe, I have."

"I shouldn't have moved us here. I should have taken that job in Kansas. Maybe things would have been different."

Andrew was angry. "I don't need to be some pathetic kid who lost his mother."

"No, but I'm going to lose you, though." He shook his head. "I thought once we got a fresh start, you weren't going to turn out this way."

Andrew laughed. "I'm just like mom. I get it. You fell in love with an alcoholic, and I became one. I'm just someone you want to fucking forget," he said.

Mark stepped closer to his son. "I would never say that I want to forget you. I just wish you didn't get caught back up in this mess."

"Dad, I don't want to be some fucking freak anymore. Do you know how freeing it is that I can be whomever I want here? No one here knows what I fucking did that night. No one knows that my rock bottom was destroying her grave. I can just be me."

"But you're becoming a drunk again."

"Maybe that's what I'm meant to be," Andrew said. "I spent every night having the image of Mom's dead body in my mind. I see her weak body, and that last smile before she passed away when I close my eyes."

Mark felt his heartbreak. Mark was at work when he got the phone call from Andrew telling him that Taylor had passed. "I wish I had been there with you."

Andrew felt the tears fall down his face. "You weren't, and you'll never understand the fucking shit that I have to put up with. You can continue to believe that you're this amazing father, but you didn't stop that from happening to me."

Mark walked closer to his son. "I'm sorry. I wish I could take it all away from you."

"But you're judging me for actually being a teenager."

"You aren't one, Andrew. You don't get to run into the world with no fears. You don't get to drink and think it's all games to you. You have a problem like your mother. You're escaping from a tragedy."

Andrew laughed. "You learn that from your lovely parenting sessions? How to deal with an alcoholic son?"

"I'm just being honest with you."

"And I'm telling you that I'm finally happy."

"No, you're not. I can see in your eyes how unhappy you are. Are you even getting back into photography? I know how much you and your mother-" Mark began to say.

"You mean, before she figured out that spending time with your son cut into her drinking? Yeah, I loved photography with her, too. It's such a shame we would have bonded more on the bottle than the camera," Andrew said. He grew up loving to take photos with his mom, but she became more and more distant.

"You hate her, don't you?"

"Don't try to turn this into a therapy session. I've made my peace with her, and I'll never think of that bitch again."

"She was your mother!" Mark's voice was stern. "You will not disrespect her in this household."

"Why? I already destroyed her grave."

Mark slammed Andrew against the wall. He tried to keep his anger to a minimum, but he needed to discipline his son. "She was a wonderful mother. You even admitted after that night, how ashamed you were of what you did. It's why you went to rehab in the first place. This person you are right now isn't you."

"But I love him so much better this way. I don't feel anything, and it's what makes everything perfect."

"And you're turning into her." Both of their bodies deflated. It was the one truth that they both didn't want to admit. "You're turning more and more into her," Mark said. "Maybe, I failed as a parent."

This was why he wanted to continue to drink. He didn't want his dad to feel this defeated for something he had no control over. Andrew knew he was an alcoholic. He was an idiot to think he could indulge for a little bit.

"You were dealt the short end of the stick. You've done the best you could." Andrew shook his head. "We're the monsters that ruined a good man's heart." Andrew pushed his father back gently. "I need to get out of here."

Mark grabbed his son's arm. "We can fix you."

"There's nothing to fix. You've done the best you could." Andrew walked out of that door, because he couldn't see that image. He saw his father completely destroyed in front of him. His father used to have so much light in his eyes, and now, he was soulless like his mother. Andrew lost both of his parents. He headed to The Pocket because he needed to forget about everything.

Andrew, it looked like you were ready for another rock bottom. You destroyed your mother's grave first, what would you destroy this time? You were trying to start a new life. You should have learned at this school, the skeletons eventually wanted to come out and play.

Chapter 61

Andrew sat at the bar drinking himself into a blackened state. Emily had to cancel, but told the bartender to hook him up. He wished his dad didn't have to comfort him the way he did. He wanted to just forget all about his mother, but he knew that the demon would never go away.

Jasmine walked into the bar. She needed to escape from her father, and she wanted nothing more than to just have a drink. Her mind was swirling from her father lying to her, her father abusing her, and The Marked Queen knowing her truths. She shouldn't have been surprised. The Marked Queen knew everything.

She looked around at the people in the bar. She saw a bunch of creepers, but then she saw Andrew. She didn't know him well enough, but she didn't want to get hit on tonight. "This seat taken?" she asked.

Andrew turned to look at Jasmine. He vaguely remembered her from school. "You're the girl Danielle hates."

Jasmine rolled her eyes as she took a seat. "I'm glad that's my identifier with the new kid."

Andrew laughed. "It's better than being known as the kid with the dead mom." Andrew raised his glass to her.

Jasmine looked at Andrew, and she could tell that he was completely wrecked. She ordered herself a drink. "What do you mean by that statement?"

He rolled his eyes. "You think that I'm just the new kid in the school. I have it all figured out. My life's perfect."

"You go to Johnson Prep, no one's life is perfect," Jasmine said.

"But you all make it seem like it."

Jasmine took a sip of her drink once she received it. "Exactly. We all make it seem like we are perfect creatures, but we're all fucking messes. I knew you had shit wrong with you when you started hanging out with Emily."

"She's not that bad."

Jasmine looked at him. "Have you heard Matthew Ryan's story?" she asked.

"Yeah, I've heard about it."

"So clearly you're fucked up in the head if you're still hanging out with her."

"Maybe she has a bad reputation. She wants to repair everything she destroyed. She wanted to be a better human, but people won't give her a second chance."

"People might change masks, but they continue to stay the same." She finished her drink and signaled for another. "Let's be honest, she's just one more mistake until she goes to rehab."

He turned to look at Jasmine. He could see the judgment in her eyes. "I went to rehab," he said.

"You went to rehab?"

He nodded. "After I destroyed my mother's grave."

Jasmine, without thinking, reached out and squeezed his hand. "I'm sorry."

He shrugged. "My mother died of liver cancer. Shocker! She was an alcoholic." He started to laugh, but it wasn't joyful. "I guess it runs in the family. Now, I get to deal with her death and the shame from my father."

"Is that why you moved here?" she asked.

"Yeah, my dad thought I needed a fresh start. He thought if we moved to a big city, I would be under the radar."

Jasmine understood what it was like. "But you became friends with the most popular girl in the school."

"But I could be whomever I wanted to be. I didn't have to be the guy that lost his mother. I didn't have to be some tragic case. It felt good going out and being a kid again."

"But?"

"But I still watched my mother die. I'm still an alcoholic. I'm still a monster who has broken his mother and father's hearts." Andrew knew he wasn't a happy story, and he wondered if he ever would be one. He was curious if there was going to be a light at the end of the tunnel for him. If this constant state of despair would be his environment forever.

"Is that why you drink?" Jasmine asked.

He stood up. "It's the only thing I'm good at."

"Where are you going?" Jasmine asked. She didn't want him to go out on the streets this drunk.

"You don't need to worry about me. If this world takes me, then it takes me. I've enjoyed the ride, but it's time that I get off of it. Have a good night, Jasmine. I just want you to know that your life isn't the pathetic one." He pointed at himself. "It's mine." He began to tear up. He turned and walked out the door. He wanted to escape into the fresh air.

Andrew hated that he couldn't have kept the happy mask on a little bit longer. He wanted to just be normal, and he looked in the mirror knowing that he wasn't. He wanted Emily here to make him escape his misery. Andrew, you were becoming addicted to something worse than a drug… a reckless girl. You should have seen all the signs, but you would make your big moment at prom very known.

Jasmine felt her phone go off again. She looked to see it was a text from The Marked Queen.

Marked Queen: *Do you have any dirt for me, or will everyone realize how pathetic you are?*

Jasmine didn't want her secret to get out, and she knew it wasn't right. She felt guilty texting about Andrew, and what he just told her. She would sleep that night knowing she was about to cause Andrew to go even more down his spiral, but she needed to protect her secret. She had to make sure no one knew the truth.

Jasmine, we should have seen this coming. You wanted everyone to love the person you were trying to perceive. No one liked an abuse case, and we understood why you did what you did. We just hoped you could feel good about yourself once Andrew's ticking time bomb goes off. We hoped you saved yourself from the blast. The Marked Queen, prom, and everyone's secrets were coming out, we couldn't wait to see how it all turned out.

Chapter 62

Demi knocked on Andrew's front door. She was hoping she could talk to him, and get him to see that he needed to go back to rehab. Mark opened the door to see Demi standing there. "Can I help you?" he asked. He wasn't in the mood for visitors. He just wanted to know where his son was.

"I was wondering if Andrew was home."

"Are you the girl that's been destroying his life? Are you the one that caused my son to go back on this path?" Mark tried to keep it together.

"I'm actually his sponsor."

He laughed. "Then you failed." He was about to slam the door in her face, before she held the door open.

"Can I come in?" she asked. "I wanted to talk to you about him."

He shrugged. He turned and walked into the living room. He sat down on the couch in front of photo albums that showed when Andrew was little. He was such a happy little kid. "I only bring out the scotch when I really need it. I don't like to drink, since I've lived in a household full of alcoholics."

Demi smiled. She looked down at the photos of Andrew. "He looked so happy growing up."

Mark picked up the album. "He was a kid that could do anything. He was into everything, and he was determined to be good at it." He pointed to a picture of him picking up trash. "He was obsessed with the idea of being a garbage man."

Demi laughed. "He looks so cute." She turned to look at him. "When did he get into photography?"

Mark turned the page. "That was Taylor's doing. She majored in photography in college. She knew it wasn't a lucrative career, but she always craved capturing the perfect moment. That's why she's never in these photos. She was always taking them."

"Did she and Andrew have a good relationship?"

"I think better than him and I. We were a perfect little family. They would go on adventures, come back, and talk about what photos they took while I cooked dinner." Mark pulled out another photo album. In it were pictures Andrew and Taylor took together.

"When did it change?" Demi asked.

"Eighth grade. Taylor was laid off her job, and she felt like a failure. She loved being an art director, but they didn't have funds for the arts anymore. We were finically fine because of my job, but I could tell that it broke her spirits. She didn't go out with Andrew anymore on photo adventures. She stayed at home and drank."

"What happened next?" Demi asked. She knew the story, but she wanted Mark side.

"She was diagnosed with liver cancer when Andrew was a sophomore," he laughed. "She tried to be sober all of a month, and she couldn't do it. We both watched her die, and it was only six months before she passed."

"That quickly?"

"It was an aggressive cancer." He closed the photo albums. He couldn't look at them anymore. "She didn't even fight to stay alive. She accepted defeat, and I have to deal with our son thinking he wasn't good enough. He picked up the bottle after he actually watched the life in her eyes disappear." He took a sip of his scotch.

"And he never stayed the same boy again."

"I thought moving him here would be good for him. I get it's the city, but there are so many arts here. I saw him taking photos again with his friend, Tucker. I saw the happy little boy come back, but it all changed."

"Why do you think it did?"

He shrugged. "I don't know, and that's what kills me the most."

They both heard the door open. They stood up to see Andrew walk into the room. Andrew wasn't expecting to see Demi and Mark in the room. He laughed. "I knew you two would eventually meet. I guess this is my intervention."

"We just want to talk to you," Demi said.

"What about?" Andrew asked.

"About how to get you clean again. I know this isn't who you want to be."

Andrew laughed at them. "I'm actually the person I'm meant to be. You think that I deserve to be someone better. I watched my mother die, and I destroyed her memory." He shrugged. "I shouldn't be surprised. She didn't give two shits about me toward the end."

"That's not true," Mark said.

"You will always defend her, and I get that, because you were married. Let's all face reality. She left both of us because she didn't care. She would have fucking stopped drinking if she cared for us. She would have fucking gone to chemotherapy, instead of the bars."

Mark looked at him confused. "What?"

"It's why I destroyed her fucking grave. She didn't give two shits about us, dad. She just wanted a good time." He turned to walk toward the stairs. "Have fun with that bombshell." He left them trying to process it all.

Mark sat down. "She didn't try."

Demi sat down with Mark. "It's going to be okay."

He shook his head. "No, he doesn't have the fight to be sober, because his mother didn't." He threw the photo albums across the room. "She destroyed this family, and she didn't have any remorse."

"Alcoholism does that to you."

"Well it ruined my life, and it's ruining my son's." Mark had thought that she had at least tried to recover for them, but it was all a lie. She was putting up a front that she was getting better. Mark, you should have known by now, that this story wasn't about all of you being better human beings; it was about calling people out on their fucking bullshit.

Chapter 63

"What do you mean, you want nothing to do with me anymore?" Delilah asked when she walked into Principal Grand's office. She had been coming to his office a lot lately. She craved someone actually wanting her, even if it was just for her mouth. She had given up on her writing dreams since she knew it didn't matter anymore.

Principal Grand shrugged. He finally got the junior he was trying to get with to sleep with him. She was trying to get into an Ivy League school next year, and her grades weren't up to par for it. "It was fun and hot, but you're starting to get too old for me." He paused. "And needy." Delilah, you knew you hit rock bottom when your perverted high school principal was over dealing with your mess. It was a shame that you had everything going for you there for a while.

She slapped him across the face. "I'll tell people."

He laughed. "No one is going to believe you. You're just some stupid girl crying wolf." He leaned forward. "I can also reverse all those grades."

She knew then that she wouldn't be able to graduate. She was left completely useless. She turned and walked out of his office. She lost her writing, and she lost Principal Grand. She wanted to escape everything going on. She wanted to feel like she mattered again, but she didn't know how.

She needed to cut herself. She wanted nothing more than to forget about this day. She ran to the bathroom, but she bumped into Mr. Rozengota. Mr. Rozengota looked at Delilah. "What's wrong?"

She shook her head. He was her favorite teacher, and she didn't want to let him down. "Nothing, I'm just having a bad day."

He looked at her for a moment. "I doubt that you're having a bad day. I've noticed you haven't been yourself the past week. What's been going on?"

She opened her mouth and shut it. She had Flynn and Principal Grand's voices in her head telling her that no one would believe her. "I just haven't felt confident about myself."

He smiled. "You should put all these doubts into your writing. I told you that you're incredibly inspiring. You should be proud of yourself."

"I know that, but it doesn't matter anyway. No one cares what I have to say."

He raised an eyebrow. "Why do you think that? I enjoy your writing. Do your parents read your material?"

"They do, but it was a stupid dream for a silly girl." She tried to keep it together. She looked down at her feet. "No one wants to be inspired by someone like me."

He touched her shoulder. He could see that her spirit had been broken. "There always needs to be a balance of confidence and self-doubt. You and Flynn are on the opposite ends. He has too much, and you have too little."

She looked up at him. "I would never want to be like Flynn."

He crossed his arms. "Because he likes to steal ideas from you," he said.

She looked at him confused. "Why do you assume that?"

He pulled out a paper from his folder of stories. "This is the story he turned in."

Delilah looked at the story. It was the same story that she caught him stealing some of her passage. "Why do you think I wrote this?" she asked.

"I don't think you wrote all of it, but there are parts that are oddly similar to your style of writing."

"And you haven't confronted him about it."

"Well, there hasn't been an accusation or proof that he's been lying. If you want people to believe that you're a talented writer, then you have to show them," he said.

"What if no one wants to read it?" she asked.

He smiled. "Who cares if they don't want to read it? You should be proud of what you're producing to the world. You will find people that find inspiration from your body of work." He leaned forward. "Plus, I think Flynn needs to be knocked down a couple of pegs."

She laughed. "Why are you so nice to me?" Mr. Rozengota reminded Delilah so much of her father.

"Because I believe in talent. You have so much of it." He patted her on the shoulder. "You need to remember how incredible you are with your words. You shouldn't let some asshole take credit for things you've written. People need to be called out on their bullshit." He looked at his watch. "I better get going. These papers aren't going to grade themselves." He took the paper back and walked away.

She pulled out her razor thinking about going into the bathroom and finishing what she was about to do. She then thought about what Mr. Rozengota said. Flynn needed to be called out for his shit. She pulled her phone out and texted The Marked Queen. She wanted some juicy dirt, well, she was about to receive it. She knew that this was a better way to take control.

We were proud parents to see Delilah decide to grow a backbone and do something about Flynn. We hoped he was ready for his big moment at prom. Delilah, we knew you were going to be riding high from your whistleblowing, but you should remember The Marked Queen loved scandal and backstabbing. Too bad for you, you were about to receive the latter.

Chapter 64

"You enjoying this exhibit?" A guy walked up to Calvin and asked.

Calvin turned to look at him. He was dark skinned, nice smile, brown eyes, and short hair. "Yeah, I've enjoyed this freedom exhibit."

"You've been here three or four times since it's opened."

"You stalking me?" Calvin asked.

The guy laughed. "I volunteer here, and I've noticed you. I'm Terrell." He put out his hand.

"Calvin." Calvin shook his head. "I just feel at peace at this exhibit."

Terrell turned to the piece that Calvin was looking out. It was a painting of a man dancing in the rain, but the rain was the colors of LGBT rainbow. "You've been looking at this painting for some time now."

Calvin looked back at the painting instead of Terrell. He wouldn't deny that there was sexual chemistry between them. He thought Terrell was extremely attractive, but he didn't know how to move forward. "I think it's beautiful to live life the way that you want to."

Terrell raised an eyebrow. "You haven't come out of the closet yet?" he asked.

"Why would you assume I'm gay?"

"You've come to this exhibit numerous times. You looked at this piece the most. It's not that hard to figure it out." He paused. "You've also been checking out my ass."

Calvin blushed. "Sorry, I didn't mean to be rude or creepy."

Terrell laughed. He touched Calvin's arm. "Don't worry. I've been checking you out, too. How do you think I've noticed you being here all the time?"

Calvin felt his whole body vibrate. "Aren't you scared of people finding out about us?" he asked.

Terrell looked around. "You're surrounded by people that don't care who you love. I'm assuming you're in a world that it's not accepted to be gay."

"I wish it was that tragic. My parents know, and they don't care. My best friend knows, and she's ready for me to come out. I play baseball, but it's not really accepted."

"So, you want to stay in the closet?" he asked.

"I'm ready to come out and quit baseball. I have always loved the game, but I don't want to play it if I'm not allowed to be one hundred percent me."

"You don't think you can have both worlds?"

Calvin looked at Terrell. "No one can have everything they've wanted. I've tried to balance both, but I'm exhausted. I'm tired of having to hide who I am. I want to walk into a room holding the hand of the person I love," Calvin said. He had always dreamed of the day that he could walk into the room with Aman, and people wouldn't care.

"But you can't."

"He's not ready to come out," Calvin said.

Terrell's face faltered. "I should have seen that coming. No one as attractive as you should be single."

Calvin blushed and looked away. "I don't even know if we are still together anymore. He's busy trying to live his straight life, and I'm stuck in the closet."

"Why not come out on your own terms?"

Calvin shook his head. "He won't come out because of his family. He thinks that they will disown him, and he doesn't get that he'll always have me on his side."

"That's called loyalty. I still think that you need to focus on yourself. If you want to come out, then you should be out in the open. You want to feel freedom, then you shouldn't be scared of it." Terrell knew from experience how hard it is for the coming out process. He had always felt he was different, until he met a drag Queen on the subway. They talked, and he felt accepted in that world. He came out to his parents, and it took time for them to accept him for who he was.

"But what if I come out, and it blows up in my face?" Calvin asked. He knew that he would still have his family, but he was worried about his social life. He didn't want people to hold that against him, especially his teammates.

"Well, it's up to you. Do you care about what people have to say about you?" Terrell asked.

"I don't know." He only cared what Aman thought of him. They were both in this situation together. He knew that if he came out, then Aman would want nothing to do with him.

"It seems that you need to make a bold move toward what you want in life. People are scared of what their peers think, but you should say fuck it to all of them. We live in a world for one time, why not have fun with it?"

"How did you get all this confidence?" Calvin asked.

"Because you spend so much time in a small room in your mind, it's freeing when you get the whole world to see you. You feel like you finally get to spread your wings when you come out, and it's the most beautiful moment in your life. You'll always have bigots and assholes trying to bring your ass down, but you keep waving that sexy flag of yours."

Calvin laughed. "It's good to know that it gets better."

"How cliché." Terrell winked. He pulled out his business card. "Here's my number if you ever want to talk more."

"You have a business card?"

Terrell leaned forward and kissed him on the cheek. Calvin thrived in the moment, because they were out in public acting like something Calvin's always wanted. "Only when I see cute boys." Terrell turned and walked around. He spun back around for one last piece of advice. "Go bold, because you only get one entrance out of the closet. You should make it epic." Terrell didn't give Calvin a chance to respond. He walked away leaving him to think.

Calvin looked down at Terrell's number. He thought about how he could be bold about coming out. He then realized prom was in two days. "Prom." He thought that people lost something on prom, why couldn't he gain something instead?

He pulled out his phone and sent The Marked Queen a picture and text message. It looked like Calvin was learning to embrace his inner bitch. He knew that he was about to ruin someone's life, but he was tired of hiding what they shared. He knew that Aman wouldn't be pleased, but this would be the bold move to get them both to accept that they loved sucking each other off.

Calvin: *The Marked Queen. You wanted dirt, I hope this works for you. Aman and I have been secretly dating for the past year. You don't believe me look at the picture below. What's more salacious than the baseball star and vlogger getting dirty between the sheets? Hope this works for your reveal at prom. -Calvin.*

All the dirt was in, and The Marked Queen had everything she needed for her big reveal at prom. We hoped these bitches were ready, because it was about to be an epic night for all of them. The biggest moment of all, was when all these puppets were going to find out who was pulling all the strings. Enjoy the last day of peace, because once you all put on your gowns, it was execution time.

Chapter 65

"You look handsome so in your tux," Amara said, as she was fixing Aman's tie.

Aman smiled. "It's weird that I'm going to prom."

Amara smiled. "And in less than a month, you'll be graduating." She pulled him in for a hug. They might have had their disagreements over the years, but she was proud of her son. "I just want you to know that everything we've done for you is to protect you."

"I just feel like sometimes I'm trapped by your rules," Aman said.

"I know, but we are trying to get you ahead in life. There has to be sacrifices in your life. Sana's parents also have shares in a movie studio."

"Really?" Aman was shocked. Sana never said anything to him about that, and he was surprised. He had been talking about his videos with her. She even knew about his YouTube channel.

"Why do you think we set you both up?"

"I thought it was because of dad's deal with him."

"Partially. He might not agree sometimes with your chosen career path, but he's proud of what you've accomplished." She kissed him on the cheek.

Aman felt better knowing that he had his parents on his side. He wanted to come out right now, but he didn't want to ruin this moment with her. "Thank you."

"I'm going to give you some time alone. I know you have a lot of emotions going through your mind right now. Sana should be here soon." Amara kissed her son on the cheek and walked out the door.

Aman walked over to his dresser and pulled out a picture of Calvin and him. They always talked about going to prom, and it was a bit surreal that they weren't going together. He knew in the past weeks, he has fucked up his relationship with Calvin. Aman, what did you ever mean? It wasn't like you made fun of the gays, got yourself a beard, and tossed him to the side.

He pulled out his phone and sent a photo of himself to Calvin. He wanted Calvin to see his handy work, since Calvin was the one that picked out the tux. "I thought you should see me in it."

Calvin pulled out his phone to see Aman texting him. "Is that from Aman?" Audrey asked.

Calvin nodded. "Yeah, it is."

Audrey kissed Calvin on the cheek. "I'm proud of you, and what you plan to do. I think finally coming out to your classmates is something extremely brave."

"And you're okay if I don't want to play baseball anymore?"

"We don't care what you do. We just want you to be happy. Yes, you would have an easier time being a baseball star, but we get that there's more out there for you to do."

Calvin smiled weakly. "I just wish I knew what I wanted to do."

"You're a senior in high school. You should never know what to do."

Calvin laughed. "I guess I'm so used to being known as the baseball star, that it's going to be scary being labeled something else." Calvin knew that after tonight, he would have a different label. He was ready to quit baseball once the season was over, and go to college to find himself. He just didn't know what it was yet. He saw the text from Aman. He wished that Aman would have stood right next to him, and he prayed after tonight he might.

"Your label is Calvin," Audrey said. Audrey, that was so adorable, we wanted to throw up. We didn't care for this afterschool special. It was nice that this story wasn't about a boy losing everything after coming out. Well, it still could be once prom happened for Aman.

Calvin rolled his eyes. "I love you." He pulled out his phone and sent a selfie of him and his family. "We all agree you look cute," Calvin replied back.

Aman saw the picture of Calvin and his happy family. He wished that he was right there taking photos with them.

"Sana is here," Amara screamed for Aman.

Aman stood up. He fixed his tux and went downstairs to his beard, we mean girlfriend. Aman, you were in for a night you would never forget. We hoped that you would record it for your next video. Who are we kidding? Someone else did it for you. Hope you were ready for your next viral video, even if you didn't want it to be.

Chapter 66

"I've never seen someone as gorgeous as you," Erika said, walking into Delilah's room.

Delilah had decided on a canary yellow floral dress with the top being lace. She smiled and twirled for her mother. "I've never felt more beautiful in my life," she said. Delilah, you did clean up nicely, and we thought it might have had to do with your new-found confidence. We couldn't wait to see you give them hell tonight, especially that weasel, Flynn.

"Why are you wearing bracelets with the dress?" Erika said. "I think you would look far more beautiful without them." Erika tried to take them off, but she noticed the cuts. She let go of her daughter's hand.

Delilah knew that her mother had found out her secret. "I'm done with it," she said.

"You know, when I was your age I cut myself, too." Erika shook her head. "It's scary what we pass down to our kids. We think we would pass down our looks and our smarts, but sometimes, we pass down the worst parts about ourselves." Erika walked over and sat on the bed. She patted for Delilah to join her.

Great, we were getting another heartfelt story, barf. Delilah sat down next to her. "I read your short story. I was impressed with how much people could connect with the characters. I thought it was a bit repetitive, but I understand why you wrote them that way. We continue to second guess every decision and fight for toxic people. We think we can break that brick wall, but we can't."

Delilah laughed. "I think that's the first time you've actually said those words to me."

"I just wanted to protect you from this world."

"Dad told me you had a hard time."

Erika remembered being so jealous of Matt. She thought it wasn't fair how his books were selling, and she couldn't even get a meeting with someone. "I tried for so many years to become someone on my own. I thought I would be bigger than my husband." She paused. "But that was the problem right there."

"Why's that?"

"I was comparing myself to your father. He wrote action novels, and I wrote romance. We were in two different worlds, and I needed to remind myself of that." She turned to look at Delilah. "You write young adult. We are three different writers in three different worlds. I should have never tried to tell you that you were less than."

Delilah nodded. "I just want you to be proud of me. I know you were trying to help, and I assume to protect me from the mistakes you've made."

"I just don't want you to think that you can't have whatever you want." Erika stood up. "I want you to be confident in yourself."

"I don't think I'm ever going to be," Delilah said. She knew that she made a move about Flynn, but she was still worried her writing wasn't good enough. She still felt the sting from Principal Grand rejecting her. Delilah, we thought you dodged a bullet there. He was banging a junior, because you were too old for him. We would see him soon enough on Dateline.

"And I think I've contributed to that."

Delilah shook her head. "I've had these voices in my head telling me I'm not good enough my entire life. I don't think it has anything to do with you," Delilah laughed, and shook her head. "I thought it was on the right path to being happy. I was with someone I liked, I was writing, and I had good times with my friends. It still didn't matter. I cut myself because I didn't think it was all real," Delilah said. "What's wrong with me?"

Erika pulled her daughter in for a hug. "There's nothing wrong with you. You're beautiful in so many ways."

"But I'm naïve in others. The boy that I liked, was just using me for my writing."

"And it's going to happen. This world isn't all rainbows and unicorns. Once you leave high school, you leave the bubble you created for yourself. You will have to toughen up.

"I don't want to feel the urge to cut myself anymore," Delilah said.

"You will." Erika kissed her daughter on the cheek. "Have fun at prom, and I want you to know that I love you."

"I love you too," Delilah said. She was relieved that she had this moment with her mom. She knew that their relationship wasn't always the easiest, but Erika supported Delilah with everything she did.

Delilah grabbed her clutch and walked downstairs. She knew prom would be her moment to rise above the voices and doubts in her mind. She was ready to be someone other than the sad girl. Delilah, you were about to be known for so much more than the dumb girl. It was even worse, once you found out who exposed your dirty little secret. Have fun at prom, we knew we would.

Chapter 67

Andrew came down the stairs wearing his suit for prom. He knew the last time he wore it was for his mother's funeral, but he tried to ignore the thought by drinking some of his father's scotch. He thought it was funny how his father thought he hid the liquor from him.

Mark was waiting at him at the bottom of the stairs. "Please be careful tonight," Mark said. They hadn't talked about the night he and Demi confronted Andrew, and he was still trying to process what Andrew said.

"Don't worry. I'll be back before curfew."

"I meant on the drinking. Andrew, I don't want you to turn out like your mother," Mark said. "I know you've had to deal with a lot of the guilt, but I can't lose you, too." Mark looked his son in the eyes. "I need you to be stronger than this. You've come along way, and it would kill me to have to bury you, too."

Andrew looked at his father. He didn't care for this heartfelt moment. He just wanted to go dancing with the girl that he enjoyed. "What do you want me to do, dad? I can't get over what she did to me."

"So, you're becoming her?"

Andrew slammed his hand against the wall. "I am nothing like her."

Mark crossed his arms. "You're exactly like her. You're choosing alcohol over your family and life. You're choosing to give up, like she did."

"No, because I knew if I was faced with death, then I would go to rehab. I would cure myself. I'm having fun right now." Andrew knew the moment he became destructive again, then he would cut himself off. He was just drinking and forgetting his problems. Why couldn't his father understand that?

"I doubt that you will ever understand what a rock bottom is. You would have steered clear of all these people."

"Then we shouldn't have moved here. Did you honestly think this was a good place for a recovering alcoholic?" Andrew laughed. "You could have also sent me away now, but you're too much of a coward."

Mark had his own share of faults. Andrew was right. You shouldn't have moved him to New York City amid temptation. You also knew he was currently boozing, and you were sitting there complaining about it. Mark, maybe you caused this more than they did. You were his enabler.

"I thought this would be the perfect place for you to start over," Mark said.

"I don't want to be the kid that needs to go to AA meetings. I don't want to relive my mother's death, or the night I destroyed her memory. It was all over the fucking news the next morning. You think I want people to know that here?"

"You can't hide from your past."

Andrew shook his head. "I'm just trying to forget it." Andrew opened the door.

"You're going to be exactly like her if you walk out that door. Stay here and become sober with me. Let's look at rehabs together, Andrew. Let's get you back on the right path."

Andrew turned to look at his father. He smirked. "Once again, you're giving me the power of choice. You should be the one forcing me into something I don't want to do, but you'll never figure that out." Andrew walked out of the door and walked toward the car where Emily was waiting for him.

"Is everything okay?" Emily asked, when he got into the car. She could tell that he seemed bothered by something.

Andrew looked at her. He could tell her everything going on, but what was the point? He needed to keep it all to himself. "I'm fine. Do you have the flask?" he asked.

She pulled it out of her purse and handed it to him. "I thought we could loosen up before we deal with this stupid dance."

He laughed. He opened the flask and began to chug it. "Easy there. I don't want us to be the sloppy ones," Emily said.

He handed her the flask. "It just takes a lot for me to loosen up." He winked. "Let's go to this thing," he said.

Andrew, you were going to make such a splash tonight. Prom was going to be your shining moment, and we hoped you were ready for your close-up. We hoped you didn't mind if The Marked Queen does a True Hollywood Story on your behalf. We did love a good tragic moment, and what better place to have it then prom?

Chapter 68

Jasmine sat in front of her mirror putting on her make-up. She covered up the black eye her father gave her. She put concealer on the bruises on her arm, because he grabbed her too many times. She put some foundation on her neck to hide his fingerprints from choking her out.

She got up and put on her golden dress, because the black one didn't fit as much even after you tried so hard. It was a little snug, but she would be fine. It wasn't form fitting except for around the chest. She made sure she wore a dress that hid her body. We could still see the rolls, but it was your prom. We should be nice to you, right?

George walked into his daughter's room. "You look just like her when we got married."

Jasmine turned around and smiled. Her father was a good mood, and she wanted to keep it that way. She was going to win Prom Queen tonight, and she didn't need anyone trying to ruin that for her." She smiled. "Thank you. I know gold was her favorite color."

George smiled. He walked up to her. Jasmine got a little freaked out. "I'm not going to hurt you."

"It's not my fault that I can't trust you," she said.

He nodded. He knew that he has been cruel to her, and she had every right to be scared of any movement from him. "I promise that I'm trying to be good here."

"What do you want?" she asked.

He pulled out a box from his pocket. "I know that this won't fix the damage that I've caused, but I wanted to remind you that we were once a happy family. We used to get along, and there was so much laughter in this home." He opened the box to reveal a locket.

"Why are you giving me this?" she asked.

"I want to apologize."

She picked up the locket out of the box. She opened to see a picture of her mother and her while the other photo was all three of them. It was a happy family before the abuse and abandonment issues. We appreciated this version of Jasmine, instead of the girl that had it all. "It's pretty."

She turned around for her father to put it on. "I love you, even if my actions speak differently." George, we could really tell you loved your daughter when your fist and her face connected. We truly felt you were an amazing dad when you were choking her out. Don't worry, your father of the year award just got lost in the mail.

She touched the locket and turned around. "Thank you for this," she said. She walked toward the window, and she saw that Calvin was there with their car. "I need to go."

"No problem. Have a good time. I love you."

She nodded. She didn't feel the need to say it back. She didn't know how else to say those words to him. He had become a monster of nightmares, and she wasn't going to let him get that satisfaction.

Calvin was waiting for her outside the car to open the door for her. He smiled when she came outside. "You look beautiful."

She smiled. "Thank you. You don't look half bad yourself." She took her seat in the car before he closed the door.

He came around and sat next to her. They rode along to the venue without speaking to each other. Jasmine tried to open her mouth to say something, but she didn't know how to let words come out. She thought of Carter, and how easy it was to talk to him.

She pulled out her phone ready to talk to him, but she didn't know what to say. She looked at Calvin who was lost in thought. She assumed he must be nervous, and that was why he wasn't talking to her. Jasmine, he was thinking of his ex-boyfriend. He was thinking about how he was about to come out. It had nothing to do with you or your cow-like body.

She thought she had it all, but in this moment, she realized that she was truly alone in the world. She touched her locket. It might have contained happy memories, but it didn't mean they were ever going to come back. She felt like she was ready to cry, because the person that could fix it was Carter. She never felt more like herself except with him, and she didn't know if she could ever get him back.

They rode their way to prom lost in their own little worlds. Jasmine, Carter would understand soon why you were doing what you did, and so would everyone else. You wanted everyone to love you, but in a few short hours, everyone was going to pity you. You would be a Queen, but it wouldn't be the Reigning Queen.

Chapter 69

Lily walked into Danielle's room to see her putting on her prom dress. "That's a pretty dress. I thought you were wearing a baby blue dress, not a black one," Lily walked over and examined the dress.

Danielle turned around. "I thought baby blue might be too innocent. I thought I would look better in black." Danielle smiled.

Lily looked closer, and saw the price tag still attached. "You know the price tag is still attached, right?" Lily reached over to grab it.

"Mom, I got it."

Lily grabbed the price tag and ripped it off the dress. She looked at how much it cost. "Two thousand dollars. Danielle, we don't have that kind of money."

Danielle might as well tell her mom the truth. "We do now, that dad's giving me money."

Lily crossed her arms. "What do you mean?"

"Dad and I made an agreement that he would give me money if I went to a couple of charity events."

"Is that why you've been skipping out of work lately?"

"Yeah, I just wanted people to know that I had money again. I've been having parties at dad's condo, going on shopping sprees, and going to fancy restaurants." Danielle understood that it was wrong for her mother to be kept in the dark, but she knew her mother wouldn't approve.

"Danielle, you shouldn't be talking to that man anymore. I don't understand why you can't accept that we are poor."

"Because it's shameful. I don't want to be looked at as less than in front of all my friends."

Lily thought she taught her daughter better. "Danielle, I left my marriage because I was unhappy. I could have stayed safe with the money, or I could go out on my own. I thought I was being an inspiration to you. I wanted you to look up to me as a woman that took charge of her life."

"But why would you leave? I get you were unhappy, but you ruined my reputation."

Lily laughed. "Reputation. Do you think it's going to matter in a couple of months once you graduated? The only thing that matters is the person you become. Are you so focused on making sure people don't know your poor, you're willing to do anything for it?" Lily asked.

She should probably tell her mother how she backstabbed her best friend and lost her boyfriend to protect her reputation. "Yes, I am."

Lily walked over and pulled out the baby blue dress Danielle had designed. "I saw all the talent and hard work you put in this dress. I saw how much you bonded over it with Dan." She turned to look at her. "Is Dan okay with your new wealth?"

"We broke up, because he didn't like who I was becoming," Danielle said.

Lily nodded. "I would like to say that I'm surprised, but I remember how you were when you would go to Dolce after school. You were barely passing class, and now you are. You are one of the top of your class, and you're planning to go to fashion school." She put the dress on the bed. "There's no talent in picking out a pretty thing." Lily walked toward the door.

"I'm not ashamed of what I've done. I did it so I could be successful in this life."

Lily turned around. "You're going to realize that it's not worth it, if you have no one standing beside you. You're going to realize one day soon that all of this is bullshit. I hope you can accept yourself once it's all said and done." She walked to the door and paused. "I thought the dress you made was prettier. The one you have on looks tacky." She walked out of the door leaving Danielle to her thoughts.

Danielle ignored her mother's hurt words as she grabbed her purse. She was waiting for the limo her father rented for her. She was going to prom with no friends or date. Did this Queen really think that was so wise? She needed someone to protect her when The Marked Queen made her attack on the kingdom. It was sad that Danielle didn't realize her rule was about to be over.

She felt her phone go off, assuming it was her limo driver. It was another message from our one and truly.

Marked Queen: *Prom is such a magical night. Full of lost virginities, broken hearts, and bullshit promises of the future. Thanks to you backstabbers, this will be the most memorable prom ever. You guys gave me a mouth full of cavities from all the sweet and delicious scandals you spilled. So, enjoy putting on your tacky dresses, getting drunk with your so-called friends, and believing your secrets are going to the grave. Because at the end of this prom, Carrie is going to look like a Disney movie once I'm done with you bitches.*

Chapter 70

The event we had all been waiting for, boys and girls is finally here. We had learned all about their pathetic attempts to keep their images intact. Prom was a night to remember. It was why in every cliché high school drama, it ended at prom. This might have been the big dance, but no one was going to remember who spiked the punch, who wore that ugly pink dress, or which couple fucked in the bathroom. Johnson Prep class of the year two thousand and eighteen was going to be remembered as The Marked Queen reveal, all the truth bombs that were dropped, and the aftermath of the destruction. Hoped you enjoyed your time bitches, because we would.

Delilah walked into prom nervous and proud. She didn't know when The Marked Queen would strike, or even if she would reveal what she had sent her. She looked around for her friends who were already sitting at a table in the corner.

She started walking over to them, when she bumped into Flynn. Flynn was with some sophomore, and she shouldn't have been surprised. He liked to pray on the weak and naïve. "Delilah, you look beautiful."

She gave him a soft smile. "You clean up very nice yourself."

It was quiet for a moment. "I hope you're not mad at me anymore," Flynn said. "It was nothing personal. I was just trying to get ahead and win that scholarship."

Delilah touched him on the shoulder. "There are no hard feelings. We have to do what we need to." She gave him a smile. "Enjoy your night. I hope it's one for the history books." She walked away from him. Delilah, we are really enjoying this bitchy side of you.

Delilah walked up to her table, which consisted of all The Marked Queen puppets: Danielle, Andrew, Jasmine, Aman, Calvin, Emily, and Sana. She took a seat next to Danielle.

"Dan didn't show up?" Delilah asked.

Danielle was still reeling from her mother's conversation. "He hasn't returned any of my texts, but I'm not worried about that right now." She showed her the mass text from The Marked Queen. "Do you think she's going to pull something tonight?"

Delilah shrugged. "She said she was going to make us remember tonight. I don't think she would bluff," she said.

Danielle was worried. She had made a mistake, and she was looking right at the person she was about to backstab. Didn't it suck that you were looking right into Bambi's eyes, Danielle? You might have at least had her turn around before executing her. Oh well, we couldn't wait for that cat fight.

"I'll be right back." She grabbed Calvin. "I need to talk to you," she whispered.

"He's here with me," Jasmine said. She was upset that Calvin was ignoring her, and the limo ride over here was extremely awkward. She turned to see Carter with some girl, and it killed her. She regretted coming with Calvin, but she wanted to win Prom Queen.

Danielle grabbed a roll off the table. "Here, have a fucking dinner roll. It will keep you distracted for a couple of minutes."

"Be nice, Danielle," Calvin said. He stood up. "I need some time away from here." Calvin was too busy staring at Aman and Sana. It was awkward for the love triangle. Aman was trying to ignore Calvin's stares, while Sana was trying to give him a hand job under the table. Sana, you should have known that it wasn't you that he was getting hard for. Keep stroking that gay dick, girl.

"I need a drink," Andrew said, getting up.

Emily pulled him down. "We already finished the flask, and you're getting drunk real fast." Emily wanted to have a good time, but she was worried about Andrew. He had downed the flask she poured for them in the car on the way here. She could tell that he didn't have a limit.

Delilah placed a glass of water in front of him. "Why not have some water?" she suggested.

Andrew rolled his eyes. "Sober me up. Whatever this is fucking stupid." He grabbed the water and began to drink it.

Danielle and Calvin walked to a corner to talk in private. "Do you honestly think that The Marked Queen is going to reveal herself tonight?" she asked.

Calvin looked at her, and he had never seen someone this worried. "Why?"

She couldn't get the talk with her mom out of her head. She was going to ruin a friendship over keeping her secret safe. "I sent The Marked Queen some dirt on Delilah." Danielle knew she could only tell Calvin.

"What did you tell her?" Calvin said.

She looked away from him. "That she's sleeping with Principal Grand and that she cuts herself."

"Danielle!" Calvin knew that was really fucked up.

She looked at Calvin. "I know. I fucked up, and she's never going to forgive me. What am I going to do?"

"You need to tell her before The Marked Queen does. You have to do some damage control, or you're going to be fucked." He paused. "I told The Marked Queen about Aman and me."

Danielle bugged out. "Calvin, are you serious?"

He shrugged. "I'm ready to come out, and I want him to be out, too."

"You can't force someone out of the closet. He's never going to forgive you."

"At least I didn't expose someone sleeping with the principal."

Danielle waved her hands in the air. "Okay, we're both bad people. How do we fix it?" Danielle asked. She knew they were running out of time, and she didn't want all hell to break loose. Danielle, why would you ruin our fun?

Danielle and Calvin were about to say something, until Principal Grand spoke. "Can I get all of the royal courts on stage, please?"

"I guess we don't have time," Calvin said.

"Fuck." Danielle knew that she was walking up to her execution, but she didn't even know when it was going to happen. She walked on stage with Calvin, Jasmine, Delilah, Aman, and Eddie.

Danielle, Delilah, and Jasmine on one side while Calvin, Aman, and Eddie were on the other side. "Now, before we announce who will be King and Queen, there is a video montage first."

The video started off about Danielle with her fashion, Delilah with her writing, Jasmine with her studies, Calvin with baseball, Aman with vlogging, and Eddie with football. The video ended with all six of them in a group shot together.

Principal Grand smiled. "Well, that was something." People started applauding. "Now it's time to announce your Prom King and Queen." Principal Grand opened the envelope. "Prom King and Queen of Johnson Prep 2018 are..." Principal Grand didn't get to announce, because the projector started displaying another video.

Everyone turned to the screen and saw the new video. Everyone in the royal court except, Eddie's, heart dropped. It started out with Delilah's scandal being revealed in the form of a photo. The photo you might ask was a screenshot of Danielle spilling Delilah's dirty secret to The Marked Queen. Delilah turned to look at Danielle.

"Someone turn this off!" Principal Grand screamed, because he couldn't believe that this was happening. He was being exposed, and he didn't know from who.

The next was of Andrew. It was another screenshot of Jasmine's text to The Marked Queen. Jasmine turned to look at Andrew. She could tell that he was livid. What set him off the most, were the photos in the local newspaper of his mother's destroyed grave. Andrew was filled with rage, and he didn't know how to feel.

The next was for Flynn. It was a photo of Delilah's work next to Flynn's, exposing that he had taken material from her story to add to his. Delilah was pissed and hurt about Danielle's betrayal, but she had a moment of gratification.

The next one was of Aman and Calvin. Aman and Calvin turned to each other. It was a photo of them kissing and a screenshot of Calvin telling The Marked Queen about their relationship. "How could you?" Aman felt completely betrayed by Calvin. Calvin wanted to feel remorse, but he felt free that it was finally out.

Then we had Jasmine's dirty little secret. "I gave you Andrew!" she screamed, as she saw the photo of her father hitting her, and her puking in the bathroom. The caption was our favorite. "Maybe if she lost the weight faster, then her father wouldn't have hurt her."

The final one, was for the main Queen herself. It was a photo of Danielle's real house. "Looks like this bitch was just a knock off." It also had photos of her sewing her clothes from the window. "She believed she was Cinderella, but she would never fit into the glass slipper." People laughed at that caption. Danielle felt mortified.

The lights in the room turned off. A spotlight had turned on toward the entrance. They saw her walk into the room, and everyone gasped at who entered. She walked into prom like the perfect villain. She knew the royal court was beneath her. Why have a plastic tiara, when your name would already be infamous? She headed straight toward her favorite subjects. Her dress was as red as the spilled blood of her victims. She knew no one expected her to be The Marked Queen, and that was what made this reveal so juicy. She grabbed a glass of sparkling cider off the table. She toasted to the puppets she had grown so fond of over the past year. "Hello, bitches," Bethany said, as she took a sip of sweet satisfaction.

Chapter 71

The lights turned on. Principal Grand ran off the stage, but no one else moved. Everyone had been tortured, inspired, and entertained by The Marked Queen all year. They had no clue that it was Bethany who was behind all this entertainment. We would like to give a round of applause to Bethany, because none of us saw this coming. We thought you were above it all, but you were the fucking mastermind behind it. Well done, bitch.

Danielle and the rest of the group followed her. "You're The Marked Queen?" Danielle couldn't believe it. "How?"

Bethany took a sip of her cider. "Easy. I knew damn well you all would be scared to be exposed. I pinned you against each other, and I got exactly what I wanted. I also had help." Tucker and Susan came walking beside them.

"Susan?" Jasmine felt betrayed. "I thought I was your best friend."

"I knew you needed to be knocked down for all the shit you did to me," Susan said. "I wanted you to go back to being yourself. I thought this would repair our friendship."

"Well you ruined mine," Danielle said, looking at them.

"You did that all on your own," Delilah said. "How could you do that to me?" Delilah shook her head and felt like a complete fool. She ran off.

"Delilah, wait!" Danielle screamed, going after her. "I'm sorry."

"Why would you keep the fact that you're poor from me?" Delilah asked.

"Because I was ashamed. I didn't want you to think less of me. I thought I could keep up the appearance."

Delilah shook her head. "We were supposed to be best friends. I told you about Principal Grand and me cutting myself, because I thought you could keep that a secret. I guess I was lying to myself that we were friends. I never want to speak to you again," Delilah said, and turned to walk away. She was done having people use her, and it killed her to cut Danielle out of her life.

Danielle stood there ready to cry. She might have been in a thousand-dollar gown, but she felt for the first time like she didn't belong there. She had destroyed a friendship over what? She lost a friendship, boyfriend, and a reputation that was now tarnished.

Sana stormed up to Aman and Calvin. "You're gay?" she asked.

"It's a misunderstanding. We kissed once, but that was it."

"Don't lie," Bethany said.

Aman turned to look at her. "You stay out of it."

Sana rolled her eyes. "Whatever. I'm out of here. It explains why you couldn't get it up." Sana stormed off.

Aman grabbed Calvin, and pulled him to the side. He didn't want to have this conversation in front of Bethany. "Why would you expose us?"

"Because I was tired of being in the closet. I want us to both be out."

"That wasn't your decision to make. I don't have a safety net like you. I'm stuck alone with the consequences."

Calvin went to grab Aman's hand. "You have me."

Aman backed up. "I can't trust you."

Calvin was angry. "And you had me stuck in a fucking cage. I told you a million times how unhappy I was in our situation. You told me to suck it up, and it wasn't right. It might have been fucked up to expose both of us, but it was fucked up that you kept me as your prisoner."

"Well, you're free now because we're done." Aman never wanted to see Calvin again. He had to explain to the world about his relationship with Calvin. He thought he could continue to live in this perfect bubble, but it had just burst. He didn't know what he was going to do.

Calvin watched the love of his life walk away from him. He wanted to feel hurt or betrayed, but he felt more glorious feelings. He finally was out, and he could spread his wings. It was the first time that he truly felt like himself, and he regretted nothing.

"Why would you expose all of our secrets?" Jasmine asked, looking at Bethany.

"I've watched for years now, as you all indulge in backstabbing, alcohol, promiscuity, and lack of self-responsibility. You acted like you were untouchable, and it wasn't fair. You act like when you made a mistake, you didn't have to be judged for it, while others were." She nodded to Tucker. "None of you were perfect, and I had to call you out on your bullshit. Accept that the wallflowers have revolted against the royal court. Enjoy the gallows; that's where you were better suited."

She looked at Andrew who was having a drunken rage. He was screaming about his mother, and Emily was trying to calm him down. "Why bring him into this? He didn't do anything."

"Because he was my cautionary tale. I wanted people to see what your kind does to innocent people like him. You caused him to be like this."

Jasmine shook her head. "No, you did. You revealed his darkest secrets to the world."

"If I recall, you were the one that exposed it to save yours." She nodded to her. "Here's the simple truth for you to understand. I was never going to expose any of your secrets. I gave you a choice. You could expose a secret for me and save your secret, or I expose yours. Every single person I marked, chose to expose someone else's secret. You all were ready to backstab each other, and none of you took the higher road." She turned to look at Andrew. "He's like this because you all created that monster. I just put a light on it." She placed her glass down. "Enjoy the rest of your night, because I will." She grabbed Tucker's hand, and they walked out of prom leaving it in utter chaos.

Bethany, we still were in awe of your determination. You ruined lives, destroyed friendships, and exposed some nasty truths. You were one cold-hearted bitch, and we inspired to be you. We were glad you made this story the way it was, and we wondered what would happen to your puppets next. We hoped they didn't learn from these lessons, because we wanted you to stick around.

Chapter 72

"Get her off the screen!" Andrew screamed. He was thrashing, causing glasses to fall to the ground.

"It's going to be okay," Emily said. She had never seen Andrew like this, and she didn't know what to do. "Take a breath."

He turned to look at Emily. "You're just like her. You're making me this monster that I don't want to be. I don't want to end up like her." He ran his fingers through his hair. "I just wanted to have fun. I wanted to forget about all of this."

"It's okay that you're mother died. She wouldn't want you like this," Emily said.

That enraged Andrew more. He slapped her across the face. "You don't know what she wanted, bitch," Andrew said.

Calvin came running and grabbed Andrew. He tried to break free, but he couldn't. Danielle walked over, too. She looked at Emily. "Are you okay?"

Emily nodded. "I didn't mean to upset him. Is he going to be okay?"

"We will take care of it. Figure out how to turn off the monitor." Danielle knew that once the pictures were taken off the screen, that things would be okay. Emily left to get the images off the loop. People started leaving, because they had no clue what was going on. They got the show they were hoping for.

Danielle turned to Andrew. She touched his face. "Andrew, it's going to be okay. I need you to take a deep breath. Can you do that for me?"

He shook his head. "I'm turning into her. I destroyed lives just like she did." Andrew saw that image, and it hit him. He had become her, and it killed him the most. He had caused so much pain to his father, and he stopped fighting to be a better person.

"Andrew, you can still fix it. Your mother didn't learn her lesson. You have the chance."

The tears fell down his face. "Why did I turn out like this? Why couldn't I have accepted who I was?" He broke down in sobs. "Maybe things would have been better."

Danielle and Calvin looked at each other. They knew those questions were also ones they had. "Because we all make mistakes. We think this is the best way for us to live in. We want to believe people love the fake us, and they could never appreciate the scars behind the mask."

Andrew began to calm himself down. "I need to apologize to him. I need to make things right." He shook his head. "I won't turn into her. I won't give up." Andrew knew that he couldn't be a bomb like his mother. He couldn't let himself check out without any remorse."

"I'll take him home," Jasmine said. "It's the least I can do after what I did." She saw Andrew become destructive, and her guilt had formed.

Danielle wanted to make a snarky comment, but Danielle did the same thing to Delilah. "Thank you."

Jasmine grabbed Andrew's hand. He was subdued, and he was going in and out of consciousness. The alcohol had taken over. Jasmine escorted him out of the room, leaving Danielle and Calvin to look at each other. "We ruined people's lives," Calvin said.

Danielle gave him a weak smile. "For our own selfish game."

"He's never going to speak to me again." It hit Calvin that he and Aman were completely over. He fought so hard for them to stay together. He manipulated, cried, screamed, and prayed they would overcome this. He was fighting a brick wall, and sadly the brick wall wouldn't budge. "I caused all of this."

Danielle shook her head. "He wouldn't give you anything you needed. You had to accept his rules, and that's not a relationship. Calvin, you're going to find someone that will love you for the flaws you have. The one thing you can take from all of this is, you're finally free. You don't have to hide anymore. Calvin, I love you so much."

Calvin pulled her into a hug. "I love you, too. I don't see you as a cruel bitch. I get that you wanted to keep your reputation intact."

She leaned back. "I ruined my friendship with Delilah, I lost my relationship with Dan, and I lost the respect from my mother. I don't think they can be repaired."

"Did you learn from this?"

She shrugged. "Yes, but what I sacrificed it all for was pointless. It's out that I'm poor. Now, I have to deal with that and having no one in my corner."

"You still have me," Calvin said.

Danielle was grateful she had one person that wouldn't abandon her. They looked around at the empty prom venue. "She really knew how to ruin a moment, didn't she?"

Calvin laughed. "Yeah." He paused. "Do you want to see who won Prom King and Queen?" he asked.

She shook her head. "I want to go home and forget about this stupid night." Calvin grabbed her hand and they walked out of the dancehall. There had been reveals, ruined friendships, and shattered hearts. We hoped the kids learned from their mistakes. Danielle, we loved you being our Queen, but it was time you were dethroned. We hoped you would enjoy your time as a civilian. We prayed you fixed those broken relationships, but we didn't care for a happy ending if you asked us.

Chapter 73

"Hey everyone, so the past couple of days have been crazy since prom. The Marked Queen, AKA Bethany, exposed some secrets about people. She thought that her life was pathetic, and she needed to spread lies about everyone." Aman turned to Sana who was standing next to him. "One of those secrets she exposed was about Calvin and me. There was a photo of us kissing. Yes, we did share a kiss, but not a relationship. He was questioning his sexuality, and I decided to let him kiss me to help him. I didn't know that he was taking a photo of us, and that was where the photo came from." Aman leaned over and kissed Sana on the lips. "This is my girlfriend, and the person that I truly want to be with." Aman and Sana then went on to talk about their relationship, for the next twenty minutes.

Calvin shut it off after they started talking about their relationship. He saw a text from Aman. "I'm sorry that I have to lie about our relationship. My parents found out about the photo, and I had to come up with something. I hope you find love in your new-found freedom, but I can't walk side by side with you. I'll always love you, and maybe one day we can be together."

Calvin deleted the text and Aman's number. He deleted all the pictures of them off his phone. He took in a deep breath, and he smiled. He was finally out and proud. He walked down the halls to see people staring at him. He knew they were whispering about him coming out, and that was okay. He felt guilty for exposing him and Aman like that, but he wasn't upset about the aftermath.

He felt his phone go off, and he saw that it was a text from Terrell.

Terrell: *Are you asking me out on a date?*

Calvin was ready to explore his sexuality openly, and he couldn't think of anyone else he wanted to explore it with.

Calvin: *I'm single, and I hope you are, too.*
Terrell: *But you're still in the closet?*
Calvin: *Not anymore.*
Terrell: *Well, then I'll see you Friday.*

"Someone has a giant smile on their face," Danielle said.

Calvin looked up to see her walking up to him. "Yeah, I have a date with a boy Friday night."

Danielle smiled. She was so proud of her best friend. He finally was coming out of his shell, and she couldn't wait to see his growth. "Tell me all about it when it happens."

He laughed. "You'd be the first to know." He looked at his phone. "I better get to baseball practice. I'll see you around."

Danielle waved him off, as she tried to go talk to Delilah. "Good luck with that."

Calvin walked toward the gym. He felt a ball of nerves, because he didn't know how people were going to respond to him being gay. He had kept it a secret for so long. He had accepted he would walk away from baseball today if they didn't accept it. He opened the doors to the locker rooms. People were putting on their gear and turned to see Calvin walk in.

They shrugged and went back to putting on their clothes, like nothing dramatic was happening. Calvin felt indifferent, because no one said anything to him. Ian walked up to him. He was the pitcher Calvin worked with the most. "Dude, we aren't going to have a coming out party for you. We don't care you're gay. You better help us win states, or we will kick your ass." Ian tapped him on the chest and walked away.

Calvin chuckled, and he walked over to put on his catcher gear. Aw, Calvin got exactly what he wanted. Well, he didn't get everything. He was free of the prison of coming out and he was free from Aman. We were on the edge of our seats waiting to see all of Calvin's new love tales. We were hoping for the good ones, and expecting the bad ones. Have fun in the world of gay, because it was so much bitchier than the straight one.

Chapter 74

"Delilah, please talk to me. I know that I messed up, but I can fix it," Danielle said. She had tried to make things right between them, but Delilah had blocked all contact.

Delilah looked at her locker, which had whore spray-painted across it. For a bunch of kids who had wealth, this wasn't that original. They should have bought a skywriter to blast that in the sky. It was just a suggestion. "Did they spray paint anything across your locker?" Delilah asked. She didn't even look at Danielle.

"No."

Delilah opened her locker, grabbed some books, and closed it again. "Exactly. Principal Grand is under review. They aren't going to find anything, because there wasn't any proof except for your text. I'm assuming you'll have your interview soon."

"I can lie and say I made it up," Danielle said. She wanted her best friend back more than anything. "I fucked up, and I know that. I was scared of people finding out my secret."

Delilah raised a hand in the air. "I don't care. I'm over your bullshit, and I'm moving on. Have a good life, Danielle. I want nothing to do with you. A friend would have told me that she was poor, and she wouldn't have backstabbed me. Did you know Calvin was gay?" she asked.

"Yes."

"But you decided my secret was more scandalous," Delilah laughed. "It's fine. I never thought we were friends in the first place." Delilah brushed past Danielle to get to class. She was going to keep her head low and focus on her writing.

Delilah walked into Mr. Rozengota's room. Flynn was standing there getting a stern talking to by Mr. Rozengota. He grabbed the paper and walked toward the door. "Thanks to you, I might not graduate now. I'm going to fail this class."

"Maybe you shouldn't have used my fucking story for your own gain."

"You're such a bitch," Flynn said.

Delilah smiled. "I'll be a bitch, but I'm tired of people walking all over me."

"At least I didn't sleep with the principal."

Delilah rolled her eyes. "You're just mad I didn't put out for you." She shrugged. "Maybe, if you had been a better writer, I would have dropped my panties for you." She walked past him, and was proud of herself. Damn, Delilah, we are soaking in this version of you. We loved that the self-harming girl is becoming a bad-ass bitch.

Delilah walked up to Mr. Rozengota. She handed in her story to be submitted for the scholarship contest. "I have been expecting this from you," he said.

"I had to fix a couple of things, but I'm ready."

"I'm ready to see what you do in this world."

Delilah thought of all the people that betrayed her, and she was going to use that as inspiration in her new stories. She wasn't going to let them hurt her anymore. She was tired of people thinking of her as weak. She was ready to show the world what she was capable of. "Me too," she said. We had a feeling Delilah was about to become the villain, but that would be too obvious, wouldn't it?

Chapter 75

Jasmine felt a wave of nerves surging through her body. She saw Carter standing alone at his locker, and she had to talk to him before she left. Jasmine walked over to him. "Can I talk to you?"

Carter turned to Jasmine. He had a mix of emotions when seeing her face. He had been spending every day since prom wanting to talk to her. He saw the photos of her father hitting her. He was so angry that she chose Calvin as her prom date, but he wanted to protect her.

"I'm sorry," Jasmine said. "I let the idea of being Prom Queen get into my head. I shouldn't have been so obsessed with people trying to love me." She smiled. "I met this guy on the track field, and he instantly swept me off my feet. He has an adorable little sister, and I could see myself being with him. He wasn't popular, and I was an idiot to make that seem like a deal breaker."

Carter looked at Jasmine's apology, and he just wanted to shut her up. He pulled her in for a kiss. He didn't care about any of that right now. He just wanted to kiss the girl that has been on his mind ever since he saw her at prom. He saw how beautiful she was, and he wanted to be with her. "Jasmine, I don't care about prom anymore. What I care about is you. Are you safe at home?"

Jasmine smiled. "I'm leaving for Europe."

"What?" Carter was shocked.

"I sent the photo to my mother. She sent it off to her lawyers. My father agreed to let me live with her in Europe, and give my mother a divorce for the photo not to come out."

"So, Bethany did you a favor?"

Jasmine rolled her eyes. "I would never give that bitch any form of gratitude. She can go fuck herself, if you ask me."

Carter thought about what would happen to them. "What about us?"

She shrugged. "I don't know, but I need to go be on my own right now. I can't be here. I need to find happiness in myself, and I think that's going to be in Europe. I just need to be with my mom. I've thought for the longest time that she didn't want me, and I need to reconnect with her again."

Carter pulled her in for one final kiss. It was filled with goodbye and hope. "Remember me," Carter said.

"I will." She kissed him on the cheek and walked away from him. She knew that maybe when she got back from Europe, that things could work out between them, but she just needed her mom right now.

She saw Danielle standing alone. She walked up to her. She needed to say some final words to Danielle before she went away. "So, you're poor?" Jasmine asked.

Danielle looked up from her phone. She didn't have the patience to deal with Jasmine right now. Danielle crossed her arms. "And your father beats you."

Jasmine laughed. "I guess we come from two fucked up households."

"Shitty dads, if you ask me," Danielle said.

"It was nice being your enemy, but I guess you have a new rival." Jasmine turned to look at Bethany.

Danielle looked to see Bethany by her locker. "I guess I do."

"I'll see you around," Jasmine said.

"Where you off to?" Danielle asked.

"Europe. I'm spending time with my mom. I'm taking my finals early, and I probably won't be back for graduation. Enjoy it without me."

"Have all the pastries you want. You deserve it," Danielle said.

"At least I can afford it," Jasmine replied. They laughed and hugged one last time. It was sweet to see two bitches getting along. They were no longer fighting for the kingdom because they lost. They could hug it out as two peasants. We enjoyed their fighting and witty banter. We wanted to barf at all the feelings, but it was the ending of this story. It had to end on a happy note, right?

Jasmine walked toward the entrance of the school. She had fought for so long to be loved by her peers. She wanted people to see her as a strong person, but she ended up failing herself. She was weak, fat, annoying, and worthless. Those were her thoughts, not ours. She needed to go away to work on herself, and it wasn't at Johnson Prep. We will miss our favorite fat girl. We were proud of you for stepping away, Fatty Jazzy. We hoped you loved Europe, because we would forget all about you soon enough.

Chapter 76

"This is the best option for you," Demi said to Andrew. Andrew, Mark, and Demi were in Andrew's living room. Andrew's bags were packed. He was going to Michigan to a retreat for sober living. Andrew needed to get professional help. He knew he wasn't strong enough to apologize to the people that he hurt during his drunken rampage. He thought he would sober up first, and then come back to apologize.

"Do you think I'm a coward?" Andrew asked Demi and Mark.

Mark shook his head. "No, you're realizing that you aren't strong enough." Mark pulled him into a hug. "I can't tell you how proud I am that you're getting the help you need. Your mom would have never done this."

"I just don't want to fail you like she did. I saw that picture of her on that screen, and I knew I had become her." Andrew didn't really remember prom, but he knew he flipped out. He hit Emily, and he went off on the people that tried to take care of him.

"You're fixing your demons right now. It's the best thing you can do for yourself. This place will get you on the right path. You're willing to accept everything now?" Demi asked.

"I think I tried too long to be a normal teenager, and I'm not one. I've lost my mom to alcoholism, and I almost lost myself to it, too."

Demi smiled. "That's the first step."

Andrew looked at his father. "I'm sorry. Please don't hate me."

Mark shook his head. "I could never hate you. I just want the best for you. I'm sorry that I brought you here, and I'm praying that you get what you need in Michigan."

"Me too," Andrew said.

Demi opened the door for Andrew. Andrew and Mark shared one last hug, as Andrew walked out the door to a new life for him. Andrew, we hoped that you got what you needed in Michigan. We loved the rock bottom story that you were. We wished it ended more tragic, because that was far more entertaining than a happy story, but we were proud you were going on your own. We hoped that once you were back to make those apologies, that you didn't fall back into the hole. Here was to hoping we get more scandals and meltdowns from you in the future.

Chapter 77

"Packing up all your things?" Lily asked.

"Just the things that I bought from dad's credit card. He can give them to his wife. She might be too big for them, but I don't want them anymore." Danielle had accepted she wasn't rich anymore. There was no fight left in her. She realized she had made a fucking mess of everything around her. She lost a boyfriend and a best friend. It wasn't a good feeling to have.

Lily walked over and sat on the bed. "Things will work out."

"Mom, I'm not sure. Dan hasn't spoken to me, and Delilah wants nothing to do with me."

Lily reached out and grabbed Danielle's hand. "You still have your mother in your corner. It might seem scary, but you're going to get through it. It's how I survived this whole time."

"Do you ever regret leaving?" Danielle asked. She was worried about turning her back on her father. This was her lifeline to wealth, but she was about to cut it. She didn't know if she was going to be able to handle it.

Lily shook her head. "No, I think it was best for me to leave. Danielle, I wasn't a role model or a mother to you. I let the nannies take care of you. I was so wrapped up in who had the better parties, the better clothes, and the better homes. I lost sight of who I was as a person and woman. I didn't want you to turn out that way."

"I was for a while."

"You're a teenager, and I'm a grown ass adult. I think there's some room for error on your side of things." She stood up. "I also wouldn't worry about Dan and Delilah. I think they will eventually forgive you." She walked out the door before Danielle could say anything.

Danielle had too many emotions in her mind. The one thing that kept her calm was sewing. She had a final interview with Parsons in a couple of days, and she wanted to focus on that. She sat down in front of her sewing machine. She threaded the machine and grabbed the fabric. She wasn't trying to create anything right then, she just wanted to hear the sound that brought her some humbleness.

"You know it's been a while since I've heard that sound," Dan said, walking into Danielle's room.

Danielle stood up. "Dan, what are you doing here?" she asked.

"Your mom asked me to come over to talk to you. She said you had a change of heart, and I had to see for myself." Dan looked over to see a box filled with designer dresses. "So, you're giving up the wannabe socialite lifestyle?"

Danielle nodded. "I don't have to pretend that I'm rich. People know that I live here now. It's not worth fighting people on anymore."

"I guess that makes me happy." He walked over and pulled her in close. "I've missed this version of you."

"Well, it's going to take some time for me to get used to her," Danielle said. She didn't know how to accept her poverty level status. We thought it better suited you. Danielle, you needed to be humble, and this was exactly what the doctor ordered.

Dan leaned down and kissed Danielle on the lips. "I'll be by your side as you figure it out."

"I've done terrible things that I'm not proud of," Danielle said. She still couldn't get the anger from Delilah out of her mind. "I've hurt one of my closest friends, and I don't know if she's ever going to forgive me."

"True friendship will be mended over time," Dan said. Dan, you were still a little slow to the game. When one friend backstabbed another friend, the victim got revenge. Danielle, you needed to watch your back, because you have a target on it now. Delilah was no longer the weak sidekick. She has become a full-fledged woman. We hoped you were ready for your new rivalry, and we weren't talking about with Bethany.

"I guess." Danielle wasn't so sure. "At least I have you."

"Exactly." Dan and Danielle kissed. They embraced this moment of tranquility with each other. Danielle had no clue what to expect, but we were only a month away from graduation. We wondered if when you walked across that aisle to get your diploma, that you would fix mended friendships, earn a better reputation, and become a better human being overall. We guessed we had to sit back and wait to see how your story unfolded. Danielle, we enjoyed you being our Queen for as long as you were, but now you got to have your romance with the stable boy. We would say you could run off into the sunset, but we knew damn well the other bitches weren't done with you just yet.

Chapter 78

"Should we be worried?" Tucker asked Bethany. "People are staring at us." He was worried people would get their revenge on them.

"What if this was a mistake?" Susan asked. She thought the idea was perfect for the time being, but she wasn't so sure anymore. She didn't want people to hate her. She just wanted everyone to get along.

Bethany raised her hand. "You two need to calm down. We are untouchable now. They know we were responsible for The Marked Queen. They fear and admire us. I don't need you two having a breakdown. We knew what we were doing, and we are going to stick to it." Bethany knew her boyfriend and Susan needed calming.

This was where Bethany wanted to truly be. She created The Marked Queen to take her rightful spot at the top of the social food chain. She knew damn well that this was long in the making, and she thought the crown fit her the best. "We rule this school, my dears."

Tucker and Susan looked at each other. They smiled at the realization that no one could touch them. They were no longer the outcasts of the school. They were high school royalty, and they smiled basking in the glory.

Bethany looked around at her newly conquered kingdom. People feared her as she walked by, and this was why her reveal needed to happen. Bethany felt her phone vibrate. She saw it was a text from an anonymous number.

Unknown Number: *Our sweet wallflower Bethany, no one would have expected you were the lady in red, but at Johnson Prep, we did love a good surprise. I hope you're enjoying your rule, because it will be short lived. You should have learned that every Queen has to be ready for an attack, and I'm planning my retaliation. Poor sweet Marked Queen, you should have realized that you created more enemies than allies. Your skeletons are about to come out and stab you in the back. You might have thought you were the best bitch, but that title goes to the legend named Karma. Have fun sweetie, while it lasts. -The Revenged Queen.*

Bethany looked around. She felt her heart drop to her stomach. She felt the same fear she imposed on all her lovely puppets. We hoped you kept your secrets close to your chest, Bethany. It looked like this Queen didn't realize that once you take your seat at the throne, all the other Queens around would kill you for it. Good luck, bitch, and may the blood bath continue.